Fire

Also by L. C. Tyler

A Cruel Necessity
A Masterpiece of Corruption
The Plague Road

Fire

L. C. Tyler

Constable • London

CONSTABLE

First published in Great Britain in 2017 by Constable

A CIP catalogue record for this book
is available from the British Library.

ISBN: 978-1-47212-288-9

Typeset in Adobe Caslon by SX Composing DTP, Rayleigh, Essex
Printed and bound in Great Britain by CPI Group (UK) Ltd, Croydon CR0 4YY

Papers used by Constable are from well-managed forests and
other responsible sources.

MIX
Paper from
responsible sources
FSC® C104740
FSC
www.fsc.org

Constable
An imprint of
Little, Brown Book Group
Carmelite House
50 Victoria Embankment
London EC4Y 0DZ

An Hachette UK Company
www.hachette.co.uk

www.littlebrown.co.uk

To the firefighters of London

Some Persons in this Book

John Grey – Me. The narrator of this sorry tale of deceit and duplicity, a lawyer of several years' standing but still, for reasons that need not concern us now, willing to undertake dangerous and poorly paid work spying for . . .

Henry Bennet, Baron Arlington – Secretary of State for the Southern Department and government spymaster, a man vain enough to wear a glossy cosmetic patch on his nose, responsible for detecting and preventing the treasons of men such as . . .

Monsieur Peidloe, Robert Hubert, Peter Smith and Ebenezer Jones (some of which names may actually be their real ones) in order to protect the interests of his royal master . . .

King Charles II – who has been restored to the throne these six years, and whose devotion to duty I am beginning to doubt in view of the time he spends horse racing, yachting and consorting with his various whores (Catholic and Protestant) and in view of his poor choice of advisers, including my Lord Arlington and Arlington's protégé . . .

Sir Thomas Clifford – who does not affect a nose patch of any sort but does own a blond wig, which is almost as ostentatious, though less reprehensible than his adherence to False Popish Doctrines, unlike . . .

Anthony Ashley Cooper, Lord Ashley – as good and staunch a Protestant as you are likely to meet and, I think, one of the few honest men surrounding the King, as is . . .

Mr Joseph Williamson – Arlington's wise and little-appreciated deputy, who is second in my trust only to . . .

Will Atkins – my clerk and loyal servant, whose only faults are that he sometimes thinks he is my mother (who is another person entirely) and that he chides me both for my very moderate consumption of wine and for being careless enough never to have married . . .

Aminta, Lady Pole – my childhood friend, now a distinguished London poet and playwright and the widow of . . .

Roger, Viscount Pole – about whom the only good thing I can say is that he is dead, once secretary to my stepfather . . .

Colonel Payne – who formerly served under Cromwell and earned in the process enough money to purchase the manor of Clavershall West, which was more than sufficient inducement for . . .

Mistress Payne, formerly Mistress Grey, that is to say my actual mother – to marry him, thus gaining for herself the large house and deer park that she had coveted all her life and which was formerly occupied by . . .

Sir Felix Clifford – bankrupt cavalier with no discernible morals, distant kin of Sir Thomas Clifford, father to Aminta,

Lady Pole, and very close friend – worryingly close friend – of my mother's in the year or so before I was born, which is a matter of continuing concern for . . .

me, **John Grey** – whose already troubled sleep will shortly be disturbed by the ringing of bells and the shouts of 'Fire!'

Prologue

Dawn broke, just before midnight and much too far to the south. At first it was just a faint pink underscoring of the starry black. Slowly it grew, broader, higher, redder, bleeding up into the sky.

Bateson (it was generally agreed he had never possessed or needed a Christian name) watched and thought it looked promising. Very promising indeed. He rubbed his hands and turned to his newest volunteer.

'See over there, Jem?' he said. 'That's the first thing that God created, that is. Fire.'

Jem frowned. He made no claim to be a theologian, but he'd once been made to write out the first page of the Bible as a punishment. 'I thought it was Light that God created first?'

'One and the same, lad,' said Bateson, extending a large and calloused hand towards the shimmering, rose-coloured streak. 'Light and fire? One's every bit as good as the other.'

Jem nodded. Bateson's word, amongst the firefighters of Clerkenwell, was law – both Civil and Canon. The Bible was mistaken. God had delayed creating light until he'd sorted out fire.

'They told me how we'd wasted our money,' Bateson continued. 'Told me how we'd never have a fire big enough here in Clerkenwell. Men with buckets, they said. And a few brass water squirts. That's all you need, they said. Plus long hooks to pull down the burning buildings what sadly can't be saved, even by us. That's how fires have been fought ever since . . . ever since there *were* fires and firefighters like us to fight them. But see that pretty, dancing glow over there . . . ? Now we'll have a chance to show the lot of them – the Mayor, the aldermen, the magistrates, the King, the Duke of York – we'll show them just what the Beast can do. My Beast.'

They both turned in respectful silence to the machine beside them, the machine that rose at least a foot above their heads, the epitome of modern, seventeenth-century engineering. There it was with its vast, shining wooden reservoir, its leather hoses, the pair of elegantly curved, brass-bound pumping handles, and the four great iron-shod wheels on which it would, now it had finally been summoned, roll down towards a grateful City.

'That,' said Bateson proudly, 'is progress. That is modernity. That can do the work of sixty ordinary firemen with leather buckets and brass squirts.'

Jem nodded. This assertion too was difficult to contradict. Forty, sixty, a hundred – who could say? The Beast had never been put to the test. They had saddle-soaped the leather, polished the wood, scoured the bright yellow metal, oiled the axles with handfuls of thick, clinging grease – but until tonight it had been a thing to admire and wonder at. Until tonight there had been no fire worthy of it.

Somewhere, not too far off, a muffled church bell had started to toll. It was the call to arms for the remaining Clerkenwell firefighters – those who lived further out in the parish.

Bateson should have been cursing and swearing, demanding to know where the missing men were, threatening to hang the last to arrive, urging them on towards the distant fire that seemed to be growing by the minute. But he was displaying a strange, almost frightening, charity towards them.

'It must be quite a big one if they've called for the Beast,' said Jem conversationally. 'I mean, they've sent all the way up to Clerkenwell for us to come and help the City volunteers.'

'City firefighters? Couldn't piss out a lump of damp coal in a china pot. Of course they've sent for us.'

Bateson looked southeastwards again towards the City and shook his head. His countenance was intended to convey wistful sadness but, for all that, inwardly he rejoiced and his heart was exceeding glad.

'So, should we fill the tank up and go and help them?' asked Jem.

'Fill it up? *Fill it up?* You haven't done this sort of work before, have you?'

'No, sir,' said Jem meekly.

'What sort of work have you done exactly?'

It was the question Jem had learned to dread. It was the question he hoped nobody would ever ask him.

'Transportation, Mr Bateson sir,' he said.

'Carter?'

'Yes, sir. Until recently.'

'Well, that's useful. Now we're having to move the Beast. And it must have been pleasant enough work for you. I'll wager you've seen every county in England.'

'No, sir. Our work was mainly in London.'

'Still, you were out on the road, meeting all sorts of folk. Gossiping. Telling a merry yarn.'

Actually, thought Jem, he had met only one sort of customer and they hadn't been very talkative.

'Yes, Mr Bateson sir,' he said, hoping to terminate the conversation without his new employer backing away in abject terror, as people often did when he was more specific about his previous job. He artfully offered Bateson the opportunity to change the subject back to his incompetence – a small price to pay. 'So we don't need to fill up with water then?' he asked.

'How much do you think that mighty engine weighs when empty?' asked Bateson.

Jem considered carefully, measuring the great bulk of the wooden cylinder with his eye and converting that stupendous volume into tons and hundredweight and pounds and ounces. 'A lot?' he hazarded.

'Precisely. A lot. And how much do you think it would weigh full of water?'

'A shit of a lot?'

'Even more than that, lad. If we had the horses to shift it – and we don't – the leather harnesses would snap like pack thread as they took the strain.'

Jem whistled between his teeth. 'So we fill it when we get to the fire, then? Well, there'll be no shortage of what we need in the City tonight.' Jem nodded in the direction of the New River Head – Clerkenwell's famed cistern, into which the New River discharged the health-giving waters of Hertfordshire for the benefit of any Londoner who would pay to avoid drinking the Thames. For over fifty years water had flowed peacefully 'mid verdant fields, all the way along the New River to Clerkenwell, then gushed through the elm pipes that ran ever downwards from the New River Head into the City, splitting over and over again into smaller lead quills that took the water right into people's homes. Not to a nearby pump but, marvellous to relate, actually *into people's homes*. Now, on a Sunday night, the stopcocks controlling the flow would be wide open, and water would be flooding down to London, filling each householder's own small cistern for the many tasks that would require water on the following morning.

Bateson coughed and, for a moment, looked uncharacteristically embarrassed.

'Water's off,' he said.

'Off?' said Jem.

'What are you? Mr Echo? Yes, it's off. It's not running. The pipes are dry. Every blessed one of them.'

'But ...'

'But *why?* Is that your next question? The reason, Mr Echo, is that one of the Directors has, in his great wisdom, turned the stopcocks in the pumping house and gone away with the key.'

'He's turned it off the same night we have a fire?'

'Well, to be fair to the man, I doubt if he actually knew there'd be a fire tonight. They've sent somebody out to find him and retrieve it. When they do, doubtless we'll get the taps turned on smartish. In the meantime, the water stays up here in Clerkenwell. Every last drop of it.'

'So, what are we to do?'

'Well, I don't know if you've ever been to the City, Jem, but when you get there you'll see this big wet thing, near a quarter of a mile wide and a couple of hundred miles long. It's called the Thames and has all the water in it that you'll need. Not even the Beast can drink the Thames dry.'

'But ... ?' Jem paused and looked at Bateson.

'But what? Is that your entire question or is there anything to follow?'

'Sorry, Mr Bateson, I thought you might want to interrupt me again. As is your right. *But* we'll need to go all the way down to the river to fill the Beast up.'

'On the contrary, Jem. Just think. What's at the end of London Bridge?'

'An inn?'

'Yes. But what else?'

'Houses?'

'Yes, but what else?'

'Streets?'

'Yes, but what else?'

'The heads of traitors on poles?'

'Who will help us put out the fire?'

'Probably not.'

'Just so that London does not burn down before you guess correctly, at the northern end of London Bridge there is a waterwheel. Its purpose is to pump water *up* into the City, just as the New River brings it *down*. It doesn't taste as sweet as New River water, but Thames water's fine for putting out fires. You just have to dig up a pipe, knock a bloody great hole in it, grab a bucket or two and fill up the tank. Then you put the fire out and wait for the praise that will be rightly yours and mine and all the other volunteer firefighters'. The innkeepers will force you to drink their finest ale and the girls will do anything you ask them to do, and teach you some things you haven't even thought of, you being still quite young and innocent.'

The educational side of the work was something that Jem had not previously considered.

'We'd better go then,' he said. He looked round the as yet empty yard. 'When the others arrive, of course.'

'Plenty of time,' said Bateson, with the strange and wholly unprecedented patience that he had been showing ever since the bells had started ringing. 'The others have been sent for. They'll come in their own good time. Ben's knocking them up, in a polite and considerate way, just in case they haven't heard the church bells ringing. *Plenty* of time. Those girls won't be going anywhere.'

At least he hoped there was plenty of time. Bateson had been eager not to start too soon. If he arrived early then the fire would scarcely have got going – it would be a waste of the Beast's wondrous capability, a travesty of what its maiden outing should be. Of course, he was equally aware of the dreadful danger of waiting too long: when they got there the fire might have already gone out. The departure time, the speed with which they proceeded – these were important decisions, not to be taken lightly. He looked at the horizon and was dismayed to see that the glow in the sky already seemed, to his expert gaze, to have diminished a little.

'It's getting bigger,' said Jem. 'That's for sure.'

Bateson laughed at his new assistant's inexperience. 'Trick of the light,' he said. 'It's nothing, that one. The Great Fire of 1666? No such luck.'

The Beast trundled onwards through the dark streets, six horses straining at the shaft, a dozen or so human attendants bearing torches to light its way. Ahead, as if in answer to Bateson's silent prayers, the red glow was spreading. Definitely spreading. This was a fire worth going to. They pressed forwards, guided by the light in the southeast, and before long they could smell the smoke and hear the sharp cracking as still the distant flames gorged themselves on walls and floors.

There was a steady trickle of traffic heading in the other direction – tired people with smoke-blackened faces, dressed in whatever clothes they had been able to find in the dark, on foot and carrying hastily gathered bundles. From them Bateson learned that the fire was hard by London Bridge. Bateson had studied the combustibility of all parts of the City and knew that the houses down there were wattle-and-daub hovels that would burn like tinder after the long dry summer. The lanes were narrow. The nimble flames would leap from house to house with alarming speed and dexterity.

'Well, it's easy enough to tell which way we should go tonight,' said Walter to Jem, pointing to the glow ahead of them.

Walter was a little more senior, having volunteered to be a fireman a few months before. He'd actually put out a small fire, though not one to which the Beast had been invited.

'I know the route into the City well enough,' said Jem unthinkingly. 'We're heading straight for London Bridge. I used to come this way a lot at night.'

'What were you doing then?'

Jem cursed his overeager tongue. 'I was in charge of a cart,' he said.

'Carrying all sorts of things, I suppose?'

'No, just one sort of thing,' said Jem. 'Same every night.'

'At night? Why not during the day?'

'There were reasons.'

'What reasons? Why would you just carry things at night? Unless ...' Walter put his head on one side, as if thinking. This usually proved very little, but there was a danger even Walter might accidentally hit on the truth.

Jem took a deep breath and looked around. Nobody was paying much attention to him. Best just to tell Walter quickly and swear him to silence. 'Look,' he whispered. 'I'll explain if you promise not to tell anyone . . .'

'Of course I won't,' said Walter. 'Cross my heart.'

So Jem told him.

'*A Dead Cart?*' yelled Walter, at what was probably the top of his voice.

Jem looked around again. Everybody was now paying a great deal of attention to him. But none of the team was quite as close to him as they had been a couple of seconds ago.

'It wasn't easy to find work during the Plague Time,' Jem said as the others backed away. 'I didn't have much choice.'

'You did have the choice of not coming and working with us afterwards,' said one of the men very reasonably.

'I don't do it now. It's . . . it's like seasonal work,' said Jem. 'They lay you off once the Plague's over. Until the next one anyway.'

'So,' said Walter, who was not noted for being quick in any sense, 'you loaded dead bodies onto the cart and took them to the plague pits? You touched their puss and sores with your hands?'

The gaze of a dozen or so men turned from Jem's face to his hands. For a moment Jem glanced at them too.

'Yes,' said Jem, instinctively rubbing his palms against his breeches.

'Enough!' growled Bateson, turning round from his position at the very front of the machine. Walter, he thought, failed to qualify as the least intelligent member of the team only when they had a horse that was especially slow on the uptake. 'If he'd caught the Plague he'd have been dead for over a year. And he can't go back to his old job even if he wanted to. I need him. I'm beginning to think we'll need all the men we can get.'

He was glad that the Beast would have its rightful chance to show what it could do, but was worried that he didn't have enough men with him. Four to work the pumps. Two to hold the hose. Six – better still, eight – to look to the refilling of the cistern with leather buckets. Four, maybe more, to use the great iron hooks and pull down burning walls. Two at the very least to watch that the fire didn't work its way round behind them while they laboured and cut off their escape route. One, if at all possible, to help rescue the trapped women and children. That made . . . He had only ten fingers and had used them all up. Hopefully there would be men there already – albeit merely City firefighters – who might lend a hand.

A burning wisp of something floated down from the dark sky and settled on the ground not far off, where it smouldered and turned from orange to dark red to grey.

'Wind's getting up,' said Bateson, with a worried glance at the rags of scudding, moonlit cloud. 'Come on, men, more speed. God has finally vouchsafed unto us the fire we have all prayed for.'

'Time to stop praying then,' muttered Jem. But the noise of the fire was already so loud that nobody heard him.

The lanes narrowed as they approached the bridge. The old half-timbered houses leaned out towards them from both sides of the street, as if trying to clutch them as they passed under their crooked, jutting upper floors. When the road was straight for a few yards it wasn't too bad, but manoeuvring round corners took time. The Beast's builders had not felt it necessary to give it a tight turning circle. Several times their way was blocked completely by loaded carts, pushed by householders desperate to get their goods away safely, and only explicit and personal threats of violence served to give the great machine the priority it deserved.

The hot, acrid smoke was getting thicker. Jem could feel it singe his nostrils as he breathed it in. Behind the dark, unlit and largely abandoned buildings silhouetted in front of them, the sky glowed fiery orange and vermillion. Over their heads, rising higher and higher in the superheated air, drifted burning sparks the size of dinner plates. They needed to find where the water pipes were, and quickly. A man with a heavily loaded wheelbarrow was approaching. His nose and mouth were covered with a scarf to protect them against the smoke. Hopefully he'd know.

'Pipes?' responded the man, lowering his scarf a little. 'They're under your feet. But there's no water in them. We've had nothing from the New River all night.'

'I know that. But the waterwheel by the Bridge . . .'

The man shook his head. 'Look down there,' he said, not unkindly.

Bateson squinted. 'You mean . . .'

'That fire you can see over there is London Bridge burning down. The waterwheel's made of wood. So work out for yourself why there's no water in the pipes.'

'Shit,' said Bateson. 'Where do I get water then?'

'Well,' said the man. 'If you go a bit further you'll come to this big wet thing . . .'

'So, I'll have to fill up the machine directly from the Thames?'

'If you'd like water, that's all there is. There were men with chains of buckets, bringing it up and chucking it onto the houses – not that it made any difference. They've all run off now.'

'Cowards,' muttered Bateson.

'No, they just needed to save their own goods before their houses burnt down too. I've rescued what I can from my place, so I'm off to my cousin in Holborn. There's no fighting it, good sir, not with this wind. The water was turning into steam in midair. If I were you I'd just save that nice new machine of yours. Wait until you've got a fire that's small enough for it. There's nothing to be done. Not down there.' He took up the handles of his barrow again.

'Stay, my good man! Now all of us are here, we can protect your own home and those of your neighbours. You look strong. We'll need help with the pumps.'

'My house – or my landlord's house, as I now prefer to think of it – is a heap of glowing ashes. My landlord may feel that the house is no longer in the state it was when I signed the lease, and I'm not planning to hang around to pay dilapidations. If you wanted my help, you should have been here an hour ago. Anyway, if I come with you, I'll have to leave this barrow here in the street. I doubt it will still be full when I return.'

'I am sure that the Lord Mayor would compensate you . . .'

The man laughed, then, having breathed in more smoke than he intended, simply coughed the remainder of his contempt for the City authorities.

Bateson, grim-faced, turned to his team. He straightened his back and held his head high. 'Press on, lads,' he said. 'Press on down to the river. We'll show them what the Clerkenwell men can do.'

'Good luck,' said the man, setting the heavy cart in motion again. 'The fire's in Pudding Lane and the wharves by the bridge. Lots of tar and oil stored down there. It's all burning up nicely for you.'

'Where's Pudding Lane?' Bateson called to the retreating figure.

'Straight ahead. Just follow the smoke.'

They followed the smoke. When they finally got sight of the river, the scene in front of them was lit, almost like day. The whole of the north bank of the river seemed bathed in a flickering orange glow. Only the south bank, on the far side of the broad stream, was cool, dark and untroubled, though the windowpanes of the low houses sparkled with a borrowed light. The dirty, fast-flowing water rippled yellow and brown and crimson. All of the houses at the north end of London's only bridge were in flames. The shape of the great waterwheel could still just be made out, a bright glowing circle, like a dying Catherine Wheel. But the biggest and reddest flames issued from the riverside warehouses. Clouds of dark, oily smoke elbowed each other in their race up into the sky.

'Pitch for waterproofing the ships,' said Bateson enviously. 'Timber. Coal. Everything a young, ambitious fire could ever dream of.'

'Who's putting it out, Mr Bateson sir?' asked Jem, pulling down the scarf that was covering his mouth.

'Just us apparently,' said Bateson.

'Thought so. Didn't see anyone else, but it seemed best to ask. Where's Pudding Lane?'

Bateson waved his hand vaguely towards the middle of the inferno.

'Shall we fill the cistern then?' asked Walter. 'We can take buckets down to the river.'

'We're still too far from the fire and from the water. We'll need to get the engine closer to both.'

'Closer to *that*?' said Walter, indicating the blazing wharves. Unquestioning though he usually was of Bateson's commands, even he could see a problem. From here, over a hundred yards away, the heat already wrapped itself around you like a blanket. You could taste the cinders on your tongue.

'That hose can squirt water twenty yards,' said Bateson, the sweat pouring down his scarlet cheeks. 'Maybe thirty if the wind is right. You can't take the horses any closer than we are. God alone knows why they haven't bolted already. You'll have to push the machine from here by hand. At least it's downhill to the river. You'll need to use the ropes to slow it down as you get to the water though.'

'What?' asked Walter.

The noise was growing. A deep-throated roar as one building after another and its contents were consumed. Jem wondered, even if they could get close enough, even if they could refill the tank nonstop, whether they could make any difference to anything. But Bateson thought otherwise. His face had taken on the colour of the fire. His eyes were feverish and bright. His hair was grey with ash. He had become, as far as was possible, a physical part of the conflagration.

'I said, *down to the water*,' yelled Bateson. 'As close as you can get it.'

Then, through the smoke, a small group of dejected men appeared bit by bit, plodding towards them. They were covered with smuts of soot and their fine coats were singed by the fire. Their lace cravats were askew. One had lost his hat. The hat of another was gently smouldering, unnoticed by its owner. But they retained a sense of their own importance.

'You, sir! Is that the Clerkenwell engine?' demanded the man in the smoking hat.

'It is, sir. And who might you be?' asked Bateson.

'Sir Thomas Bloodworth. Lord Mayor of this City. You took your time, I must say. We sent for you almost two hours ago.'

'We came as fast as we could, my Lord.'

Bloodworth took from his pocket a large silver watch and pointed to it as proof of their tardiness. 'Not fast enough by an hour at least. We could have still used your machine even five and twenty minutes ago, but now . . .'

They all turned, with a sense of awe, towards the vast sheet of fire, towering above them. A hundred machines would scarcely have been equal to the task, and they had one with no water in it.

'We did our best, sir. Can't do more. How many men do you have fighting the fire now?'

'None,' said the Mayor. 'Not a single blasted one. Nobody will stay once the fire nears their own house. Those whose houses are close but not already burning are packing their goods. Those further off wait and watch – they won't come with me for fear that they won't be able to return in time to save what they can. Those safe outside the City walls say I have no jurisdiction to call upon them.'

'The London fire engine?'

'It caught fire. The buckets that filled it were all leaking anyway. Leather buckets, left in the church tower for years to dry out and crack . . .'

'Well, we're here now, sir.'

'Yes, so you are. At least your men won't run off to Clerkenwell, I suppose. Not yet. And your engine? Where have you positioned it?'

They peered into the smoke that was now swirling along the river bank.

'Must be over there by now, sir.'

Then they all heard the sound, the one that none of them would ever forget to their dying day; muffled, it is true, by the many other sounds, but still unmistakable as that of a large object entering the river.

'What was that?" asked Bloodworth.

'Could be all sorts of things, my Lord. But hopefully not what I think it was,' said Bateson.

The smoke parted enough for them to see the river again. The Beast was still afloat, but had started to drift slowly with the current towards Gravesend and the sea. It looked smaller than Bateson remembered it; but the empty chamber, brightly polished and well caulked, kept it bobbing in the tide. Then, mercifully, the smoke billowed in front of them again.

After a short while Walter reappeared.

'I see you managed to get the engine close to the water,' said Bateson. 'Well done, lad.'

Even the horses, had they been present, would have detected the danger in Bateson's voice and backed away, ears flattened, nostrils flaring.

'Thank you, Mr Bateson,' said Walter, his fingers massaging the soft, warm cap he held in his hands. 'We did our best, sir. And, as you so often tell us, you cannot do more.'

Chapter One

I am uncertain what has woken me: the harsh smell of burning or the incessant pealing of bells or the pounding at my door. I rub my eyes and, from my bed, try to look out of my window. It is still night-time but there is a glow in the sky that suggests morning cannot be far off. A glow in the east.

'Yes?' I call out. 'What is it?"

'Fire, Mr Grey, sir,' says Will, cautiously opening the door. The dim recesses of the room are lit feebly by his single, flickering candle. 'There's a fire in the City. Big one.'

I rub my eyes again and sit up. My clerk is in his nightgown, bare-legged but awake and alert. I think he may have been up for some time.

'Yes, of course,' I say, though I have no idea what fire he is talking about.

'Are you all right, sir?'

'I'm fine, Will. Why shouldn't I be?'

Will says nothing.

'Will, if I want to drink a bottle of wine of an evening, it's nobody's business but my own.'

'Two bottles, sir.'

'Does that make it your business?'

'No, sir.'

'If I'm ever drunk in court, in front of a judge, to the detriment of my clients, that will be your concern.'

'Yes, sir.'

'But I'm not in court. I'm in my own chambers in Lincoln's Inn. I work hard, Will. Since the Plague ended, my clients have returned, and a satisfying number have chosen to sue each other. I have in no way discouraged them. The realisation that death may strike at any time has caused many of them to rewrite their wills. I have advised them on how to bring joy or despair to their surviving kin through the simple expedient of a well-drafted codicil. The tread of feet on my staircase is never-ending. I should be permitted, once the last of them has departed and paid you my fee, *to drink a bottle of wine.*'

'Yes, sir. The empties are still on the table if you'd like to count them.'

'All right, two bottles. No more of this, Will – you're making my head ache.'

I do, of course, understand that the throbbing I can feel has little to do with Will. And actually my head is much less painful now than it was last month. That too was my fault. I need no reminder, but still I touch my cheek gently with my fingers and feel the hard edges of the scar that I shall probably bear for life. My fingers move slowly up my face until I can use them to massage my temples. Then, with a great effort, I slowly swing my legs over the side of the bed and stand. As I do so, Will holds out, quite unnecessarily, an arm to steady me. I ignore both him and the gentle swaying of the floor and walk over to the open window. I clutch the sill with both hands and remain there for a moment, trying to take in everything in front of me. The sleeping city is dark, except for the terrible red glow in the distance. The air is cool but the sharp smell of fire is unmistakable. There is the distant crack of burning timber and there are unaccustomed cries in place of the usual night-time silence.

'It started over by the Tower, sir,' says Will. 'Pudding Lane. Now London Bridge is burning. The waterwheel's gone. It's the biggest fire for a very long time – bigger even than 1654.'

'Who says?'

'Nightwatchman, sir. Called up at three o'clock. He remembers 1654 very well. You would still have been at the University then, sir. He says there's no water from the New River to fight it – the French have turned off the supply.'

'The French? Why would they want do that?'

'Because we're at war with them, sir.'

'He should be attending to his duties, not gossiping with you.'

'I think they get lonely, sir. Out all night. Nightwatchmen, I mean, not the French. Never met one who wouldn't stop and tell a body some news.'

'And they've been ringing the church bells?'

'Yes, sir. For over an hour. They're calling for men to help fight the fire—'

'I'd better go then and see if I can help.'

The wind is getting up – not exactly a gale, but strong enough. It is blowing in from the west. If Will's talkative nightwatchman is to be believed, then the fire will be edging towards the Tower of London and away from us. It still seems reassuringly distant, anyway. And however big it grows, it cannot possibly trouble us on this side of the massively thick city wall, not here in comfortable, lawyerly Lincoln's Inn.

'They won't be expecting gentlemen to go and fight the fire, sir. Just tradesmen and labourers and the like. Anyway, it can be dangerous work.'

'Good,' I say. 'That's the sort of work that would amuse me.'

I rub my temples again, hard with the palms of both hands. It dulls the ache for a moment. What was I saying?

'Are you sure you're all right, sir?' says Will.

I do not reply, nor do I glance at the bottles on the table. I breathe in the night air. The wind carries to me the scent of burning wood and pitch and other things I cannot identify. I need to get my breeches on and find my coat and stockings and shoes, which are somewhere in the candle-dim room.

'Why not wait until it is light, sir?'

'Because I'm going now,' I say.

'Of course, sir. One of your stockings is on the chair and one is in the fireplace, sir.'

I say nothing.

'Is it because of her, Mr Grey?' asks Will, retrieving the stocking from the ashy hearth.

'Who?' I say.

'My Lady Pole,' says Will, though we both know he doesn't need to answer my question. It's unlikely to be because of my mother or Lady Castlemaine.

'Why should my going out have any relevance to Lady Pole?' I ask, taking the proffered stocking from Will's respectful hand.

'No reason. But you've accepted more work from Lord Arlington in the last few months. The sort of work you'd have been wiser to turn down . . .'

'I still fail to see what that too has to do with Lady Pole.'

He looks at me, perhaps taking in the livid red mark on my cheek.

'She hasn't visited you lately. Even though she's back in London.'

'I haven't invited her,' I say.

'That would be why then,' says Will.

Well, he's wrong there. The lack of an invitation never stopped Aminta Pole doing anything.

'Anyway, she's busy writing plays,' I add.

'I went to see one of her comedies – before they closed the theatres because of the Plague last year.' Will pauses to see if I'll ask which one. When I don't, he adds very cautiously: '*The African Prince.*'

'*The Moroccan Prince,*' I say.

'So it was. I hope you don't mind me mentioning it. Under the circumstances . . .'

'Had you not mentioned it, your discretion would have done you credit. But you don't need to account to me for your pleasures, any more than I need to account to you for mine.'

Will finds my hat, brushes it on his sleeve and hands it to me.

'I'd always hoped that the two of you would marry,' Will continues, showing he has in fact considerably less tact than he imagines. 'You and Lady Pole. Now she's a widow and you had a second chance of proposing to her. Which you decided not to do. For very good reasons, I'm sure. But you always seemed to like each other. And your families approved. Your mother likes her very much indeed. And *her* father, Sir Felix, always says . . .' Will glances at me and realises that, however many of my relations he brings into the discussion, it will change nothing. 'Not that it's any of my business, of course, sir.'

'That's right,' I say. 'It isn't. Not yours. Not my family's. Not her family's. Just my business and hers. I'm going out, Will. I may be a long time.'

'Do you go to Lord Arlington, sir?'

'I'm not looking for any more work from Lord Arlington,' I say. 'Not until the scars have healed from the last job he gave me.'

'It was at least a clean wound, sir. That sort of scar does heal.'

'Yes,' I say. 'That sort of scar does.'

I enter the City through Ludgate, passing under the statue of Queen Elizabeth, who looks down unconcerned at the stream of people leaving her capital by moonlight and heading out into the country. When this street was last this crowded, they were fleeing the Plague. Now, only a year later, they are fleeing again. There are no guards on the gates. They too have gone. The crowd presses on unchecked, tripping over itself in its haste.

'Where's the fire?' I ask one man.

He lowers the scarf over his face. 'Fire? Lord bless you, sir, it's everywhere. I live just down by the bridge. When it started I moved my goods to my brother's house in the next street, thinking that safe enough. Now his house is in flames too, and the next three streets beyond. They say it's the French, sir. They started it with fireballs. There are gangs of men out now hunting for them. I hope you're not French at all yourself, sir. It wouldn't be safe to go that way if you are.'

'I'm not,' I say.

'Well, you look normal, but I thought I'd ask anyway. No offence. But I'd still come away, sir. There's nothing for you in the City. Dear old London is lost, and there's naught to be done about it.'

'Do they not need men to fight the fire?'

'They do indeed sir,' he says. 'But if you go they will still have only one. The City firemen are fled and the Clerkenwell men stand by the Thames abusing each other for reasons I cannot tell.'

'Is the Lord Mayor not on hand directing affairs?'

'He would if he had anyone to direct. The dry season ... the wind ... the lack of water ... ill fortune ... it's too big for anyone. When the wind drops, the fire will die down, as all fires do. Or it will reach some broad thoroughfare and not be able to leap across. Or perhaps all London will burn to the ground. Who can say what God's will may prove to be? Come away now, sir. Have some care for your own life.'

I look towards the glowing horizon. 'It's my life,' I say, 'and I'll take as much or as little care as I wish.'

'Oh, I see. Well, in that case, you're going the right way,' he says.

For a while I follow the backstreets, avoiding the fleeing carts and the wagons. Though not a Londoner by birth, I know the City well. In my work for Arlington, obscure alleyways often serve me better than more frequented routes. Tonight the fire lights up even the narrowest and deepest of lanes with a strange crimson radiance. I have no need of a lantern. I turn a corner close to St Paul's and almost trip over two of my fellow citizens. The one who isn't dead looks up at me in alarm.

'Can I help in any way?' I ask.

The dead man does not respond but the living one jumps quickly to his feet. His face too is covered with a scarf, as tonight's fashion seems to be. His clothes are covered in smuts. Both things suggest he has come from the fire, but the panic I glimpse in his eyes relates to something else. He is holding an object in his hands, but before I can see exactly what it is, he backs away into the shadows, then he turns on his heel and runs. There seems little point in calling out to him to stop – if he had really wished to remain and be questioned then doubtless he would have done so.

I look at the figure sprawled across the road. Already a thin layer of ash is covering his body. His stillness, the awkwardness of his position, the hurried manner of his friend's departure – these things have already informed me he will not rise again of his own accord. But, dead though he is, he may still have something he wishes to tell me. I kneel beside him, exactly as his companion had been doing when I interrupted him, and place a hand on his chest. There is no heartbeat, but there is a great deal of warm blood from a very large wound – too large a wound for a sword or dagger to have made, but which in the shadows and under the ash I had not noticed.

This is not the first time that I have, in the course of my work, crouched beside a dead body. I have seen men with their throats cut and men stabbed through the chest and through the back. I have seen men shot. I have seen men strangled. I have seen men so slashed by cavalry sabres that they should not have been alive, and yet they were. Wounds as large as this tend to be made by a musket ball leaving the body. I examine his chest more closely, then roll him over and observe the much smaller wound in his back. Yes, shot from behind without doubt. Now I look at it, probably a pistol ball rather than a musket ball. Perhaps I should have paid more attention to what the other man was carrying. I allow the body to return to its former ungainly position. He is, or perhaps I should say was, a tall man, dressed in a wool suit – of a rust colour under the pale ash – and yellow stockings that are still bright. He has a broad-brimmed hat, which lies close by. One hand is flung forward, the other clenched tight, close to his body. His face, like his now-vanished companion's, is much blackened with smuts of soot and there are burn marks on his clothes. He too has come from the fire and probably in haste. Now he lies peacefully waiting for the flames to catch him up again.

And it may not be long before they do so. If I am to discover more then I must work fast. I pull out his two pockets. One has a blue velvet purse with a few coins in it – also still warm from his recently living body. If this was a robbery, then I have interrupted it just before the work was complete. I place the purse in my own breeches. It may help identify him or it may not, but it will certainly not be there in an hour's time if I leave it where it is. The other pocket is empty. It is odd that he has come out with so little, but perhaps he had reasons for carrying nothing that might identify him, or perhaps his now absent companion is looking after his other possessions for him. I regard him again, lying slantways across the road. He is too large to carry, and in any case I have nowhere to carry him to. He must bide where he is for the moment. Apologetically I wipe my bloody hands on his breeches and say a brief prayer for him. Then I stand. I have done what little I can for a murdered man in a burning City.

When I find a magistrate, I shall report this. I do not expect to find one soon, but turning the next corner I come face to face with just such a person. Unfortunately, a group of Londoners has found him first, and I think they have plans to kill him very soon.

Chapter Two

My magistrate seems surprisingly unconcerned to be threatened by half a dozen armed ruffians, but whether he is wise in that view remains to be seen. His back is against the wall, but he stands defiantly facing them. One of the gang has drawn his sword. Two of the others have rough cudgels, raised, ready to strike. There are, I realise, many reasons why I cannot just pass this by. I must speak to these people tactfully; but, before I do, I think I may draw my own sword. It often helps.

'Can I be of assistance?' I ask politely.

The men turn. The noise of the fire had prevented them hearing either my footsteps or the rasp of clean white metal against a scabbard, and they are surprised to see a lawyer menacing them with a blade that, like everything else tonight, reflects back the distant fire. Even in this red half-light, the quality of the steel is apparent. I think however that my face is not well lit because they merely glance at it and make no comment.

'We've caught this fellow,' says the man with the cheap sword, squinting at me. 'One of the fire-raisers without a doubt. Found him sneaking out of the house yonder, where that French whore lives. It's the French who've started this.'

One of the men with cudgels nods. 'This is no English fire,' he says. 'Look at that red. Like a cardinal's robe, sir. That's a Catholic fire if ever I saw one – the exact same colour as Hell itself.'

The others nod. Everyone knows that Hell, like London tonight, is red and full of Frenchmen.

The old man shrugs. 'If I've been with a French whore all night, then neither of us will have had much time for fire-raising. I'd scarcely waste my money paying her to do it. And she does nothing free of charge. Believe me, I've asked her.'

'Keep quiet, you,' responds the man with the thirty-Shilling sword. I hope he won't endanger himself by actually trying to use it. He turns back to me. 'We're taking him to a magistrate, sir. But he won't go.'

'That's true enough,' says the old man. 'I won't go.'

'He *is* a magistrate,' I say. 'Or at least, he used to be one. Anyway, you can see that he's English. Why would he wish to burn down his own city?'

'Oh, I'm no Londoner,' the old man says cheerfully. 'It matters very little to me whether this city burns or not. Especially since it is home to fools such as these. But since I have indeed been in the house yonder, I couldn't have started a fire on the other side of the city. I have an alibi. I have done my best to explain this to you, gentlemen. Perhaps, since we have been joined by a lawyer, you'll listen to him.'

'I said to keep quiet,' the man with the sword warns again. 'I won't tell you again.'

The old man nods. That suits him. He would be happy not to be told again.

'He clearly presents no danger to anyone,' I say. 'You can leave him to me. Your time would be better spent in fighting the fire.'

'No point in fighting a fire that springs up again wherever the French throw in another fireball. We don't need any lawyer's help, young sir. We'll deal with this fire-raiser on our own, and if he won't come to the magistrate, then we'll give him London justice here and now at the point of a sword.'

They have not queried how the old gentleman knows I am a lawyer, nor how I know he is a former magistrate. If they asked themselves that, then they might see why I am not leaving without him.

'You misunderstand me,' I say. 'I was not offering legal advice. And, even if you felt in need of it, you wouldn't be able to afford me.'

I think there may have been something in my tone that they did not like. 'I hope you aren't a French sympathiser, young sir,' says the man with the sword. He gives me a crooked smile. 'French sympathisers get the same treatment as Frenchmen, eh lads?' Deciding that I am outnumbered, he starts towards me in a leisurely manner. The old man watches on with no more concern than before. His confidence in me is flattering, but may yet prove unjustified.

I decide that perhaps after all I can offer them a little legal advice *pro bono*. 'Take one more step,' I say, 'and you'll find yourself gutted and trussed like a turkey. Of course, you are entitled to seek a second opinion if you wish.'

The man stops suddenly, a pace or so away, and for a moment they all look at me uncertainly, taking in my black doublet, black breeches, black stockings, black hat and my face. Yes, the moonlight must have caught it, because they look especially at my face. One or two start to back away. That's always good.

'There's only one of him and six of us,' says the man with the sword. He smiles, showing some crooked yellow teeth. Then he yelps like a pig, drops his weapon and clutches his bloody hand.

Lord Arlington, when he is pleased to employ my services, rarely offers me anything other than the agreed fee for the job. On one occasion, however, he kindly blackmailed a fencing master, who had committed some minor treason, into giving me free tuition. It has proved invaluable on several occasions. So many people own swords but have no idea how to use them. 'Strike before they even know they're in a fight' was one of his better pieces of advice. 'Never trust Arlington further than you can see him' was another – though I knew that already.

'What did the lawyer do?' somebody asked.

'He stabbed me before I was properly prepared,' said the man with the bleeding hand. 'A scurvy coward's trick.'

'I apologise unreservedly,' I say. 'But I never gave any undertakings as to my courage or character. Now, do the rest of you think you can do any better than your overly trusting friend? If not, this elderly former magistrate is mine, I think.'

The wounded man clutches his hand, though I fear it may take a great deal more than that to stop the flow of blood from between his fingers. He may have saved a trifle on legal fees but he'll need to pay a surgeon. They're not cheap. 'The old man's yours then,' he says. 'If you want him so much. But next time we'll be ready for you – won't we, boys?' He turns to his friends for confirmation, but they show less enthusiasm than he was hoping for.

'You'd better take your sword,' I say. 'You may need it.'

He swallows hard, then edges forward, crouches and

cautiously reaches out his left hand, never taking his eyes off me for a second. The blade grates on the cobblestones as he draws it slowly towards him, then he is suddenly upright and holding it. Just for a moment he seems to be contemplating striking me, but we both now know how inadvisable that would be. Especially with his left hand. He opens his mouth as if to offer a final threat, glances again at my cheek, then thinks better of that too.

'I hope you'll remember that we did catch the old gentleman first,' says one of his friends. 'If there's any reward—'

'There's no reward,' I say. 'Not for him.'

They back rather than walk away. The man with the cheap sword is leaning heavily on his companion's shoulder now. He is shivering, though it is a warm night. I think they should get him to a surgeon soon. When they have all finally turned the corner, the old man raises his hat to me.

'Well done, John,' he says. 'I would have expected nothing less of you.'

'You might have drawn your own sword, Sir Felix,' I say.

'I was thinking about it. I thought about it very seriously. Then you arrived and it seemed more amusing to find out how you would get rid of them. What on earth have you done to your face? I think it was that that undid them more than your swordsmanship. I wouldn't care to fight a man who looks like you do either.'

'It's a scratch – in the course of duty. It will heal.'

'You should be asking Arlington for more money if that's what happens to you when you work for him – I'm assuming it wasn't inflicted on you by some solicitor in court?'

'No,' I say. 'It wasn't inflicted on me in court. It was at an inn in Devon.'

'Well, I hope they find the man who did that to you.'

'They won't,' I say. 'Not where I left him.'

'I was told that you were still wasting your time working for the Lord Arlington. You have a good legal practice and an excellent clerk to help you run it. You have no need of Arlington's gold. I trust he is at least paying you well.'

'When he has any money, which is not often, he pays me what we have agreed.'

'Then my advice is that you should attend strictly to the law. Unless you want to die in the next dark alleyway my Lord Arlington sends you to grub around in.'

'We all have to die somewhere.'

'We do indeed, and I intend to die in a feather bed with a woman forty years my junior beneath me. How is your mother, by the way?'

'She is well,' I say. 'At least when I last heard. You have not seen her lately?'

'I haven't been to Essex for a while. I've been living in London. With my daughter. As I think you know.'

'Somebody told me – my clerk, I think. I hope that Aminta is well.'

'Ah, the excellent Mr Atkins. Little escapes his notice. If you came to visit us, you would find out how she was for yourself.'

'If you wish, I can escort you back to your lodgings, Sir Felix,' I say. 'These are dangerous streets.'

'That wasn't what I meant,' he says. 'I can make my own way home. I doubt that anyone will choose to attack me, unless I decide to tell them of my connections with the Kingdom of France. And if I do so decide . . . twenty years ago this sword did good service for the late King at Naseby and Marston

Moor. It will do so again. How much did that flashy piece of steel cost you? Twenty Pounds? More than that?'

'A lot more. The money wasn't wasted.'

Sir Felix Clifford looks at my face critically. 'Spending good English money on Spanish steel doesn't seem to have protected you very much so far.'

'It was somebody I trusted,' I say. 'I held my hand until I was certain he'd betrayed me.'

'Indeed? You'd have been safer running him through on a mere suspicion. I fear these nice scruples may yet prove your undoing.'

'Let us hope not,' I say. 'Well, if I cannot assist you further, I must continue my search for a magistrate – an active London one, rather than a former Justice of the Peace from Essex, however distinguished. I discovered a body back there, and he died from a bullet in the back, not from the fire.'

'How careless of him to have escaped one only to succumb to the other. But, as you say, it's a little too far from Essex and about fifteen years too late for it to be worth informing me. I'll be happy to leave it to my younger City colleagues. They'd be more used to that sort of thing anyway. I'll tell Aminta that you lovingly asked after her and sent her your fondest regards. Not, I suspect, that she'll believe me, but it is always worth trying.'

Chapter Three

I watch Sir Felix walk briskly away, with only the briefest of glances towards the house of the French whore, back in the direction of Westminster.

So Aminta still lives where she did before. But that is not information that will be of any practical use to me. I have no reason to pay her a visit. Will is right. I had the chance to propose to her. She was expecting me to propose to her. Our parents were expecting me to propose to her. But I didn't propose to her. I couldn't. Such non-acts have consequences that stretch into the future, and who knows how far?

But if my clerk's daily reminders of my error are not sufficient punishment, fate is always willing to give the knife another twist in the belly. It has now thrown Sir Felix and me together in a way that cannot be brushed aside easily. I have saved him the inconvenience of, and risk of arrest for, running through some ruffians who sought to delay him. That too will have consequences.

Like me, he is not unfamiliar with violent death, and we have both, in our own way, employed our swords in the service of our King. He in battle; I, as Sir Felix kindly reminded me, in less glorious circumstances in the service of Henry Bennet, the newly created Lord Arlington. Sir Felix returned from the Civil War to his home in Essex with no visible scars, though he lost a wife when my father ran off to the Spanish Netherlands with Lady Clifford. Was it when Sir Felix was fighting at Marston Moor or Naseby? One or the other. I can't remember now, though my mother might have better cause to. She has known Sir Felix well – very well indeed – since before I was born. There are many tangled strands that connect Aminta Pole and me. And tonight I have a chance to forget some of them. I have an appointment with a fire.

The smoke is beginning to resemble one of our November fogs, drifting through the streets and lanes. A dry, searing fog that cuts into my lungs and makes my eyes water. The buildings ahead of me are nothing more than shapes – depth and distance no longer apply. Figures emerge from the miasma as if in a dream. They seem to pass silently, their footsteps as light as the pale ash that is constantly falling, but that is because nothing as inconsequential as a footstep could be heard above the roar of this furnace. And yet, on the easternmost horizon, I see the sky lightening. Somewhere outside this nightmare, all across late-summer England, dawn is breaking.

When I finally reach the river, I am greeted by a sight that I have never seen before. In the distance, across the broad Thames, a bloody sun is rising behind the mean, low rooftops of the south bank. But I see it only in patches, as the swirling grey smoke hides, reveals and then hides the scene again. Everything on the north bank, from the Tower to the other side of London Bridge, is in flames, fanned by a prodigious wind; a vast sheet of flame that rises higher than the rooftops, almost as high as the steeples – not individual houses, not single streets, but a whole city under a great arc of fire. The river is full of boats, carrying people's goods to safety. But the streets here are empty. Everyone has fled. Nobody is trying to stop this glowing wall from advancing and devouring parish after historic parish.

Behind me, westwards, the City is still whole but, even as I watch, the fire appears as if from nowhere at the very top of the steeple of a nearby church, licking the brass weathervane. The flame seems curious, as if it is looking speculatively for new streets to burn. For several minutes a bright tongue streams in the wind. Next, smoke starts to emerge through the gaps in the tiles, first as a trickle, then as a vast cloud. Finally the steeple collapses in on itself with a crash that I hear even above the general rumble of the inferno. I think it has been the victim of wind-borne sparks, but it is easy to see why Londoners believe in fire-raisers amongst them when the fire leaps from street to street in this fashion.

I was presumptuous to think that the bells were summoning me in person, and I have spent too much of my time going east when I should have just gone west. I know only one person who can authorise the action that is needed. The King will still be in bed with Lady Castlemaine. The Duke of Albemarle is away fighting the Dutch, with whom we are also at war. That just leaves the aforementioned Henry Bennet, Baron Arlington, Secretary of State for the Southern Department and spymaster to His Majesty. If anyone can charm or blackmail a few people into dealing with the fire, it will be him.

Chapter Four

Arlington has been up and about for some time, it would seem. He is already dressed in a doublet and breeches of wine-coloured silk, with a large lace cravat, newly tied and blindingly white. A fresh black patch has been applied to the bridge of his nose, concealing – so he wishes us to believe – a wound sustained in the King's service some years ago. I wonder what he would say if I applied a similar one to my cheek? He is a man sensible of his own worth and not somebody to be mocked lightly, or at all. He can make or break a career, as he frequently reminds me. Still, a black patch on my cheek might be considered becoming. I shall see tomorrow if I can find anywhere to buy one.

'You're covered in ash,' is his first remark to me.

'It's the fire,' I say. 'There's one in the City.'

'Yes, they woke me up at three this morning to tell me. The bells have been ringing ever since, damn them.'

'Nobody is answering,' I say. 'Nobody is fighting the fire. We'll all be covered in ash soon if the King does not act.'

'It won't jump the City walls,' he says with a sniff. 'No fire

40

has ever done that. And if this one does, it will stop at the Fleet River. It can't reach us here in Westminster.'

'So it won't inconvenience the Palace, you mean? That is your only concern this morning, my Lord?'

'Certainly not, Mr Grey. My main concern is that we seem to be losing a war we should never have got into. I am also anxious to ensure that that puffed-up ass Clarendon is removed from his post of Lord Chancellor as soon as we conveniently can. After that, however, you are correct in assuming that I should like to avoid the Palace burning down. But I am also anxious for the safety of the Tower of London on the far side of the City. Its walls should be strong enough to hold back any fire but, if they don't, then the King's supply of gunpowder will be in great danger, as will anything within a mile of the Tower if it goes off.'

'Some of that powder could be put to good use. It will be faster blowing up houses to create a firebreak than it will be pulling them down. But the King will need to order it. The Lord Mayor will not take action to pull down houses without his authorisation.'

'Bloodworth quite properly fears the financial consequences. Citizens who have lost their houses on his express orders will expect somebody to pay, and Bloodworth doesn't want to. The King, however, simply needs to promise that, in the fullness of time and when appropriate taxes can be raised, assuming of course that no greater priority arises before the money can be spent on the thing it was raised for, an element of compensation will be paid to those whose houses can be indisputably proven to have been pulled down as a safety measure rather than burnt in the normal way. That very clear and unequivocal reassurance on the part of the King will give the Lord Mayor the confidence to destroy any houses in London that may still remain standing.'

'So, you will ask the King to take action?'

'As soon as I decently can. For the moment somebody else has ownership of him. But once he is awake and has returned to his own bed, I shall most certainly call upon His Majesty and inform him of what is happening in his capital city.'

'In the meantime, can you send in soldiers to help fight the fire? The ordinary citizens are fleeing as fast as they can.'

Arlington nods. 'We can send in troops to fight the fire only with the permission of the Lord Mayor. The City is his jurisdiction. The King's men may not enter without his authority. If the fire does go beyond the walls, then that is another matter entirely. The King may order his men to put out fires in the suburbs or anywhere within the county of Middlesex without any damage to tradition or precedent.'

'But soldiers must at least be sent to maintain order. The Mayor can scarcely refuse that. The people of London are blaming the French for this. Nobody who appears in any way foreign is safe. I was obliged to save a gentleman of my acquaintance from a mob – a very small mob admittedly. They thought that he might be French and that that gave them entitlement to hang him.'

'That is a common misconception in London. It is not good law, as you are possibly aware. Anyway, since the King is half-French himself and his mother and sister reside in Paris, I doubt that he would approve. Of course, the French would be perfectly entitled to burn London if they could. Though it is easy to forget, we are now at war with them as well as with the Dutch.'

'Are you suggesting that they have indeed started this?' I ask.

'Of course not,' says Arlington. 'There is no French plot – let us be absolutely clear about that. The French have declared war only as a courtesy to the Hollanders. They have no real intention of wasting their resources attacking us. If we were looking for enemies who might have started the fire, the Dutch are far more likely, since we have recently burnt one of their towns. But they would burn somewhere unimportant like Yarmouth or Lowestoft. If they burnt London, we would be obliged to burn Amsterdam. Both sides would be put to the most ridiculous expense for no gain at all. No, it is simply that we have had the driest summer anyone can remember. There is a strong wind. There is no water from the Thames or the New River. Our enemies, real and nominal, had only to sit back and watch it happen. We English have done this ourselves, unaided, as we so often do.'

'I'd heard there was no water from the New River,' I say. 'I thought it was just a rumour.'

'If it is a rumour it is a very circumstantial one. One of the Directors of the company . . .' Arlington consults a paper beside him, '. . . John Graunt, arrived unannounced, turned the water off and left with the key. Just before the fire started.'

'The one and only key?'

'It seemed more secure that there should be just the one. To avoid unauthorised tampering with the supply. Since that is precisely what has now happened, you might actually commend their foresight in not having another cut.'

'And the sole key has been retrieved?'

'Not when I last heard.'

'Could the door not be broken down?'

'Only on the authority of a clear majority of the Directors, with a casting vote from the chairman if required. The porter would not take it upon himself to damage the door without. Again, a question of financial liability, I think. This is a cautious and prudent city.'

'Who is Graunt?'

'A newly elected Director. And a Catholic.'

'Is his religion of any significance?'

'I certainly hope not. We have reports of attacks on English Catholics as well as Frenchmen. If rumour spread that the Catholics had deliberately cut off the water supply, it would be very unhelpful. Luckily I have no reports yet of anybody being murdered, French or English.'

'Then it is my duty to report the first. I found a body in close to St Paul's.'

'A victim of the same mob you encountered?'

'I don't know who killed him, but there was a man close by who ran off when he saw me. Otherwise all I can tell you is that he was shot in the back. He carried no papers to identify him, though I have this.' I take the dead man's velvet purse from my pocket and open it. I empty the coins onto Lord Arlington's table. Golden Pistoles spill out in a stream.

'French coin,' says Arlington. 'New French coin. Very pretty indeed.'

'Then perhaps he *is* French,' I say. 'But as to whether he was killed by the mob . . . somebody certainly took a serious dislike to him and they didn't want his money.'

'Did you get a good view of the man with the gun – the one who ran away?'

I think about this. 'It was dark,' I say, 'and his face was half-covered with a scarf. I didn't see the gun well either – just that he had something in his hands.'

Arlington nods. 'Where is the body now?'

'Still in the lane a bit to the north of St Paul's, I would imagine.'

'Far from the fire?'

'The fire shouldn't have reached it yet. The wind still blows from the west. But if it changes …'

'I'll send some men to fetch it,' says Arlington. 'When I have somebody to spare.'

'I can take them to it,' I offer.

Arlington shakes his head. 'A body just north of St Paul's? It won't be difficult to find. I'll need you later for more important matters. In the meantime go home and change your suit – or at least get your man to brush the ash off it. Anyone seeing you in pale grey rather than black might suspect you were no longer a Puritan.'

'I've never been a Puritan,' I say.

'Well, at least nobody is blaming the Puritans for starting the fire,' says Arlington. 'Not yet, anyway. You should get home safely, so long as you don't speak French to anyone.'

I am tempted to reply: '*Bien sûr*, milord.' But I doubt Arlington would appreciate the joke. He'd smile if I told him that Lord Clarendon was dying of the smallpox, but otherwise he's not an easy man to amuse. I bow to his Lordship, replace my hat on my head and depart.

Chapter Five

While I have been roaming the streets and rescuing elderly cavaliers, Will has been out and rather more usefully purchased bread and cold meat, which was cleverly done, for most of London's supplies are now on fire and my walk has given me an appetite. Will shakes his head over the state of my clothes, but I assure him that there is little point in cleaning them until the fire is over. Whatever work Arlington has in mind for me will probably involve ash. Or blood. I cannot however prevent Will tutting and brushing his hands over my back and shoulders whenever I stand still long enough.

A knock at my door announces a visitor. I wonder that any citizen has time for legal action when the City is on fire – perhaps it is a landlord prudently considering how he can recoup his fire losses from his fleeing tenants. He has been well advised in consulting me in such a timely fashion.

The door opens and a shiver runs down my spine as a young woman enters. She wears a light cloak, not I think against the early morning cold, but to protect her dress against the smuts that are now falling constantly into the street. A hood covers her hair. She lowers it and shakes her golden locks free. She gives me a half-smile, as if uncertain of her welcome. There is just the trace of grey under her eyes. She looks both tired and ill at ease. I think she would rather not be here.

'My Lady Pole,' I say with great politeness. 'To what do I owe the honour of your visit?'

For a moment she says nothing, then she gives an exasperated snort. 'Oh, for goodness' sake, John! When was I ever "Lady Pole" to you? I've come to thank you. Not to ... I don't know ... to do whatever it is that makes you feel you have to address me as "Lady Pole".'

She's right, of course. She's always right. When we were younger, very much younger, she invented games that involved my having to address her as 'Your Highness' or 'Your Majesty'. And to kiss a ring made out of a daisy and plaited grass. I had to bow to her before I was allowed to speak. But that is in the distant past. I don't think I've ever called her 'Lady Pole' before, even though that's been her name for some time.

'You have nothing to thank me for,' I say.

For some reason this answer displeases her too. She definitely wishes to thank me.

'Only you, John, could save my father's life and then sulk about it,' she says.

'Sulk?'

'Yes, sulk.'

'I'm not sulking,' I say.

'Of course you are. He's sulking, isn't he, Will?'

We both turn to my clerk who, it seems, is to be the arbiter on this question. If Will imagines that his silence is tactful, then I shall shortly inform him how wrong he is.

'I thought you said you had come to thank me,' I say to Aminta. 'Not to consult my clerk on my character.'

'I do apologise, Mr Grey,' she says. 'Thank you for saving my father's life this morning. Sir Felix's French whore and I are eternally indebted to you for preserving our client and father respectively. There, I've said it. You may now carry on sulking if you wish.'

'My point,' I say very carefully, 'was that I didn't need to save his life. He was about to run the ruffians through with his own sword, an act that might have brought him to the attention of his colleagues, the City magistrates. The Earl of Rochester can kill citizens with impunity, but Sir Felix, not being a drinking companion of the King's, would have at least had to show that he killed his assailants in self-defence, which might not have been true after the first two or three. I simply provided some legal advice. No charge. It might be better if you didn't let him roam the streets at night.'

'Do you disapprove of drunken whoring in general or my father's in particular?'

'I was unaware that there was any room for debate on the matter ...'

'I see. You are the same Puritan as ever. Or ... do my eyes deceive me? Is that suit of clothes actually *grey*?'

'It's black,' says Will. 'Or it would be if he would let me brush the ash off.' For some reason Aminta can do no wrong in his eyes, but I think he needs to consider carefully which of us is paying him. Anyway, there's nothing wrong with black.

'Yes, I thought grey would be a little too daring for a Puritan,' says Aminta to Will, 'though heaping ashes upon his head must be all part of a day's work to him.'

She raises an eyebrow. I catch Will's glance and hold it well before his smile is even half-formed.

'Black is a very practical colour, my Lady,' he says stiffly. 'Especially in London, now we have all of this Newcastle sea-coal being burnt. Can I serve you some tea?'

Doubtless Will has heard somewhere that it is now considered genteel to take a morning draught of tea rather than small beer. But he does not need to concern himself with the cost of strange foreign drinks. I do. Small beer is good enough for me.

'Thank you, Will,' she says. 'Tea would be delightful.' She looks around the room as if deciding whether any of my chairs are fit to sit in, and chooses the largest. She spreads her olive-green skirts becomingly, her hand stroking the shining velvet and the gold lace with affection, and looks up at me. I have learned, over a period of some twenty years, not to trust her smiles. Any of them.

'My father says you're still working for Arlington?' she says, looking critically at my scar.

'It's nothing,' I say.

'Oh, don't worry – I think it probably improves your looks,' she says. 'Are you going to amuse me by telling me how it happened?'

She waits for my reply, head on one side, her bright blue eyes focused on my own. She is not going to be content with less than the full story. I sigh. 'My Lord Arlington sent me into the West Country. There are rumours of an uprising there – possibly Catholics, possibly extreme Protestants, but almost certainly aided by the Dutch. Or the French. Or the Spanish. Somebody called The Precious Man – probably not the name he received at his baptism – was to lead them. I needed to ask some questions. A person I thought I could trust took exception to the questions I was asking and, without consulting me, decided to prevent my return to London with the information I had gained.'

'But he did not succeed?'

'No, he did not succeed. He's dead now, so I consider the matter closed.'

'You forbid my father's innocent amusements, but you nevertheless run people through the guts for your own selfish pleasure?'

'For Arlington's selfish pleasure,' I say.

'And the information you gained was useful to Lord Arlington?'

'Not as far as I know.'

'You found The Precious Man?'

'He probably doesn't exist,' I say. 'At least half of what Arlington's agents tell him has been made up so that he will pay them.'

'And do they get paid?'

'Sometimes,' I say. 'The King doesn't give Arlington much money to run his operations.'

She shakes her head sadly. 'Aren't you getting too old to play games for Henry Bennet?'

'I'm not thirty yet.'

'But you have a successful legal practice. One of the busiest in London. As you say, Arlington can scarcely afford to pay his people. I've heard the King allows his department almost nothing – less even than he gives for Pepys's Navy Office. I'm sure that cut still looks worse than it is, John, but another inch and you'd have lost an eye. Then you wouldn't have been able to see both sides of your clients' problems, with a corresponding loss of fees.'

'Tea, my Lady,' Will announces, placing a tray on the table. That was quick anyway. He fusses round Aminta, manipulating something he calls a 'strainer', and allowing a stream of steaming amber to flow into her delicate porcelain cup.

'I assumed that you would prefer small beer, Mr Grey sir,' he says, placing a battered grey pewter tankard at my side.

'Thank you, Will,' I say. 'I would indeed prefer small beer.'

'Can you afford no better?' asks Aminta.

'His practice provides us both with a comfortable income, my Lady,' says Will. 'It is a question of taste rather than expense. Of course, a wife might be able to persuade him otherwise.'

'Then he'll need to ask some lady to marry him,' says Aminta. 'Wives do not come unbidden.'

'Don't you have some work to do, Will?' I ask pointedly.

'No, Mr Grey, sir. The books are up to date. You won't let me brush your suit, so there's nothing for the present. However, I shall withdraw and allow you and Lady Pole to converse.'

I think I would prefer it if Will's concern for my well-being stopped at invoicing my clients and serving my wine. On the other hand, I do not know of anyone with a clerk more efficient than mine. If he says the books are up to date then they are up to date. If he says I need a wife . . .

'You can brush my hat,' I say.

'Thank you, sir,' says Will. 'I should like that very much indeed.'

'So,' says Aminta, as Will departs, holding my filthy head-gear out before him, 'you have had a chance to view this fire.'

'Yes,' I say.

'My father's opinion is that it will burn itself out.'

'It would if there were no wind, or if it would please God

to rain. You will be safe in Westminster, but I think that there'll be a great loss of property if nothing is done to slow its advance in the City. Bloodworth needs to order the blowing up of houses.'

'But he won't?'

'No, until it's agreed who will pay. The word will have to come from the King.'

'And His Majesty has acted with his usual resolve and determination?'

'The King has fallen into unfortunate habits,' I say. 'It would be better if he were less under the thumb of my Lady Castlemaine and spent less time in her bed. He prefers the card table to the Council table, the racecourse to the battlefield.'

'So would I in his place. Therein, however, lies the argument against Will's advice that marriage is a sovereign remedy for all ills. Marriage has changed the King's habits in no way at all, except that he now goes home and breakfasts with his wife rather than staying to take tea with his mistress. But perhaps Will has only commoners in mind. I assume that Arlington has never offered you a title as a cheaper alternative to cash for your services?'

'He offered me a knighthood,' I say.

'That is within his gift?'

'Apparently.'

'And you said . . . ?'

'I said I had no use for one.'

'So, your wife . . . your purely theoretical wife . . . would have to be Mistress Grey? She would have no prospect of ever being Lady Grey?' She takes a sip of tea.

'That is the case.'

'Unless she already had a title of her own, of course. A lady like that would not be inconvenienced by your own lack of ambition.'

'Yes.'

'I merely hypothesise. I obviously know no woman with a title who would wish to marry you.'

'That means neither of us does,' I say.

'How pleasant it is to be able to agree on something, Mr Grey.' She puts her cup back on the table.

If I had any hope that my failure to propose to her (when she had every reason to think that I would) had ceased to matter, then I have been corrected. If I thought that the pain of our subsequent estrangement was any less, then I have been corrected too. In which case, I think this conversation has gone far enough. I have been thanked and do not especially need to be insulted as well. Or not as much as Aminta is capable of insulting me.

'I must return to Arlington,' I say. 'He is recovering a dead body for me. Please give your father my compliments and say that it was an honour to be able to assist him.'

'I shall do that, *Mr* Grey,' she says. 'My family is forever in your debt.'

'It was my pleasure, *Lady* Pole,' I say. 'I am much obliged to you for your kindness and condescension.'

She smiles as if she had just won a game of some sort, which may or may not be the case. Next time I'll have to ask her for the rules in advance.

Chapter Six

'It would have been better,' I say, 'if I had accompanied your men, my Lord. They might then have found the body.'

Arlington glares at me across his nose patch. He doesn't agree.

'They spent as much time on it as was worthwhile,' he says. 'When half the City is in flames, one body is less important than you seem to think. Your description of its location was more than adequate.'

'Are you saying the body had vanished into thin air?'

'The fire has spread westwards towards St Paul's. Streets that were there yesterday are no longer there today. You can scarcely blame me for that, Mr Grey. It may be that when we have extinguished the fire or it has burnt itself out . . .'

He pauses. We both know the fire has shown no sign of wishing to be extinguished. Houses have been pulled down. Gaps have been created. But it was left too late: with growing confidence, the fire has jumped them all. The rumours of fire-raisers continue to run in the City, and Londoners still see the French as a more immediate threat than the flames. The troops sent in by the King, and led by the Duke of York, have spent all their time trying to maintain order. The Duke has conducted himself bravely, but already I have heard it said that he was seen to smile with satisfaction at the sight of London's destruction. Because everyone knows he's a secret Catholic. Whatever he does in the next few days will be wrong.

'I could go even now if you would let me have a couple of men to assist,' I say. 'I do not understand—'

'Mr Grey, my men were as thorough as they needed to be.'

'But consider, my Lord, it was the body of a Frenchman—'

'The body of a man with French gold in his pocket.'

'An Englishman with his pockets stuffed with French gold is scarcely less worrying—' I say.

Arlington holds up his hand. 'Mr Grey, let us leave the rabble to believe in plots if they wish. They know no better. We, I think, are above that sort of thing. The French are at best our reluctant enemies. They seem to have slipped into an alliance with the Dutch purely by oversight. Our informants at Versailles tell us that His Majesty of France is somewhat embarrassed by the position he finds himself in, and is anxious to disentangle himself from his uncouth, Republican Dutch friends as soon as he can. It is unlikely that he would endanger his cousin of England by starting a fire so close to His Majesty's principal Palace. Let me be frank with you, Mr Grey. I blame nobody except Bloodworth for the position we find ourselves in, and even he could not have been expected to know that a small fire in Pudding Lane would grow into this.'

Through the tall, narrow frame we can see the cobbled Palace courtyard below, where ladies-in-waiting take the air in their morning finery, only slightly troubled by the sharp smell of London burning to the ground and the occasional, annoying smut descending from the sky. The fire might be in another country.

'So there are to be no arrests?'

'We have had to arrest a number of men for their own protection. Your offer to accompany my men in search of the body is kind but, rather than hunt for a dead man who happened to have French gold about him, you might like to interview one of the prisoners for me.'

'Interviewing a prisoner? Surely that will wait?'

'I am particularly anxious that it is done now and that you should do it. It would place me greatly in your debt.'

I look at Arlington suspiciously. Obviously he'd rather be in my debt than pay me. But I'm surprised he's ready to admit even that.

'Of course. If I can be of service I shall be delighted to assist you,' I say. 'Who do you want me to interview?'

'The Mr Graunt that I spoke of – the newly appointed Director of the New River Company. As I say, on the night that the fire started, the water supply from the New River Head was inexplicably turned off.'

'It is odd, I agree, but more likely to be incompetence than treason.'

Arlington smiles. I have said something he agrees with. 'That would, of course, be entirely for you to decide. Mr Graunt is, as I have said, a Catholic. Everything he does or thinks is therefore potentially treason . . . or certainly that is the vulgar and popular view. I am pleased, however, to see that you will approach the problem with an open mind – that he is innocent unless proved overwhelmingly and unavoidably guilty. I shall of course not try to influence you in any way.'

Well, at least I'm being left in no doubt what my conclusion should be.

'Where can I find him?' I say.

'He is being held in Clerkenwell, at the New River Company's Water House.'

'I shall go there at once.'

'I could of course pay you ... but, as an English gentleman, you might feel that it would be wrong to charge the King at a time like this.'

'I'm a lawyer. I work only if I'm paid.'

Arlington looks displeased. He was relying on my considering myself a gentleman. 'Very well,' he says. 'The usual rate, though payment may have to be delayed if any of the cost of this fire falls to the Exchequer.'

'It is always an honour and pleasure to serve the King's Most Excellent Majesty,' I say.

Chapter Seven

The Water House in Clerkenwell is a substantial brick building and the residence of the chief officer of the New River Company. Graunt is imprisoned in a high-ceilinged drawing room, with comfortable chairs and a bottle of Canary on the table. He has opened a window, since the air here is fresher and more pleasant than in the City. Not everything in Clerkenwell is ash-grey, and outside there lingers the faint scent of roses. The prospect – the round pond and the lush green trees beyond – is reassuringly rural.

'Yes, I inspected the stopcocks,' says the prisoner, concentrating carefully on pouring himself another glass of the pale yellow wine. 'I'm a new Director and I wished to ensure that I understood my business properly. But I didn't turn them off. Why should I? What would be the point of that?' He finally looks up at me, inviting my agreement.

'You took away the key however,' I say.

If I were not a lawyer I might almost be taken in by the bland smile he gives me in reply.

'I simply forgot to return it to the porter. I hadn't realised there was only one key. An unfortunate arrangement. I shall question it at the next board meeting, I can promise you that, Mr Grey.'

'So, were the stopcocks on or off when you left, Mr Graunt?'

'Off, I assume. I mean, I couldn't really tell, just looking at them. But they were off when the porter broke the door down, so they must have been off when I left. I wasn't to know that there would be a fire. Does anyone say that I did know?'

'No, they haven't. Not yet. But they may. Could anyone else have got into the room before you?'

'Yes, in the same way I did – by getting the key from the porter's lodge. When he isn't there you can just take it off the hook, if you know which key you need and nobody else has it.'

'And does the porter say anyone did that?'

'Not as far as I know. But, forgive me – I am forgetting my manners – can I offer you some of this wine?'

Will's disapproving face flashes before me for an instant. 'Thank you,' I say.

I watch him pour. His hand, quite steady before, now shakes slightly. He pushes the glass in my direction.

'Thank you,' I say again. 'Now, could we please return to what you were doing on the night that the fire began?'

'Of course. I really wish I could tell you more, Mr Grey, but the facts are very much as I've already related. I obtained the keys, opened up, inspected the stopcocks, locked the door again and departed. By oversight, I took the key with me. *Mea culpa*, Mr Grey. *Mea maxima culpa.*'

'You went home?'

'No, I went to an inn close by – or reasonably close by – where I remained until some time after midnight. Later, I cannot recall when, I went home. I remember seeing a glow in the distance and wondering what it was. Does that help establish when it might have been? No? Well, when I did get home, I was told that a man had called enquiring about the key, which I discovered that I still had in my pocket. I returned here as quickly as I could. They had – as was proper – already broken down the door; but any delay in doing so is scarcely my fault since I wasn't there. Later I was told that I was under arrest, which did not seem altogether necessary, as I explained at the time. If it is no trouble for you, then the sooner we can deal with this matter the better.'

'I'm sorry it has been necessary to detain you.'

'It is no great inconvenience, I suppose. As you can see, the hardships of prison are much exaggerated.'

'And you are a Catholic, Mr Graunt?' I ask.

His smile is a little more strained than it was before. He swallows hard.

'I am proud to say I am. It is not illegal. There is no requirement for Directors here to be Protestants.'

'It is at the moment quite dangerous to be a Catholic.'

'It seems perfectly safe here.'

I stand, my glass of wine still untouched on the table.

'For the moment,' I say.

I again take a roundabout route back to Westminster, travelling southeast to the Tower. Arlington will be more than happy that I have uncovered nothing in Clerkenwell that he cannot cover up if he wishes. If I can view the fire, I may also report to him how things fare in the City. It proves, however, impossible to enter through Aldgate as I had planned. The road is blocked with carts, some (full) trying to leave London while others (empty) try to enter and profit from the rapidly increasing prices for transporting goods. The good citizens curse each other thoroughly, but no malison they might lay on each other could exceed the reality of what has already happened to them. Beyond the walls, inside the City, the fire continues to grow. The noise of destruction is now almost deafening. It is as if a thousand carts with iron-shod wheels are rattling across the cobbles. I follow the ancient City wall along Houndsditch. Even the ivy covering it is baking and shrivelling in the heat. Eventually, having traced the outer arc of the City's defences, I find myself in Moor Fields.

Here is desolation of another kind. The large open space has started to fill with shelters made out of bleached sailcloth and old bedsheets and planks and packing cases of every sort. Already the shelters are taking on the ashen colour of the rest of London. Families driven from their homes and with nowhere else to go have got this far and sunk wearily to the ground. From there they stare back in bewilderment at the destruction of everything they have ever known. People who have come home safe from the Civil Wars and survived the Plague now know without the shadow of a doubt that they are ruined. They are too exhausted even to weep at their misfortune. They can only wonder at how cruelly their future has been snatched from them. They look upwards at the smoke swirling high above them and clutch to their chests the few items that they have been able to save. Somebody must be to blame. Soon they will decide who it is. A foreign Papist would fit the bill nicely.

On my return to Westminster, there is no Arlington to report to. Joseph Williamson, Arlington's right-hand man, is there, however. He's an old friend. I tell him what little I have found out.

'My Lord is in consultation with the King,' he says, 'but I am about to speak to the man who ought to know more than anyone about the origin of the fire. Perhaps you would like to accompany me?'

Thomas Farynor is not a happy man. His house has, after all, just burnt down. That he has the distinction of owning the very first house to burn is, it seems, little consolation to him.

He rises reluctantly from his seat as we enter the room. Like Graunt's, his temporary prison is not wholly uncomfortable – a small, windowless, oak-panelled anteroom in the Palace, furnished with several chairs. But he is exhausted and Arlington has not thought to provide him with Canary, as the New River Company Directors have for Graunt. He still wears the clothes he escaped from his house in – a nightshirt tucked untidily into a pair of breeches, and bare feet in his much-mended shoes. Those may now be his only possessions.

'You may sit, Mr Farynor,' says Williamson. 'You're amongst friends here.' There is slightly more trace of his Cumberland accent than usual. He is, in this way, telling Farynor that he is a straightforward, plain-dealing sort of man; the sort of man that Farynor can be entirely open with. Farynor would do well to be cautious.

'It wasn't my fault, Mr Williamson,' says Farynor, getting straight to the point.

'We haven't said it was, Mr Farynor,' says Williamson.

'What am I doing here then?' Farynor has the air of a hunted beast, uncertain whether to flee or to charge, head down, at his tormentors.

'London is being reduced to ashes,' Williamson explains patiently. 'I imagine you know that. The fire started at your bakery in Pudding Lane. Both Mayor Bloodworth and your neighbours testify to that. There is no doubt. There is no point in trying to convince us otherwise. It is an established fact. Now, there are those who say that it is the work of the French or the Dutch and that their agents continue to start new fires as we put out the old ones. To fight such a fire, constantly renewed by malicious hands, is not easy. We need to know what we are dealing with, Mr Farynor. Is it one fire that started in Pudding Lane, or is it many, started all over the City? If you were to tell us that the fire was a result of an accident in your shop, then it would be a great relief to a lot of people. We could stop looking for conspirators. We could fight the fire we see, not the fire we imagine. I would try to ensure that you suffered no ill consequences for being truthful. Accidents happen.'

Williamson smiles at Farynor in a friendly way. Farynor returns the smile for a moment, then his expression changes. He is a hunted beast again.

'It was the French,' he says.

'The French set fire to your shop?' asks Williamson with friendly curiosity. 'The whole French nation?'

'Some of them.'

'You know that for fact, Mr Farynor?'

'A man who was watching – he told me he had seen a Frenchman start it.'

'He could tell he was French just by looking at him?'

'Yes.'

'And where can we find this helpful witness?'

'I don't know. He left – while I was trying to fight the fire.'

'How very inconvenient for you, Mr Farynor.'

'It's true.'

'I haven't yet said you are lying. Save your indignation for when I do.'

Farynor scowls at Williamson. 'I'm the King's baker,' he says defiantly. 'His Majesty will vouch for the quality of my work. And he will protect me from false accusations.'

'I am aware that you have sold hardtack to the Navy Victualling Office for use on His Majesty's ships. I am not aware that the King knows you personally or enjoys hardtack himself. If you started the fire, it is unlikely that the King will try to prove you did not. You are not important enough for the King to lie about you. You are scarcely important enough for him to tell the truth about you. For more reasons than I can list now, you would be unwise to count on the King's personal intervention on your behalf. None of that is, however, important. As I say, accidents happen in bakers' shops, Mr Farynor. It is not uncommon. You have much need of your oven and it doubtless requires a great deal of kindling and faggots to keep it running. You are, I am sure, very careful – but you cannot be expected to watch your family and your servants all the time. Perhaps one of them was less careful than you and overlooked the embers still glowing in the oven . . . perhaps they left a pile of kindling nearby . . . perhaps there was an unfortunate spark from the one to the other?'

'I would do no such thing, sir, nor would my servants. I know my responsibilities towards my neighbours. I am a liveryman of the Worshipful Company of Bakers – a skilled master baker. I would never do such a thing. Never.'

'Not intentionally,' says Williamson soothingly. 'I am not accusing you of burning down a great city for your own amusement. I am merely suggesting to you that it is *possible* that the fire began because of the carelessness of one of your apprentices . . .'

'I have no apprentices. There's just me and my daughter and my manservant and my maid. Look, I closed my shop at eight o'clock on Saturday night. The oven was stone cold. I checked it carefully, then filled it with faggots ready for the morning.'

'Do bakers' ovens ever really get stone-cold?' asks Williamson. Farynor narrows his eyes. 'Mine does.'

'Does it? And the fire in your own kitchen? How was that?'

'Long since gone out. There were a few embers, but I raked them up. And the floor in that room is brick, so even if there'd been a spark or two, it would have made no difference. My daughter Hanna checked the whole house at midnight – when she needed a candle she couldn't find a trace of a flame anywhere in the house to light it with, and that's the honest truth.'

Williamson is aware of only one sort of truth and is suspicious of those who distinguish between the honest and other forms of it. But he nods in a friendly way. 'And then?' he asks.

'And then, about an hour later, my man woke me up to say that the ground floor was full of smoke. I'd been sound asleep, you see – he had to shake me several times. I went down and you couldn't breathe in my sitting room – horrid black smoke – so we went back upstairs quickly and yelled out of the window for help.'

'But none came?'

'None at all. Drunk or asleep or both, everyone out there. So we crawled out of my chamber window and along the eaves of the house and into the chamber of my neighbour. All except my maid, who was afraid to come with us.'

'And who we must assume perished.'

'Unless she escaped some other way.'

'Let us hope that she did, though I am not sure what way you think that might be if the sitting room was on fire.'

'I haven't seen her, so I don't know.'

'Of course not. You don't know. And what happened next, Mr Farynor?'

'London burnt down. But *I* didn't start the fire. You can't blame me. The witness said *he saw a Frenchman starting the fire* and that is what must have happened, because nobody . . . nobody at all . . . could have taken greater care than I did.'

'Indeed,' says Williamson. 'Your diligence is noted and will be reported to the King. You are a marvel amongst bakers.'

'Is that all?' asks Farynor suspiciously.

'For the moment,' says Williamson.

'So,' says Williamson, once Farynor has been released, 'that seems very straightforward. The difficulty with which his man raised him suggests that Mr Farynor may have had more ale than was good for him before he went to bed. But, drunk or sober, I do not doubt that he failed to rake out his oven properly, and that there were glowing embers somewhere in it when he loaded it with faggots. The faggots caught fire, the oven door was open, there was kindling piled close by . . .'

'But he fears that there may be a cost in admitting that,' I say.

'Let us be fair,' say Williamson. 'If he was as drunk as I think he may have been, then he may not remember that or anything else. In the absence of facts, he is merely giving himself the benefit of the doubt, to which we are all entitled. The anonymous witness who spotted the French fire-raiser is a nice touch on Farynor's part because so many people do believe in them. Had Farynor provided the slightest proof that it was the work of our enemies, then I would have so advised the King and we would have taken action accordingly and sought to arrest every Frenchman and Dutchman in London. But it is simple incompetence and laziness that we are fighting against – Farynor's and his neighbours' and Bloodworth's. As you may know, the King has already given instructions that houses may be blown up to create firebreaks. That will rectify matters somewhat. We can save the Tower and the Palace and most of the suburbs. It's a pity about the rest of London, but it is a large city and we must be content with whatever God has chosen to leave us.'

Over the next few days I am kept busy by Arlington and Williamson. The King makes a public proclamation that the fire is not the work of our enemies. So certain are we that the destruction of the City is an unfortunate accident that my next visit to Arlington's office delivers something of a surprise.

'We have apparently caught the man who started it all,' says Arlington. 'I'd like you to talk to him.'

'Farynor?' I ask. 'I've already interviewed him with Mr Williamson. He denies it.'

'No, not Farynor. A Frenchman,' says Arlington. 'His name is Robert Hubert. He is a watchmaker. He was arrested yesterday heading for Harwich. The authorities at Romford, rightly equating foreignness and guilt, stopped him and sent him back to us under guard.'

'And he denies it too, I assume?'

'No, quite the reverse. He's admitted everything. Conspiring with our enemies. Setting fire to the City. Oh, and murdering one of his co-conspirators. I think you'll find him more than obliging.'

Chapter Eight

Hubert is being held in a gaol just across the river in Southwark. Now that the fire has died down, it is easier to find a waterman to row me across. For the past four days, citizens have been fleeing the fire and every boat was laden with their goods. Now the river is almost deserted.

As we skim across the Thames, a melancholy sight greets our eyes. All along the north bank of the river, from the Temple almost as far as the Tower, are jagged, sooty ruins, from which plumes of smoke still rise lazily into the blue sky. Here and there I can see brilliant flashes of red, where the embers smoulder on or small fires continue to burn harmlessly in cellars. Apart from the flames and the deep blue of the sky, London is a city with no colour at all. This is a strange landscape of stones piled randomly on stones, such as I have seen in the mountainous regions of the north that Williamson comes from but never here in the soft, green south. It is not the heaps of smoking rubble, however, that strike you so much as the absence of the buildings that, less than a week ago, gave this view its whole shape and purpose. The solid stumps of the church towers remain, a lonely memorial to each ruined parish. Of the houses in between, only the blackened brick chimneys have survived; devoid of any possible purpose, they stand proud above the chaos.

I am distracted by the scene but my waterman is constantly watching the way ahead. 'Bloody crap everywhere,' he says, as he skilfully manoeuvres round a large beam floating in front of us, almost invisibly, just below the ashy surface of the water. 'Part of one of the wharves, that one, I'd think. It all washes up and down with the tide – drifts halfway to Putney as the tide comes in – back again, not that we want it, as the tide goes out. Heaps of stuff piled up against the bridge, because a lot of it just won't squeeze through the arches. Timber, furniture, virginals. It will all go eventually – that sort of thing does. But you don't want to hit it and put a hole in your boat in the meantime. Now, just look at that object over there – it's been bobbing up and down for days – it must be a fire engine. See that shiny brass handle sticking out of the water? Lord knows how that got there.'

'The empty reservoir is keeping it afloat,' I say. 'I'm surprised nobody's tried to drag it ashore and salvage the metal.'

'There are easier pickings in the City. Why go to that effort when you can go into a half-burnt house and pocket whatever you find?'

'True,' I say.

'I don't go out on the water after dark now. Too difficult to see it all. Too easy to find yourself overturned and in the Thames with the tide running fast. You'd need to be a strong swimmer to stand any chance at all. It's the last thing you'd want, sir. Watch your arm, sir, we're just coming into the steps. That will be sixpence, and cheap at the price.'

I pay the waterman a Shilling and set off, up the stone stairs, towards unburnt Southwark and White Lion Gaol.

Robert Hubert has been less well accommodated than the previous two suspects that I have visited. His cell is dry but admits little sunlight, even at this hour. The arched stone ceiling is low. On the walls are the marks made by former prisoners, counting the long days until it no longer mattered to anybody. The place seems designed to induce gloom in all who visit it. It is, however, furnished with a bed, a table and two chairs. Arlington has been known to omit several of these things if he does not wish the prisoner to feel at home.

Hubert is a little over medium height, thin and sallow. His nose is large. His dark hair is lank and unwashed. His clothes are dirty. He looks like what he is: that is to say, somebody who has been in a fire then spent two or three days on the road, trying desperately to return to France. That may well be all it takes for a London jury to convict him. He could get away with the dirt, but being French is a bad miscalculation on his part.

'I do not need you,' he says in good but heavily accented English. 'They questioned me in Romford. I have told them everything. I have nothing left to say.'

'Lord Arlington wishes me to ask you some further questions,' I say, sitting down at the other side of the table.

'Different ones?'

'Perhaps. I don't know what you were asked by the Romford magistrate,' I say.

'He took notes. You must read his notes. I told him. I set the City ablaze and I have killed Monsieur Peidloe. That is all. You cannot make me say otherwise, whatever you do.'

'Why should I wish to persuade you otherwise?'

He shrugs. It's obvious that's the sort of person I am. 'I am guilty,' he says.

I regard Hubert with some curiosity. I have examined suspects who claimed to be innocent. I have examined suspects who were prepared to tell me what I wanted to know in exchange for money. I have examined suspects who talked to us only under extreme duress to save their remaining fingers. This is very different from all of these. Here is a man who wishes to assure me of his absolute fitness for the gallows.

'Why is your face like it is?' Hubert enquires.

'I was in a fight,' I say.

'You will not find a wife with a face like that.'

He starts to hum a tune that I do not recognise. French, probably. Without knowing the words, it's difficult to be sure. I take from my bag my notebook, quill and inkhorn. I set them out on the table.

'Tell me first when you came to England,' I say. 'You speak English well enough.'

Hubert ceases to hum in mid-bar. 'I thought you wanted to know about the fire. I came to England before the fire. I did not burn any cities in France.'

'Tell me about it anyway.'

He yawns and looks around the room. There is not much to see. Eventually he turns back to me. 'Very well. I did not explain this to the magistrate so I shall say it to you. I came to England three years ago. My father is a watchmaker in Rouen. He is well respected, though I do not know why. I learned to make watches from him. But we do not get on well. He says he finds me odd. I say, very well then, if I am odd, I shall go to London. He says, yes, that is what you should do. So, I go.

In London I find a workshop and I mend watches. You are writing all of this?'

'Yes,' I say, dipping my quill into the inkpot. 'I am writing.'

'Do *you* find me odd?' he asks.

'No,' I say, looking up from my notes. 'No odder than most people I have to interview in places like this.'

'I think you do,' he says. 'I can tell from how you look at me. You think I am strange. It is always better to tell the truth.'

'Sometimes,' I say. 'It depends what the truth is. And you remained in London after you had set up your shop here?'

He frowns and doesn't reply for a long time. 'No,' he says. 'I travelled to Paris and met Monsieur Peidloe. He is a Catholic. He asked me to burn London down.'

'To burn London down? Just that?'

'Yes, it is clear enough. I think you understand me.'

'Perhaps. When did you go to Paris?'

Hubert pauses again. Perhaps he can't remember if he told them in Romford. He hums another couple of bars – I think it may be a different tune this time. He taps his finger on the table in time to neither. 'I do not recall,' he says eventually. 'But that is what he asked me to do.'

'You don't know when? Very well. I have noted that. And you said to him . . .'

'I said I should be pleased to help him if I could.'

'Why?'

Hubert smiles. That is a question he is happy with.

'He offered me gold. Twelve Pistoles.'

I do a quick calculation. 'That would be about ten Pounds of our money?'

'Yes, I think so.'

'And he paid you?'

'Not yet. But he is dead now, so I think perhaps he won't. He had the money with him, but he would not pay me, even though the City was clearly burning.'

'Is that why you killed him?' I ask. 'Because he didn't pay you?'

Hubert is silent for a minute or so. 'I do not know,' he says eventually. 'Maybe it was because he no longer interested me.'

'I don't understand.'

'Do you not? Sometimes it is like that with a watch. It cannot be mended. There is nothing to be done with it. You throw it away.'

I also make a note of these words, though I think I already have enough for any jury to convict him. A confession is a confession, when all's said and done.

'Why were you willing to work for him for so little?'

He shrugs. 'I promised him that I would. It was a promise. Promises must be kept. Especially if you swear to do it. You do as you promise, then you are safe.'

'Safe?' I check this word with him.

He nods with great certainty. 'Yes, safe. If you do as you promise you are safe. The Lord will protect me.'

'The Lord?'

'Yes, the Lord.'

He seems confident in his religion.

'You did not set fire to the City because you are a Catholic?' I ask.

'A Catholic? Monsieur Peidloe is a Catholic. I am a Protestant. A Huguenot. I have never been a Catholic. A Catholic killed my great-grandfather in 1572. That is why my family fled to Rouen. We Huguenots have not forgotten 1572.'

'The magistrate at Romford thought that you were a Catholic.'

'He is wrong. He should have asked me. I would have willingly told him about my great-grandfather if he was interested. Would he have let me travel on if I had told him that?'

'Not if you also said you were a murderer. So, you and Monsieur Peidloe came over from Paris together?'

'Yes. We came over from Paris. But I told the magistrate this.'

'Still, I need to know. When was this?'

Again a frown, as if remembering is not easy. 'About a week ago. On a ship from Sweden.'

'Sweden? Why did you go there?'

'Monsieur Peidloe had business in Sweden.'

'What sort of business?'

'I did not ask. It did not concern me.'

'What was the name of the ship you travelled on?'

Another pause for thought. 'The *Skipper*,' he says at last.

I realise I have made no notes for some time. I dip my pen in the ink again and write 'Sweden' and 'Skipper'. Hubert waits patiently, like a tethered horse, gazing at nothing in particular.

'So, it was just the two of you who were to burn down the City?'

'No, there were twenty-three of us.'

'Twenty-three?' I scribble down this very exact number. 'What are their names?'

'I do not know. They did not travel with us.'

'How do you know about them?'

'Monsieur Peidloe told me.'

'You did not mention these people to the magistrate in Romford.'

'He did not ask me about them. I thought he wasn't interested.'

My pen scratches briefly on the paper. Twenty-three conspirators. All names unknown.

'Tell me how you started the fire,' I say.

'I have told the magistrate already. I set the City ablaze.'

'Please tell me. I really don't know what you said in Romford.'

This time he is silent for so long that I think he will never speak to me again, but then he begins very quickly.

'After we arrived in London, Monsieur Peidloe obtained some fireballs. He took one himself and gave one to me and we set out into the City. Monsieur Peidloe also gave me a long pole and said that I should light the fireball and put it in through a window. I lit the ball and used the pole to drop it in the house. Then he did the same with his fireball.'

'Where was this?'

'The baker's shop in Pudding Lane.'

'Did you set fire to other buildings?'

'No, just that one I think.'

'Hoping that would be enough, by some lucky chance, to burn down the whole City?'

'Yes.'

'Didn't you think that unlikely? Didn't you expect the fire would be put out by the baker before it had taken hold? After all, once he smelt the smoke and had awakened, he would douse the fire straight away.'

'I don't know. I told you: I have never burnt down a city before. How could I tell how it is usually done?'

'Had Mr Peidloe burnt down a city before?'

'Of course. Many.'

'Which ones?'

'He did not say.'

'What happened next?'

Hubert frowns again. 'Monsieur Peidloe said that we must now go and set light to the King's Palace. So we went through London. But on the way . . . I killed him. Hard by St Paul's.'

'How did you kill him?'

'I shot him. Hard by St Paul's.'

I write down the location, since that seems important to him.

'St Paul's. I see. And after that?'

'I went back to my shop very quickly. It was not far. I decided I would return to Rouen, because maybe my father would no longer consider me odd, or maybe he would be dead. Either would be good. But when I got to Romford they arrested me and so I am in London again. I do not mind. I do not like Rouen.'

I wonder how much of this nonsense to record. Still, Arlington is paying for this and likes value for money. My pen scratches on the paper for some time. Hubert hums to himself, though I wish he wouldn't.

'Thank you,' I say eventually.

'Is that all?'

'It is enough for now,' I say.

'Can I go then? I have told the truth. I think I should like to go to Paris.'

'Well, you can't yet. But perhaps you shall very soon,' I say.

I find Arlington closeted with a gentleman I have not met before, but whom I think I recognise, having seen him from a distance, talking to the King or to the Duke of York. He is a slight man with a pale, thin face. He has a small well-trimmed moustache. A simple white cloth cravat sits, loosely tied, above a dark grey woollen suit. His face is pinched, I think with pain. Though not old, he leans heavily on his ebony stick. He is, as Lord Arlington is about to confirm, the Chancellor of the Exchequer.

'Lord Ashley, this is Mr Grey,' Arlington says as I enter the room. Arlington is already cross and I have not yet had much time to annoy him. I think he does not like Lord Ashley, though they work together for the King. 'Grey has been interviewing Hubert,' he continues, 'and can doubtless give us his views on whether we may release him or not. Mr Grey, Lord Ashley has also been interviewing witnesses at the request of His Majesty. He and Lord Hollis were stationed at Newgate during the fire and a number of suspects were brought to them and interrogated.'

'Catholics mainly,' says Lord Ashley. He smiles at me apologetically, then he grimaces as if he suffers. I think he is not entirely well.

Arlington, if he notices it at all, decides Lord Ashley's discomfort is not relevant to our discussion. 'The Chancellor is very much of your persuasion, Mr Grey,' he says lightly. 'He is a Puritan and hence he sees Catholic plots everywhere.'

'I must protest at that slander,' says Lord Ashley, slowly straightening his back and turning to me again. 'I merely followed my instructions from His Majesty. I am no Puritan, Mr Grey, and I see no more plots than I absolutely need to.'

'Then, my Lord, you are most certainly of my persuasion,' I say.

Indeed. To the extent that I know Lord Ashley, I am happy to be associated with him in any way. It was Ashley who persuaded the King, at his accession, that only the most extreme Republicans – those who had had a hand in the beheading of the King's father – were beyond forgiveness and should be executed. Many of Cromwell's former adherents should be grateful to him that they still possess their heads. He has tried to lessen the harshness of laws against Dissenters, though with less success. Younger than Arlington's arch-enemy, the Earl of Clarendon, but older than the young bucks with whom the King drinks, Ashley is the voice of reason at the Privy Council table. I am honoured to have met him, though it may be as well not to say that in Arlington's presence. Not if I wish to be employed by Arlington again.

'Your friend Arlington really has no idea what a Puritan is,' Lord Ashley says to me. 'If he'd been taught by Puritans as much as I was when I was at school and at Lincoln's Inn, he'd have a better idea of what they look like. I am happy to confirm, Mr Grey, that I see only the merest touch of the Puritan in you. And, since we can learn from all religions, I commend a little of the Puritan in any man.'

'Thank you,' I say.

'It's very pretty to see you two Puritans agreeing so well,' snaps Arlington, 'but we have work to do. Tell us, Mr Grey, what do you make of our Catholic friend Hubert?'

'First,' I say, 'he is no Catholic – he claims to be a Huguenot. He actually dislikes Catholics – one of his family was apparently killed during the St Bartholomew's Day Massacre in 1572. Second, I have no doubt whatsoever he is mad. If you listen to a few sentences, then you might believe him to be as sane as you or I. But listen to a few more and you start to have doubts. He has, he says, agreed to burn down London – and risk hanging if caught – all for twelve Pistoles or about ten English Pounds. He has, or had, twenty-three co-conspirators whom he never met and about whom he showed no curiosity. He went to Paris but doesn't know when. He went to Sweden but doesn't know why. And he has killed the man who recruited him for reasons that he cannot remember.'

'What do you think, my Lord?' says Arlington to his companion.

Ashley closes his eyes and considers for some time. 'Did he name the man he says he killed?' he asks.

'A Monsieur Peidloe, according to Hubert. He apparently had the twelve Pistoles about his person but would not hand them over.'

'And this Peidloe is the leader of the plot? Or did he report to somebody else?'

'Nobody that Hubert mentioned. He said it was Peidloe who gave him instructions.'

'Good.' Ashley nods, apparently content with this. 'But you seem to doubt he's told the truth. Maybe you're right that he's mad. Or maybe he's just being clever?'

'If he was clever he wouldn't have admitted to a murder we didn't know about.'

Ashley nods again. 'Well,' he says, 'if Hubert really murdered anyone on the first night of the fire, the body should have been discovered by now.'

'Of course, I found a body near St Paul's . . .' I begin. But perhaps that story will not reflect too well on my employer.

'You found a body?' says Lord Ashley with sudden interest. 'And did you identify whose body it was?'

Arlington does not look happy. He's been afraid the subject might arise. And he thinks he may not come out of this well. 'Mr Grey found a body in the City as he says. We have since recovered the remains of some poor person from roughly the location he described, on the edge of the burnt area, and brought it back here for examination. The ashes had finally cooled enough to send some men in. What we found was scorched and dried out. It might have been a man or a woman. There's nothing to suggest that it's Peidloe, if that's what you're thinking.'

'Really? And did he or she have twelve Pistoles about their person?' asks Ashley. 'I am merely curious. It would be a strange coincidence if they did.'

Arlington again looks at me to see if I plan further disloyalty to him. I have no strong feelings either way. Does he wish me to deny the existence of the money I gave him? It would probably be safer to do so.

'I didn't count the coins,' Arlington interrupts, before I can speak, perhaps not trusting me to lie properly.

'But there were some?' asks Lord Ashley.

'Yes. Some,' says Arlington. 'Everyone carries some money, my Lord.'

'Was it French money by any chance?'

'It may have been.'

'Do you still have it?' asks Lord Ashley.

'Of course,' Arlington says. 'What would you expect me to do with it, sir? Give it to the poor?'

He goes to a drawer and comes back with the blue velvet purse. He spills out a golden stream onto the table. It does not take too long to count with Lord Ashley's thin fingers.

'Eleven Pistoles,' says Ashley.

'One short then, my Lord,' says Arlington, with a note of triumph.

'Close enough though,' says Ashley. 'Might we be permitted to see the body?'

Time for me to intervene, I think.

'I doubt that we would learn much from it, my Lord,' I say.

'You are too modest,' says Lord Ashley. He turns to Arlington. 'I've heard that your Mr Grey is skilled in discovering how a man has died. I'd be curious to see him at work. I'm sure he will find some way of amusing us.'

Arlington scowls at me again. He wishes me to know that whatever comes of this is entirely my fault. 'Follow me,' he says to Lord Ashley. 'It's in the cellar.'

Chapter Nine

Arlington was right. The corpse before us, lit by the torches held in iron wall sconces, could have been anyone – man or woman. Lord Ashley too is right. It is not entirely without interest, and I may be able to tell at least if it is indeed the person I found. The body is scorched, blackened, desiccated. It gives off no odour other than that of the fire. The eyes, the lips, the ears – all of these have vanished, along with (if it is the same man) the doublet, breeches and yellow stockings that I saw. The corpse bares its white teeth at us defiantly. The arms are held up in front, fists clenched, as if to defend himself, or herself, from a blow. The knees are bent, as if ready for action. Fire does that to a corpse.

'So, what if anything can we learn from this, Mr Grey?' asks Arlington with a note of sarcasm. 'Lord Ashley would like you to entertain him, though reading this puzzle will I think be beyond even you.'

I take a deep breath. With my expertise thus challenged, I must put on a good show for the two gentlemen.

'What we can learn mainly, my Lord, is that bodies should

be collected promptly, before vital evidence is lost,' I reply.

'Bravely said, Mr Grey,' says Lord Ashley. 'But that is very true, is it not, Lord Arlington?'

'If Mr Grey tells us so,' Arlington mutters behind his teeth. 'But I suspect that is all this corpse will reveal.'

I nod. Nevertheless I do examine the body more closely. The skin is like hard, brittle leather. I think, however, that I can still make out where a pistol ball left the body. I doubt if many men were shot that night by St Paul's. I mention this in passing. Lord Ashley seems more pleased than Lord Arlington.

'So, this would in fact appear to be the man you found?' asks Ashley. 'If the wounds made by the entry and exit of the ball are still clear.'

Arlington coughs. Perhaps the greasy smoke from the torches bothers him.

'I could of course be mistaken,' I say.

Then I see something more interesting. Something far more conclusive. Very carefully I prise open one of the clenched fists. Within the cracked bones and carbonised skin rests a single gold coin, still shining brightly in the torchlight, unblemished by the fire. The light down here is not good, but I think this is a Pistole.

'I make that twelve, then,' says Lord Ashley. He smiles at Arlington.

'Well,' I say, 'that coin, the brother of the rest, would certainly seem to confirm that this is the person I found.'

'Thank you, Mr Grey,' says Lord Ashley. 'So, Peidloe was supposed to be giving Hubert twelve Pistoles and we have discovered that this man had precisely that number. Hubert says he killed a man, and this person is undoubtedly dead – unless you would like to argue otherwise, my Lord?'

Arlington flashes a look of annoyance in Ashley's direction.

'Mr Grey saw the killer,' says Arlington. 'I think he will be able to confirm that he did not resemble Hubert in any way.'

'Really?' says Ashley, with some interest. 'You saw him clearly?'

'I saw a man standing by the body,' I say. 'But only briefly and in the dark. All I can say is that I think Hubert is taller than the man I saw. And Hubert showed no sign of recognising me when I visited him. He might have remembered the scar on my face, if nothing else.'

Ashley makes no comment but Arlington smiles. 'In short, Mr Grey saw somebody else entirely,' he says. 'And Hubert didn't mention shooting a man in the back, did he? It was an obvious thing to have confessed to, when you think about it.'

They both look at me. There is an unmistakable tension in the room. Although these two great men are allies some of the time, for the rest of the time they are rivals for the King's attention and his favour. Arlington wishes to close the matter quietly, just as the King does. Lord Ashley's lively mind would prefer to keep his options open.

'No,' I say. 'He said nothing about shooting Peidloe in the back. We can't be sure that he is Peidloe and there is certainly no proof that Hubert killed him.'

'You think so? In spite of the coin in his hand?' asks Lord Ashley.

Not really. I rather think the twelve Pistoles change everything. The sum is too exact, the coincidence is too great. I'm just not sure why Arlington doesn't think that too.

'Of course that's what Grey thinks,' says Arlington. 'That's what he just told you.' His look defies any contradiction, especially from one of his own agents.

'So, no French plot then, Mr Grey?' asks Lord Ashley. I sense his disappointment in me. I'm rather disappointed in myself.

'I'm sorry, Lord Ashley,' I say. 'There is no firm evidence to support one. This corpse could be anybody at all.'

Arlington nods in approval. I am lying blatantly for his benefit. That's more like it. 'I think we might return to my office?' he says.

Lord Ashley ignores that suggestion. 'It would certainly be convenient for the King if that were the case, my Lord,' he says, shifting his weight on his stick. 'I believe that His Majesty has already denied any possibility of a plot – Catholic or foreign – that might conceivably involve his brother, the Duke of York. I can see why it would be awkward for you and certain other ministers of the Crown if the charred remains in front of us proved to be the same Peidloe that Hubert admits to murdering. So, how fortunate you are to be blessed with an agent who supports your contention. Otherwise I might think I was right and you were wrong.'

'The Duke of York is not a Catholic,' says Arlington.

'I didn't say he was.'

'You implied it.'

'Very well, I implied it,' says Lord Ashley. 'He isn't a Catholic yet – not publicly. But we both know he wishes to declare himself one as soon as he conveniently can. Or should I not say that in front of Mr Grey? He seems like a man who can be trusted with secrets.'

'Of course he is a man who can be trusted with secrets,' says Arlington. 'That's why I employ him. That's why I sent him to interview Hubert. If we can't trust Grey, we can't trust anyone.'

Lord Ashley turns his thin, pale face to me and nods. I think he is in more pain than he wishes to admit to Arlington.

'Then let Grey and me interview Hubert again. Let us question him on his purported killing of Peidloe. We know a lot more now than we did when Grey questioned Hubert earlier. It should be relatively easy to catch him out if he is lying. But if Hubert can, with a little prompting, be persuaded to describe exactly how and why he killed Peidloe, then perhaps he is telling the truth after all.'

Arlington looks startled. He had not expected this sudden burst of energy from this slight, undeniably sick man.

'I would have thought your time was better spent elsewhere, my Lord,' says Arlington. 'Grey can go himself and make further enquiries. He would be . . . faster than you.'

Lord Ashley gives Arlington a crooked smile. Could it be that he is enjoying this? 'My stick carries me as fast as I need to go. The King asked me to take statements at Newgate. For completeness I should like to speak to this man as well.'

Arlington is not pleased. He is expecting me to do something about it – maybe kick Lord Ashley's stick away from him, if that would stop him going to Southwark.

'Lord Arlington is right, sir,' I say to Lord Ashley. 'I can deal with this on my own. There is no need to trouble yourself.'

Lord Ashley seems not to hear me. 'Are you saying, my Lord, that you would prefer me not to have the opportunity to speak to this man Hubert? That it might in some way be better if I did not? If so, though I do not understand your reasons, I shall of course bow to your wishes.'

'I say nothing of the sort,' snaps Arlington. 'It is entirely your decision whether you waste your time.'

'In that case, Mr Grey, I shall meet you at the Whitehall Stairs at ten tomorrow morning,' says Lord Ashley. 'I'll have my very strongest stick in my hand. You don't need to fear that I'll fall behind. I like to think I can keep up with anyone – however fast they believe they are.'

And the Chancellor of the Exchequer winks at me and smiles.

'I'd be careful if I were you, sir,' says Will. 'When two great lords decide to have a duel, then standing in between them is not a good and safe place to be. You may take a bullet intended for one, or you may take a bullet intended for the other, but you take the bullet for all that. Two bullets if you're unlucky.'

'Lord Ashley suspects Arlington of hiding something,' I say. 'So, frankly, do I. Arlington denied that the fire was a Catholic plot long before he had any evidence one way or the other.'

'My Lord Arlington often does keep things to himself, sir,' says Will. 'He failed to mention that the last job he gave you might in some way be dangerous. It would have been helpful if he had been more informative. I'm sure he means well; but Lord Arlington expects you to tell him everything you know and tells you as little as he can in return.'

That is as neat a summary of my affairs as I have heard in a long time, but I have no wish to be lectured on my dealings with His Majesty's Secretary of State, any more than I wish to be reminded how many bottles of wine I have drunk.

'Indeed?' I say.

'It's what you always tell me, sir, and I'm sure you wouldn't deceive me.'

Will's face reveals nothing except respect. He is showing more tact with me than I showed with Arlington. Perhaps

I do have something to learn from him in dealing with my master.

'So, what is Lord Arlington hiding this time?' I ask.

'You've said, sir, that Hubert is a Frenchman and that, if he has done what he says he has done, then it would be firm evidence of a French plot, the existence of which the King has most emphatically denied. Lord Arlington is the loyal servant of the King, and hence of his brother the Duke. He might wish that Hubert should be found innocent or mad or, better still, quietly vanish before he can incriminate himself further. He needs somebody to prove his contention for him and to blame if any part of his scheme goes wrong. That's you, sir.'

Again, I cannot fault Will's summary. 'Arlington sees it as his job to accommodate the King in every way,' I say. 'If he can't be the King's wisest minister, then he'll certainly be the most flexible one. But Lord Ashley isn't afraid of speaking the truth to the King when necessary. If I were the King, I'd listen to Ashley. Arlington is, however, my employer.'

'A position that, speaking as *your* employee, I understand very well. But I think, sir, that Lord Ashley will find a way to talk to Hubert, whether you help him or not. He already seems to have the King's authority to speak to any prisoners taken during the fire. And he is one of the cleverest men at court. My advice would be to accompany him. At the very worst, you can let Lord Arlington know what has happened. Lord Arlington may be grateful for that. But that's only my opinion, sir. You must do as you think best.'

'Thank you, Will,' I say. 'I'm sure that is good advice. I won't need you again today. You may go and enjoy the rest of the evening as you please.'

'Thank *you*, sir.' Will coughs and shuffles his feet. 'There was one other thing, sir. Immediately before I go, as it were.'

'Yes?' I say.

'Lady Pole, sir,' he says. He awaits my reaction but, since I throw nothing large or heavy at him, he continues cautiously. 'Lady Pole called and, since you were away on business then, she wondered if you could attend upon her this evening at her lodgings.'

'Did she say why?'

'Not exactly.'

'For goodness' sake, Will, what did she say? Is she in trouble?'

'She? No, sir. I don't think so. I'm not supposed to say, but I think her father may be. That's what she implied. Of course, if you're busy, I could go and tell them . . .'

'No, I'll go,' I say.

Aminta stands, twisting a small lace-bordered kerchief in her hands.

'I am sorry to have called you away from your business,' she says, almost apologetically.

I wait to see if she will address me as 'John' or 'Mr Grey', but that seems to be the end of the sentence.

'I am sorry I was not at my chambers when you called earlier,' I say. Nothing notable occurs to fill the long pause that ensues, so I add: 'What can I do for you then?'

'Arlington has asked you to make enquiries about the causes of the fire?'

'Yes.'

'And you have spoken to Mr Graunt, one of the Directors of the New River Company?'

'Yes. I'm not sure how you know . . .'

'I'll come to that. Does Lord Arlington really suspect that Mr Graunt was part of some conspiracy?'

'His conduct was unfortunate – to go off with the only key on the very evening that water was so urgently needed. That was not helpful. And he was not comfortable with some of the questions I asked him. In short, there's something odd about his account of what he did. But Arlington wants me to keep an open mind, so I have.'

'You know he is a Catholic?' asks Aminta.

'So I understand. But half of the King's ministers are Catholics or sympathise with the Catholics. Why are you so concerned for Mr Graunt?'

I feel a sudden and completely unaccountable pang of jealousy.

'I'm not,' says Aminta. 'It's simply that my father is also a Director of the company.'

I had not known that, but then there is no reason why I should. None at all.

'The Directors, as a body, are not accused of cutting off the supply of water deliberately. Quite the reverse. Once the error was detected, all efforts were made to turn the water on again, at the expense of a perfectly good door. Your father is only one of a number of trustees, and I can personally vouch for the fact that he was nowhere near Clerkenwell when the fire occurred. I saw him. There is also a French lady who might be produced in evidence.'

'Thank you. I'd prefer not to produce her unless we have to. But there is a further complicating factor in that my father personally recommended Mr Graunt to be a Director. He assured the other trustees that Graunt was suitable for the post.'

I nod thoughtfully. 'There is a slight awkwardness there but, whatever Graunt did or didn't do, nobody could dispute your father's loyalty to the Crown. He bankrupted himself, and indeed you, supporting the King's father during the late wars. That is as well documented as you could wish. After the war was lost, he was obliged to sell the manor to pay the fines imposed by Parliament on Royalists. Hence my stepfather now possessing it, of course.'

'For which the King has shown little gratitude,' says Aminta. 'Most of those he now favours swore allegiance to Cromwell in their time – even Albemarle and Buckingham. Previous service to the Stuarts, however ruinous, is not a golden key giving admission to the King's future favour, nor is it a mitigating factor when accused of a present treason.'

She's right about Buckingham, who not only deserted the King but also married the daughter of one of Cromwell's generals, just so that there was no doubt how he felt about things. And, now I come to think of it, Lord Ashley served in the Royalist Army, then the Army of Parliament, then worked willingly for Cromwell after the war. As indeed I did myself. Most of us have served many masters in our time, and it is unreasonable for Aminta to blame me, even if my family came out of it well enough. Hers is one of the few to have remained defiantly loyal to the King throughout his defeat and exile. The Restoration has been strangely little help to her. Or to her family. That's why her father is merely an ex-magistrate, and no longer lord of the manor as he was when I was a boy. My formerly Republican stepfather, conversely, is now both of those things under the rule of his newly restored Majesty, King Charles, having switched sides and become a royalist just in time.

'Sir Felix has surely done nothing to require mitigation,' I say. 'He is no traitor.'

'All Catholics are now suspected of treason,' she says. 'And on the night the fire began, he was undoubtedly consorting with one.'

'So was the King,' I say. 'Unless Lady Castlemaine has converted to Protestantism.'

'Don't joke about it,' says Aminta.

'What do you want me to do then?' I ask.

'If, in your investigations, you need to say anything about the management of the New River Company, I should be grateful if you did not mention my father's name in any way. It would also be better, under the circumstances, if you didn't say that you saw him in the City, close to where the fire began.'

'I doubt that I should need to mention him in either capacity,' I say.

'I need more than your doubts.'

'Very well. I promise not to.'

'Thank you,' she says. She reaches out a small, soft hand and places it briefly but firmly on my arm. I feel the warmth of her touch, and a deep sense of loss when she finally takes her hand away.

I wonder whether to leave now, but something makes me say: 'Lord Ashley thinks that Arlington is trying to cover up a Catholic plot.'

'If there were such a thing, that is what Lord Arlington would instinctively do. Given the choice between night and day, my Lord will invariably opt for night. It's where he feels comfortable. The King rather likes the night as well.'

'The King has surrounded himself with sycophants and

rogues,' I say. 'My Lord Ashley may be the only honest man amongst them.'

'Then I wonder how long the sycophants and rogues will tolerate Ashley's presence at court? If Ashley claims there is a plot in the rather intemperate way he has, and you can find Arlington plausible evidence that there was no such thing, then Ashley will look a fool and his days of influence may be numbered.'

'My Lord Ashley is a sick man,' I say. 'It might not take much to force him out.'

'Is Graunt the only suspect?'

'Joseph Williamson blames the King's biscuit-maker, who in turn denies everything. But they've also arrested a man named Hubert for starting the fire. He conversely admits his guilt – both to the fire and to killing a Mr Peidloe. I don't believe a word of it, but if the King wants a scapegoat, he has a willing volunteer. I never saw a man so anxious to hang.'

'Does the King want a scapegoat?'

'Not at the moment, or Arlington would have had Hubert hanged on the spot. Fortunately for Hubert, it would suit the King better if he were innocent.'

'And that's what you think?' asks Aminta.

'I think Hubert's mad, not dangerous,' I say. 'Anyway, I may actually have seen Peidloe's killer – if so, he didn't look much like Hubert. But it's not quite that simple. Amongst the many impossible things Hubert's said, there does seem to be remarkable coincidence. On the night of the fire, somebody was undoubtedly murdered. And Hubert knew not only that a man had been killed, but also that he'd been shot near St Paul's and precisely how much money he had in his purse. That may take some explaining away.'

'Which pleases Ashley?'

'He wants the truth,' I say.

'I think the truth may be too dangerous a thing to possess – possibly even for Ashley, but definitely for you.'

'That's what Will said.'

'You admire Ashley, don't you?'

'He is one of the King's more reasonable ministers,' I reply. 'He's decent and honest.'

'And ruthless.'

'When he's in the right.'

'Well, you can't afford to throw in your lot with Ashley just because you think he may be in the right. You're Arlington's creature, in case you have forgotten. And the more wrong Arlington is, the more he needs you.'

'Will said that too. More or less.'

'Then you should listen to your clerk,' says Aminta. 'He understands Arlington.'

'I grant you Will's no fool,' I say, 'but he still doesn't know the ways of the royal court.'

'Compared with Arlington or Clarendon, I am afraid you too are still a novice around the royal court,' she says. 'But my family have been courtiers, on and off, for generations. If you need advice on the court, you can always ask me.'

She's right. The Greys have never had much time for following kings around, but Sir Felix served at the previous King's court and his father served at the court of King James. Sir Felix also knew the present King when he was in exile, as did Aminta. They may lack cash, but they probably know or are related to most of the King's ministers, including Clarendon.

'Can I do that?' I ask.

'If you can overcome your stiff-necked Puritan pride suffi-
ciently, yes, you can.'

'I'll do my best,' I say. 'And I'll not mention your father's
name to Arlington.'

'Thank you . . . John,' she says.

Was I wise to make that promise? Well, I've done it now and,
as Hubert has pointed out, it's usually safer to keep promises
than break them. And, as Sir Felix explained to anybody who
would listen, he wouldn't have had much opportunity for
treason anyway.

'It is my pleasure, Aminta,' I say.

Chapter Ten

The sun is rising again over the smoke-blackened corpse of London. Like the gentleman we viewed yesterday in a palace cellar, it stretches thin, carbonised fingers up into the sky. And, like the corpse, I suspect it still clutches a gold coin or two, hidden from our sight. There are already stories of gangs that haunt the ruins, digging dangerously at night in smoking and abandoned cellars for whatever treasure was left behind. For the moment, however, there is an eerie stillness to the scene. In what is left of the once bustling streets, nobody moves. No cat prowls. No rat scurries. No dog pisses on the warm masonry. Even the birds dare not land on their old perches for fear of scorching their wings.

Lord Ashley and I stand on Whitehall Stairs, on the river side of the Palace, waiting for a wherry to carry us across. The only bridge in London is still smouldering gently at its northern end.

'Your master Arlington seems to doubt the possibility of there being a Catholic plot,' he says.

'Not the possibility, my Lord, just the advisability of there being one at the moment. He is quite aware that these things happen. A few years ago, the country seemed united in welcoming King Charles back to the throne. But since then his Majesty has succeeded in convincing many people that some other king, or no king at all, may be better. In his role as his Majesty's spymaster, Lord Arlington receives constant reports of plots by the Catholics or the Dutch or the Fifth Monarchy Men or disaffected Republicans.'

'We must take such reports seriously,' says Lord Ashley. He painfully straightens his back and turns towards the river, where a boat is approaching us.

'Of course,' I say. 'That is, in essence, my job. But, when investigated, few of the plots reported to us prove to be more than an overheard conversation in a tavern on a day when there is little else to report. An agent with nothing to tell us is an agent that we are paying needlessly, and our agents know that as well as we do. Lord Arlington will require a lot more evidence than he has now before he feels that it is worth spending money investigating this further – quite rightly.'

'Your loyalty to Arlington does you credit,' says Lord Ashley, turning to face me again. 'But we both know that there are other reasons why Arlington might not wish to discover a plot. He and his faction have strong Catholic sympathies.'

'I must protest, my Lord . . .' I say.

'Then do protest, by all means. I won't stop you. When I say your loyalty does you credit, I am paying you a great compliment, Mr Grey. There is little enough loyalty at the court in these days. Arlington lost no time in unseating old Sir Edward Nicholas and sending him into retirement, even though Sir Edward had served the King devotedly, and largely unpaid, all through his time in exile. Arlington and his faction would like to see Lord Chancellor Clarendon gone, even though Clarendon has been as loyal a servant of the Crown as any man this century. I know because Arlington has asked for my help with this design more than once. But at the same time I know that Arlington would bring me down tomorrow if he could find a way to do it. Gratitude is rare nowadays, Mr Grey. I admire you for being prepared to stand by a man who is as wrong-headed as your master. I mean that. It is not my intention to make you break any confidences or to be in any way disloyal.'

'Thank you, my Lord,' I say, as loyally as I need to.

'It is the least I can do for the only truly honest man I have met in a long time,' says Ashley, though as a courtier his opportunities for meeting honest men will have been limited. 'Well, here's our boatman. Do not let him charge you more than sixpence. It's a corrupt and deceitful age in which we live.'

'Another visitor for Mr Hubert?' asks the guard. 'Considering he's a murdering Papist, he has many friends.'

'He has had an earlier visitor?' I ask, surprised. 'Who was that?'

'I think he said his name was Smith. A man carrying a basket, in any case, and a neighbour of Mr Hubert's. Do not worry, sir – we checked the basket and it contained nothing but food and drink, which we also checked carefully. The cheese was excellent.'

'Fear not. We can ask Hubert about him,' Ashley whispers to me as we are led across the courtyard. 'But what the guard says is very likely to be true. Smith is simply a friend of Hubert's and nothing more. You'd starve in here if you had nobody to bring you food. Hubert has lived in London. We should not be amazed that his neighbours are a little concerned for his welfare.'

*

Hubert looks up as we enter his cell. I am of no greater interest than I was before. When I introduce Lord Ashley, Hubert simply nods and says: 'Yes, of course.' He seems unimpressed that my companion could save him or help condemn him to the gallows. He clearly feels he has already told me all I need to know, but he is at least prepared to consider my enquiry about Mr Smith.

'That is correct,' he says. 'My neighbour came both yesterday and this morning. It is allowed.'

'You have many friends who visit you?' I ask.

'I still have two friends. He is one of them.'

'Where does Mr Smith live?'

'Close to my shop.'

'I'll ask after him,' I say.

'If you wish,' says Hubert generously. 'But his house has been burnt to the ground. He told me. I do not know where you would find him now. Perhaps outside the City. He has a red face.'

'Red?'

'Bright red, but only half of it. The other half is like yours, but without the scar. I would rather have a half-red face than a scar.'

'Did you tell him why you are here?' I ask.

'Yes. He knows. I have killed Mr Peidloe.'

'Did that trouble him?'

'No. I think he was pleased. Why not?'

I exchange glances with Ashley, who simply raises his eyebrows. Hubert has one of the two chairs in the room. I offered the other to Lord Ashley, but he scorned to sit in spite of the discomfort that I see he is still in. We are both therefore standing, looking down on Hubert, an arrangement that Hubert seems to find perfectly acceptable.

'Now then, Mr Hubert,' says Ashley, 'you claim to have started the fire. Where exactly did you start it? You just need to tell the truth – you understand that, don't you? You know you can trust me.'

I look at Ashley. I too wish to know the truth, but I am not sure that Hubert does understand what will happen to him if he continues to admit to murder and arson. I wonder therefore if Ashley's reassurance is playing fairly with him. But, as Aminta said, my Lord Ashley can be ruthless in his search for the truth. Hubert, never having met Ashley before, simply smiles at him. I fear he may be about to dig his grave.

'Yes, I know that,' Hubert says. 'I can trust you. I have already told you that I shall tell the truth, just as you ask. It was my doing. I started the fire at the King's baker's in Pudding Lane. Then I shot Monsieur Peidloe in the back.'

Well, this is more circumstantial than his last confession.

'Are you certain?' I interrupt. 'You said nothing before about shooting him in the back. Why are you remembering these details only now?'

'You did not say you were interested in how I shot him,' says Hubert. 'But now you do, and I tell you that is how it was.'

'So,' says Lord Ashley very carefully, 'Mr Grey is right. You should say *only what is true*. And you are telling us that you started the fire, yes?'

'Yes. I started it. With Monsieur Peidloe. Surely you know that?'

'Of course. I just have to ask so that we are certain what you are telling us. Then you went with Mr Peidloe to Westminster?'

'We did not get there,' says Hubert. 'I killed him. Hard by St Paul's. You know that too, I think.'

Lord Ashley smiles at this rebuke. 'Please remember, Mr Hubert, that I do not necessarily know what you have told Mr Grey or the magistrate at Romford. However, I understand what you are saying. You killed Mr Peidloe.'

Hubert nods. 'I asked him for money. He would not give it to me. Perhaps I became angry. He took out a coin and said that was all I would receive. I shot him in the back with the coin still clasped in his hand. I did not remember before but I do now.'

Lord Ashley turns and looks at me. Telling us that Peidloe was shot in the back might be a lucky guess, but I agree that it would be remarkable if Hubert had invented the small detail of the coin in his fist.

'Did Mr Peidloe say who he worked for?' I ask.

'Worked for?'

'Who told him to burn London?'

'I cannot tell you their names.'

'But you know them?' I ask.

There is a very long pause.

'No,' he says.

'Were they Catholics?'

'Yes, of course. They are evil people. They killed my great-grandfather.'

I look at Hubert, sitting before us, quite expressionless. I think his madness may yet save him from the gallows, but equally it may not.

'You realise,' I say, 'that if you continue to say that you set fire to London you will be hanged?'

Hubert looks at us both blankly. The prospect of hanging

might worry some people, but not Hubert. I might as well have said that it would cost him tuppence.

'Will I?' He looks at me, then at Ashley.

'Yes,' I say. 'It will not be pleasant for you.'

'Pleasant? No, perhaps it will not be, but I cannot tell you,' Hubert says. 'I cannot tell you any more. I think you are trying to trick me, Mr Grey, but it will not work. I am safe without your help. Safe in the hands of the Lord. Please go now. I have nothing more for you.'

'What do you think of that?' asks Ashley as we cross the yard, towards the main gate of the gaol.

'I still think he's mad,' I say. 'He believes that God will save him and that allows him to lie without any danger to his person.'

'It could still be the truth,' says Ashley. 'Perhaps he thinks a pretence of madness will save him.'

'I agree that he might hope to escape by convincing a judge he was mad, but then why confess at all? He wasn't caught in the act. Denying everything would be a much safer course of action.'

'That is very true. But if he is wholly innocent, why does he know so much? He knew about the coin, Mr Grey. How could he, when we ourselves did not know until last night? And he knew Peidloe was shot in the back. How would he know that?'

'I think his visitor may provide a clue,' I say. 'What if Peter Smith told him – about Pudding Lane, about how Peidloe was shot, about the coins in his purse? There's something odd about Smith's visits. He's been burnt out of his home and ruined, but he has the money to buy food for a neighbour?'

Lord Ashley nods. 'Such generosity is surely not unknown, even in these times? Still, let us assume that Smith did come here, under the pretence of bringing food, but with the real intention of telling Hubert how to reply to our questions. We must then ask how Smith would know the manner of Peidloe's death, or about the coin in his hand, or even what our questions would be.'

'At least three of us knew,' I say. 'Somebody could have told Smith.'

'True. And there were more than three of us,' says Lord Ashley. 'In addition to you, me and Arlington, there was the guard at the door when we met. And we mustn't forget the men who found Peidloe and carried him back. You are right. Before we jump to too many conclusions, we should indeed consider that there are several who would have known, and that one of them might have somehow discovered Smith was to visit Hubert, located him wherever it is he is now living, and told him what he needed to know. But what is more likely? That Hubert did indeed shoot Peidloe with the coin in his hand, having first set fire to the City, or that he has learned about it all by some tortuous route we can only guess at? Before this meeting I wasn't sure, but now I think we should put Hubert before a judge and jury.'

I begin to feel sorry for Hubert, caught between Ashley and Arlington. I respect Ashley's devotion to the truth every bit as much as I deplore Arlington's desire to cover up anything that might be inconvenient for the King. And yet, it may be possible to reveal the plot, as Ashley wishes, without destroying this poor madman. Contrary to what he believes, I think Hubert is without a friend in the world.

'If I could talk to Smith, perhaps I could find out more,' I say.

Lord Ashley shakes his head. 'I admire you, Mr Grey. What does it take to make you give up a lost cause?'

'I never give up,' I say. 'It's why Arlington pays me.'

As we leave the prison, Lord Ashley leans for a moment on his stick and says to the guard. 'If a Mr Smith comes to visit Mr Hubert again, kindly ask him to go and see Mr Grey at Lincoln's Inn.'

'Mr Smith?' says the guard thoughtfully. 'Not sure I know anyone of that name.'

'You mentioned him when we arrived.'

'Smith? My memory's not what it was, sir. Unless there's something to ease it, of course.'

Ashley hands him a coin.

'Ah yes, Mr *Smith*,' the guard says. 'Perhaps I do recall him – now I think a little more on the matter. A birthmark on his face perhaps? I'll do as your Lordship requests. I am your Lordship's and Mr Grey's most obedient servant.'

'It is,' says Ashley as we emerge into the street again, 'a grasping and corrupt world. Fortunately we both understand how it works. That always helps, I find.'

Though I had thought Arlington had expressly approved Lord Ashley's accompanying me, there seems to be no aspect of the visit that is not wholly my fault.

'Ashley is not to be trusted,' says Arlington. 'You said: Hubert is mad. That is clear to you and to me. Why could you not persuade Ashley to accept one simple fact? That man simply wishes to make trouble for me and for the Duke and for the King. I begin to suspect he is a secret ally of that pompous ass Clarendon. If so, he and Clarendon can fall together, for all I care. Not that I predict a long career for my Lord Ashley, whatever he does. He is, in spite of considerable competition, the most hated man at court.'

It is difficult to see how Lord Ashley's improbable alliance with Clarendon, if true, would inconvenience Clarendon's son-in-law, the Duke of York. But I do not think that logic plays much part in Arlington's denunciation. He hates Ashley almost as much as he hates Clarendon. Lord Ashley couldn't buy a new piss-pot without Arlington questioning his motive for doing so.

'I think, my Lord, that he merely wishes to discover the truth.'

'Truth!' Arlington spits this foul insult back at me. 'What would Ashley know about the truth? You are aware, I suppose, that he fought for Parliament during the war? One day he was fighting for the King in Dorset; the next he was fighting against him. He didn't discover he was a Royalist again until he fell out with Cromwell. Ashley has principles only when it suits him to have principles.'

I am not sure that his conversion to Republicanism was as sudden as Arlington implies. But there is no doubt that he fought for Parliament, and was for a while a member of Cromwell's Council.

'He has been consistently loyal to the State, my Lord. It is just that the State has had different masters over the past few years.'

'That thought is very close to treason, Mr Grey.'

I suppose it is. Should I also tell him how much better his Parliamentary predecessor, John Thurloe, was at running an intelligence operation? Thurloe lives in obscurity in Lincoln's Inn now. I see him sometimes, grey-haired and defeated, walking in the gardens because he has nothing else to do. One day that will be Clarendon. One day that will be Arlington.

'I bow to your greater knowledge, my Lord,' I say.

'You'd be very wise to do so,' he says. 'Unless you share Hubert's desire to have your guts ripped out by the public hangman. So, what did Ashley ask Hubert? I hope you took notes.'

I nod. 'He enquired mainly about Peidloe's death, as you would expect. He stressed that Hubert should trust him.'

'And did Hubert trust him?'

'He thinks Ashley is his friend,' I say.

Arlington smiles for the first time. 'Proof, if any were still required, of his madness. Ashley will have him hanged if he can – being Ashley's friend won't save him. What else did Hubert have to say for himself, apart from his strange delusion concerning my Lord Ashley?'

'Hubert knew that Peidloe was shot in the back.'

'He didn't say that before. Still, it had to be one or the other – back or front.'

'He also knew about the coin in Peidloe's hand . . .'

Arlington's jaw drops visibly. 'But he can't possibly . . .'

'Of course, somebody else may have told him all of these things.'

'Obviously,' he says. 'But who? You mean Ashley?'

'I was with Lord Ashley,' I say. 'It would have been impossible for him to have done it without my knowing. But there was a man who visited Hubert in gaol. He's called Smith. He may have coached him on all his answers – for example that the fire began in Pudding Lane – that is well known. But I am not sure how Smith could have found out about the coin. Do you have a Mr Smith working for you?'

'Not at present. Not under that name,' says Arlington thoughtfully. 'But men of that type rarely work under their own names. And Hubert still claims to have done this himself?'

'Yes,' I say.

'The man is determined to have himself hanged,' says Arlington. He seems to like Hubert a little less than he did.

'Of course, I don't believe him,' I say.

'Nor do I.' Arlington sits there for a moment, staring into mid-distance and tapping his finger against the table. '*Could* it have been Hubert you saw on the night of the fire? If it was, it's better we know so that we can decide what to do about it.'

'Seeing him a second time today, I really don't think it could have been. But it was dark, so on the other hand—'

Arlington shakes his head. It's not that hand he's interested in. 'You're right. Smith has somehow fed him the information he needed. We just have to find out how Smith knows.'

'Lord Ashley asked the guard to send Smith to us, if he returned to the gaol.'

Arlington's finger taps the table again, while he works out how this very reasonable request might be to Ashley's discredit. 'Speak to Smith then,' he says eventually. 'If you can find him, and if you think he has anything to tell us. But Ashley intends some trickery – mark my words. And I need you to stop him. Deceive him however you wish. Tell him what you like. Spy on him in his bed or on his close-stool if that's what is required. Use anything short of bribery, because I can't afford it. Just prevent him drumming up some phantom army of Catholic conspirators and presenting them to the citizens of London as the friends of the Duke of York.'

'What if Lord Ashley is right?' I ask. 'What if there is a plot? What if Hubert is, unwittingly or not, part of it?'

'Let me assure you there is no plot,' says Arlington. 'You need not waste your time speculating further on that. Your job, Mr Grey, is to provide me with the evidence for what I have just assured you is true. Do whatever you need to do. But, at the end of it, I want no question to remain in anyone's mind. The fire was an accident.'

'And Hubert is innocent?'

'If he has to be.'

'Just out of curiosity – what if Mr Smith's evidence suggests otherwise?'

'If Smith doesn't say what he ought to, then find any reasonably priced witness who will agree with me. Anyway, Smith will have left London long ago if he has any sense. I'll wager a Guinea to a copper Farthing that you'll never find him.'

When I get home, Will is waiting for me in the hallway.

'There's a Mr Peter Smith in your chamber, sir. He's most anxious to speak to you about Mr Hubert.'

Chapter Eleven

'Sit down,' I say, because Mr Smith has risen from the seat in which he has been waiting patiently for my return. 'Has my clerk given you any refreshment?'

'He was kind enough to present me with a glass of Canary wine, sir. No thank you – I won't have another, excellent though that was. The porter at the White Lion Gaol said you wished to speak to me, sir.' He rubs his hands together, like a shopkeeper ready to serve me.

I don't know how much Lord Ashley gave the guard, but it was clearly more than enough. This is fast work. I look at Smith – short but very solid and dressed in an old velvet doublet and breeches. I think he has seen better days. His leather hat, which he removed as I entered the room, is on his lap, held in both hands. On one side of his face is a bright red birthmark. I have no doubt this is the kind neighbour that Hubert was describing.

'So, you know Mr Robert Hubert?' I ask.

'Indeed, sir. I've known him for three years or so – ever since he came over from France, in fact. He lives close to me . . . lived, I should say, because his house and mine burnt in the fire. I lost a lot of stock, sir – I'm a grocer, you see – though I managed to save most of my household goods. Mr Hubert lost everything, as far as I know.'

He rubs his hands together again and smiles. His velvet suit had almost brought to mind a down-at-the-heel Cavalier but, now he mentions it, yes, I can imagine him a grocer, about to recommend the newly arrived nutmeg and cloves to his customers.

'You have been unfortunate,' I say.

'No worse than everyone else, sir,' says Smith. 'I lost my poor wife in the Plague, sir, and two children. This year it's only my house that's gone. Not so bad, really.'

'I'm very sorry for your losses, Mr Smith.'

'Thank you, sir. But I don't want to burden you with my troubles. You wished to ask me about Mr Hubert?'

In all honesty, I really wanted to find out what sort of man Mr Smith was and whether he was likely to have passed information to Hubert. He appears as harmless and straight-forward an individual as you might hope to meet. But let's start with a question or two about Hubert, by all means. It would be helpful to understand him better.

'How do you know Mr Hubert?' I ask.

Smith leans forward. 'He's a neighbour and he's given me no trouble, but he's a peculiar fellow for all that, sir. Not much to say to you, except "good day". And such a strange way of expressing himself when he does try to say more . . . A competent watchmaker, I think, though he repairs people's watches rather than makes them, if you see what I mean. He doesn't have the money to hold hundreds of Pounds' worth of stock. A few Pounds is a lot to him. Ten would change his life . . .'

Well, that was about the sum he says he was offered to burn London to the ground.

'Does he have many friends?' I ask.

'Just me, I believe. He's not an easy man to be a friend to.'

'I can see that. He mentioned another friend though. Do you know who that might be?'

'No, sir, I don't, though I'm glad he has one.'

'Mr Hubert is a Huguenot?' I ask.

'I couldn't tell you, sir. I'm not even sure what that is.'

'A French Protestant,' I say.

Smith shakes his head doubtfully. 'I thought the French were Catholics. All I can say for sure is that he didn't attend our parish church. But since he's foreign, and doubtless has his own church and his own God, I never expected him to.'

'Did he ever talk of wanting to harm the City?'

Smith laughs. 'Had he talked of burning London down, do you not think that I would have reported it to the magistrate? But yes . . . I think he might do such a thing. He doesn't think as you or I do. And he did need money, I can tell you that.'

'So you think he's mad then?'

'No, sir, not mad exactly. Nobody would have trusted their watch to a madman. But he was – how can I put this? – hot-headed . . . capable of getting into a rage about things.'

'Could he kill somebody?'

Smith thinks hard. 'Mr Peidloe, you mean? When he told me, I didn't want to believe it, but, yes, I think he could have done that too.'

'Do you also know Mr Peidloe?'

'He talked to me about Mr Peidloe, sir, but I never met him myself. Maybe that's his other friend?'

'He spoke as if the other friend were still alive,' I say.

'What did he tell you about Peidloe, other than that he'd killed him?'

'Only that Mr Peidloe had some work for him that would bring great profit. I thought maybe he wanted to buy a watch or even two. Mr Hubert's trade was poor, as I say. His idea of great profit and yours and mine might not be the same.'

'Did no other people visit him?'

'Of course they did, sir. He mended watches.'

'I mean people with whom he might have been plotting some mischief.'

'I think sometimes he went to Mr Peidloe's house. I believe it was close by.' Smith pauses and looks at me.

'Did he say who he met there?' I ask.

'No, sir. He did not. He was quite secretive about who he met and what he did there. I never thought at the time, but perhaps I should have realised . . . I'm sorry, sir, I may have been blind to his treasons, as they now seem to me to be.'

'You weren't to know,' I say.

'No,' he says.

'Well, it was kind of you to take food to Mr Hubert,' I add. 'Especially in view of your own losses.'

'It's in the Bible, sir. "For I was an hungred, and ye gave me meat: I was thirsty, and ye gave me drink: I was a stranger, and ye took me in: naked, and ye clothed me: I was sick, and ye visited me: I was in prison, and ye came unto me." Matthew, sir. Chapter twenty-five, verse thirty-five. You'll remember that, sir.'

'Yes,' I say. 'I'll remember that. But tell me, on your visits to him in prison, did you give him only food and drink, or did you give him something else?'

He looks at me blankly. 'Are you thinking of clean linen, sir? He was much in need of it. I gave him a pair of my old stockings, though I could scarcely spare a stitch of clothing from what I saved.'

'That too does you much credit, but I'm thinking more of information. News that you might have come across? About the fire?'

I watch Smith carefully. I am used to searching for the small signs that tell me a man is not comfortable with my questions. But he just scratches his head in a puzzled way. 'I had to tell him his own house was burnt to the ground. Is that what you mean, sir?'

'So, nobody asked you to take any sort of information to him? Where the fire started, say?'

'Why should they do that, sir?'

'You said nothing about a body being found?'

He frowns. 'Body? No sir. I've heard very few died in the fire.'

'A body was found by St Paul's,' I say.

'Was it, sir?'

'With a purse full of gold.'

'I don't know anything about that, Mr Grey.'

I have not taken my eyes off Smith throughout this exchange. He is bemused by my questions but his countenance is otherwise untroubled. Either he's telling the truth or he's a very good actor.

'Thank you, Mr Smith. That is helpful,' I say. I stand and reach into my pocket. 'I am grateful to you for coming. Buy yourself some new stockings to replace those you gave to Mr Hubert.'

'Thank you,' he says, taking the coins. 'The righteous, sir, shall go away into the Life Eternal.'

'I'm not expecting to get there on the back of ten Shillings,'

I say. 'Where can I locate you if I need to ask you any further questions?'

'You can't, Mr Grey,' he says. 'I'm no longer to be found in any fixed place, because I don't have one. But if I remember anything else about Mr Hubert, I'll come and see you. You may count on that.'

'Thank you, Mr Smith,' I say. 'I'd like that very much.'

'A strange fellow,' says Will to me later. 'Quoted the Bible at me.'

'Is there anything wrong with that?'

'Not in church, I suppose. Not on a Sunday. He was just a bit too glib for my liking, sir. I thought his piety was a bit overdone.'

'You are a harsh critic,' I say. 'I agree he's a little too pious for most tastes. But I think he's a good man for all that. Not many would be as generous to others having lost their own home and their business.'

'If you say so, Mr Grey,' says Will. 'And so are you, sir. A very good man. Though perhaps too willing to believe in the goodness of others.'

I shake my head. 'I've seen enough of the badness of others not to take anything for granted,' I say. 'I'm going to get to the bottom of this, Will. I won't let Arlington bring Lord Ashley down and I won't let Hubert hang if he's innocent.'

'Of course, sir. The problem is knowing when you really are at the bottom, if you follow me. When the water's murky, it's not that easy to tell. Will you be wanting any wine tonight, sir? I can fetch one from the cellar. Or two if you wish. I think you're probably entitled to that, sir, with all you've done.'

I pause. 'No, Will,' I say. 'Thank you – but not tonight.'

Chapter Twelve

'I wasn't expecting to see you again so soon,' I say.

'I simply happened to be passing Lincoln's Inn,' says Aminta. 'But I'll go away, if my visits are too frequent, and return when I am more welcome.'

Should I say how much I want her to stay? Can I admit that even to myself?

'I'm sure that Will is already preparing you some tea,' I say. 'If you go before he is able to serve you, he will sulk all day and I need him to send out some bills for me. You may as well take a seat and tell me whatever you've come to tell me.'

'He's preparing chocolate for me,' says Aminta. 'Not tea.'

'I didn't know we had any.'

'I suggested that he bought some. It's from the West Indies.'

'I know where it's from. I have drunk it myself before now.'

'And now you have some here in your chambers. Because of me.'

'That's kind of you,' I say.

'I thought so too. If I left your domestic arrangements in your own hands, you'd drink nothing but watered-down ale in the morning and too much cheap wine in the evening. For the past ten years tea, coffee and chocolate have been on the tables of people of taste all over London. You must have noticed them, when you visited people of taste.'

'We have tea here,' I point out. 'And you drink it.'

'But you didn't have coffee or chocolate.'

'They are a passing frivolity,' I say.

'But a very pleasant one, sir,' says Will, entering with a tray bearing a steaming pot of chocolate and a china cup. 'You'll have small beer yourself, Mr Grey? Or perhaps some cheap wine?'

'No, Will, I'll have chocolate too,' I say. 'Since you have wasted my money buying it, I may as well gain some benefit from it.'

'Then I'll bring another cup at once, sir.'

'So, what have you come to tell me?' I ask Aminta. We now have the right number of cups and they have been filled with the thick, dark brown liquid. I may as well try it while it's still fashionable.

'I came to enquire if there was any news of Mr Hubert,' says Aminta. 'Or Mr Graunt. It would be good to hear, from my father's point of view, that it has been decided that there is no plot.'

'I have heard nothing further about Graunt,' I say. 'I've reported to Arlington that I think there is little point in holding him any longer. The case of Mr Hubert is different: he continues to insist that he is guilty. I had thought that a Mr Smith was feeding Hubert the information he needed to convict himself but, having met him, I don't think so. He seems a good Christian and wholly without guile, even if he is too pious for Will's taste. But that leaves me puzzled at how much Hubert knows about the fire and about the murder that took place. Hubert can't have done the things he says he's done, so he must have another source of information that I've overlooked. I am to see him again today. Arlington wishes for conclusive proof that Hubert did not start the fire. I'll get no further asking him the sort of questions you might ask a normal prisoner. So, I have proposed taking our suspect back across the river. We shall see if he really has any idea where Pudding Lane is. Perhaps he will not.'

'Does Arlington know you're taking him there?'

'No. Just that I'm questioning him again.'

'Then I would proceed with great caution. What you learn may be inconvenient, as Lord Arlington would put it. It is difficult for anyone to find their way through London, ruined as it is. If Hubert can't find Pudding Lane, it will prove little. On the other hand, if he could find the baker's shop it would simply condemn him further. Your visit could very much prove Lord Ashley's case and condemn Hubert.'

'Yes,' I say, 'I realise that. But it may also throw up something completely unexpected and save Hubert. He's going to hang if I can't do something for him. It's worth the risk to get to the truth.'

'And if it just confirms what Ashley has always said? Lord Arlington may not enjoy being proved wrong – he may even feel you have tricked him. I would be careful, John. He is not a man to cross.'

'It isn't just about Arlington's feelings. An innocent man may be about to die and it may be that a plot is being concealed. I want to know why Hubert is lying. I want to know who he's working for. I want to know what Arlington is covering up.'

'And is Lord Ashley to accompany you?' Aminta asks.

'Arlington does not wish Lord Ashley to see Hubert again. It would be difficult to disobey such an explicit instruction.'

'That's wise at least. You are going alone then?'

'The gaoler will accompany Hubert,' I say.

'And you can trust the gaoler?'

'Of course,' I say. 'Lord Ashley and I are currently bribing him more than anyone else.'

'Still he is a servant of the Crown, a fact that he may recollect at an inconvenient moment. You should not rule out his remembering his loyalties to Lord Arlington, in spite of your gold. Would it not help to have somebody with you with whom you can discuss matters more privately?'

'I could ask Will,' I say.

'I am sure that he is busy with the many tasks you have already allocated to him,' says Aminta. 'But, by a lucky chance, you now have me. In gratitude for your help with my father's various problems, I shall go with you.'

'The City is no place for a lady,' I protest. 'The roads are thick with ashes ...'

'My maid can brush my skirt afterwards.'

'And there are footpads and thieves ...'

'My father says that you are a moderately good swordsman.'

She waits for me to protest that I am a very good swordsman, thus defeating my own argument comprehensively. Sir Felix is, however, correct. I am a moderately good swordsman unfettered by any notions of fair play.

'Your father is too kind,' I say. 'But to return to your accompanying me, the ground will of course be very rough ...'

'I'm coming with you, John,' she says. 'You're just wasting time.'

I can, if I am left to fight in my own way, clear the street of half a dozen armed ruffians with a single blow of my sword. Why is it that I have never been able to stop Aminta doing anything that takes her fancy? Perhaps because we always play according to Aminta's rules and those rules change frequently.

'We'll get a ferry boat from Temple Stairs,' I say. 'It's easier if we can travel by river as far as the bridge.'

Aminta looks at me with innocent, deep blue eyes. 'I am happy to be guided by your greater wisdom in these matters, John. We shall do exactly as you say.'

Hubert and his gaoler are waiting for us, just upstream from the bridge, at the spot where the Old Swan stood until a few days ago. The sun continues to shine down on us from a cloudless sky. It will be warm work, tramping over the rubble. As we land, the smell of burnt timber rises to meet us. It is not unpleasant – the usual London odours of rotting cabbage, dung and stagnant water have been replaced by that of bright, clean charcoal. A small cloud of ash swirls along the river bank, whipped up by the breeze, causing us to cover our noses for a moment. The gaoler, his face half-hidden behind his own scarf, advances towards us down the gentle slope.

'I'm Mr Lowman, sir,' he says, lowering the scarf and shaking my hand. He's a small, neat man in a leather coat, pleased with himself and the world in general. 'I run the White Lion Gaol.'

'John Grey,' I say. 'And this is Lady Pole.'

He turns to Aminta. 'The famous playwright?' he asks. 'I'm deeply honoured to meet you, my Lady.' He makes an awkward bob of the head. He's not used to bowing to writers. Not many people are.

'Thank you,' she says. 'Well, I'm glad somebody is pleased I'm here.'

'But the City is not a safe place now,' he adds. 'Not for the likes of you, my Lady.'

'Yes, Mr Grey has already informed me that it is a haven for felons of all sorts, but with you and him to guard me, I have no fears on that score.'

'No, my Lady. Of course not. You'll be safe enough with us, while it's daylight anyway. But we must finish our work before dark. I wouldn't care to be still here when the sun goes down.'

'It's not midday yet,' I say. 'We have daylight enough.'

Lowman leans across to me and jerks his thumb in Hubert's direction. 'He's not in the most helpful of moods,' he says. 'This may take a while, sir.'

Hubert stands on the wharf, looking across the river. His face is dreamy, almost expressionless, though I think I detect a slight smile.

We too take stock of our position. My feet are firmly planted in the warm ashes of the City. I can sense the heat even through the soles of my boots. In places, smoke still climbs in thin, white rivulets. The view flickers and writhes as the heat escapes bit by bit from the charred clay on which this lost London was built. Close to where we are standing are the sad remains of what was once a church. The broken flint walls and the stone tower are caked in black soot. All over the road in front of it is a thin covering of what looks like parchment, but which I know to be melted glass from the windows. There has been no roof on this building since the early hours of Monday morning, and I doubt there will ever be one again. Most of the delicate tracery of the windows has gone with its glass, but a few thin strands of stone remain in place, like dead winter branches.

'Time of Richard the First,' says Lowman sententiously. 'Richard the Lionheart, of glorious memory, conqueror of the heathen King Saladin. That's how long that church has survived fire and storm and flood. Now look at it. Tombs of two Lord Mayors in there – or there were two; I've no idea what's left now and no plans to find out – too dangerous to meddle with it. I peeped into one church the other day and there was just a mass of melted lead from the roof – all in a heap. *Tons* of it, must have been. Good pickings there for the first man brave enough to venture in when nobody's looking – once it's all cold enough to touch. In another church, I hear they've pulled out a dead bishop from his smashed-up coffin – two hundred years old, he is. Just dry skin and bones, of course, though they say his ginger hair's almost as good as new. Stiff as a board, poor man, and stark naked for all the world to see. They've propped him up against a wall while they work out what to do with him – not that there's much you *can* do with a dead bishop. That place over there will be just the same. Full of tombs open to the bright blue sky and burnt beams and stones that have swelled and burst in the heat and heaps of melted glass – gold too, if you wanted to look for it, though it would be bad luck for all eternity if you took it away. Just half an ounce of church gold in your pocket would drag you down to Hell on Judgement Day. Never thought I'd see this, my good sir and Lady. Never thought we'd see old London brought so low. I think it must be the Dutch, don't you, sir?'

'I don't know,' I say. 'The King says it's an unfortunate accident; but then it didn't reach the Palace, so he's in a position to be charitable. How do we get to Pudding Lane?'

Lowman looks around him at the uncharted, gently

smoking chaos. 'Blessed if I've any idea,' he says. He turns to Hubert. 'So, where did you start the fire, Mr Hubert?' he asks.

Hubert turns from his long contemplation of the river. 'This way,' he says abruptly. And he sets off northwards at a steady pace, limping slightly, but with no trace of hesitation.

We cover our noses and mouths again against the dust that our feet will throw up. And we dutifully follow Hubert towards his own damnation.

The street we have reached is almost completely blocked. We have to scramble over piles of broken brick and stone. The debris is loose and treacherous. My feet slip and slide as I mount each heap and I send showers of stones before me as I descend on the other side. Even Aminta is obliged to accept a helping hand from time to time. Once more she gathers up her dusty skirts and petticoats without complaint, reaches out to me, and I pull her up onto the little mountain of detritus.

'Is this it?' I ask Lowman, who has just joined us, puffing from the exertion.

He shakes his head. 'How could any honest man say?' he replies. 'I know the City well enough – or knew it as it was until a few days ago – but this defeats even me, Mr Grey. You can get your bearings a bit from the old church towers and from the river, but the rest is gone. Look, sir, see the Thames flowing down there?'

I nod.

'Exactly,' he says. 'Before the fire you couldn't see it at all. Rows of houses and workshops and warehouses in between. Now they're vanished and you can see it all clear as clear. That's what throws you. It feels as if we're much closer to the river then we actually are. I wonder . . .'

He scrambles down and runs nimbly across the rubble to intercept the only other living creature in sight – a porter carrying a basket full of wine bottles. The man puts down his load on what was once a doorstep, thankful for an excuse to stop. He and Lowman have a whispered conversation with much pointing. Lowman struggles back up the brick heap, his boots scrunching on the broken mortar, to where we are standing.

'He's a wine porter, sir,' says Lowman in an undertone. 'He used to live close by. He's crossed this way a dozen times since the fire, rescuing some wine merchant's stock – can't get a cart or even a barrow in – and he reckons he's worked out now where most of the streets were.'

'And where is this?' I ask.

'It is Pudding Lane apparently,' Lowman whispers triumphantly. 'Hubert's come to the right place. That would be the baker's shop just over there, he says, near where you can make out another road crossing this one.'

A small group of people have now also made their way along the street and have paused at the spot indicated. It would seem the location is becoming notorious. We look at Hubert, still standing a little behind us with a dreamy expression on his face. He doesn't seem to have heard us. He can't have seen which way Lowman briefly indicated. At least, I don't think he can. But maybe he's seen the visitors, who are now pointing out to each other the main features of the ruined house. Or maybe not. I don't think that Hubert hears and sees what the rest of us do.

'Let's find out whether Mr Hubert really knows where he is then,' Lowman says. 'It's one thing to recall that Pudding Lane is inland from the river. It's another entirely to know

where the bakery is that he's supposed to have burnt down.
I think we might have a bit if fun, sir, if you'll permit it.'

Lowman calls Hubert up to us. Hubert climbs the rubble
slowly – he seems increasingly lame.

'Now Mr Hubert,' Lowman says when the four of us are
together at our vantage point. 'Where is this shop you say you
set fire to? Can you see it yet? Somewhere over there, I think?'

Lowman points out into the City, away from the bakery.

Hubert shows little interest in Lowman's crude subterfuge.
He turns slowly as if looking for any remaining trace of the
building. 'Just there,' he says, pointing to where the crowd is
inspecting the ruins. 'The shop was there.'

'You must be mistaken, Mr Hubert,' says Lowman in a
friendly fashion. 'We haven't reached Pudding Lane yet. Not
by a long way. See, we're still close to the river.'

'I am not mistaken,' says Hubert. 'Do you think I do not
know where I am? That is the house. I used to buy bread there
sometimes. I shall take you now. I shall show you where we
put the fireballs through the window.'

Hubert hobbles away down the rubble. Lowman shrugs
apologetically and once more we all follow.

It is difficult to discern where the building began and
ended, such is the jumble of tile and burnt plaster. Nothing
identifies it as a baker's shop.

'I put the fireball in through a window here,' Hubert says.

'Near the front door?' I ask.

'Yes. The front door was there. You can tell. There is a yard
at the back – in the form of a triangle and full of dry wood for
the oven. I could have just thrown it in there, but inside the
shop was better.'

Lowman looks at me. He is rather pleased that this little

outing has worked so well. He will want to take the credit for getting Hubert to incriminate himself in this way. But I cannot help but feel that our prisoner is a little too glib.

'So, how did you get here on the first night of the fire?' I ask.

There is one of his characteristic pauses. 'Monsieur Peidloe and I came from the ship,' he says to nobody in particular. 'From Sweden.'

'From which town did you sail?'

'I said: from Sweden.'

'That's not a town.'

'On the contrary. I saw many houses there.'

I am beginning to notice that the longer he has to think, the stranger the statements that follow.

'So, you mean the ship arrived the day before the fire? Where did you land?'

'I can take you there. But walking will be difficult. I do not know what it is called. It is over by the Tower.'

'We'll go by boat then,' I say.

We board another ferry at Botolph's Wharf, having clambered over more ruined walls to reach the river, and are rowed a short distance to just below the Tower of London, where St Katharine's Church and the surrounding houses still stand unburnt and whole. There is less debris on this stretch of river – fewer floating reminders of what London has lost. What has found its way between the pillars of London Bridge has continued unhindered on its way to Tilbury and the sea. But a scum of ash still sticks to the surface of the water. It is as if London will never be clean again.

Hubert, who has viewed the scene without any emotion, now points excitedly at the bank.

'St Katharine's by the Tower?' I say. 'That's where you moored?'

'Certainly,' he says.

'We'll go ashore and ask,' says Lowman. 'Somebody will remember.'

There are certainly no boats there now. We land and make enquiries about a Swedish ship, possibly called the *Skipper*. Nobody has heard of a Swedish vessel docking there lately, still less seen it. Yes, they say, they'd have remembered a boat that arrived on the night of the fire. It's not a night they're likely to forget. Lowman nods to me. A base lie from Hubert and another point to himself.

Our boatman returns us to Southwark, just by London Bridge. The incoming tide, pounded back by the bridge's massive stone buttresses, is rushing with a great roar under the narrow arches. The river flows tumultuously in reverse, back towards its source.

'Would you like to shoot the arches, sir? Two Shillings, that would be. The current is fast today, but I've done it when it's faster and still not overturned the boat. The lady might enjoy the excitement of it, sir. Or you could both walk round and take another boat on the other side if you'd like that better.'

'The lady would prefer to save her Shillings and not to get her dress soaking wet, thank you,' says Aminta. 'We'll get out here and walk round.'

We do walk round and find the upstream landing place. We watch as a party of City apprentices accepts a boatman's offer to take them through the arches. Their craft pitches alarmingly as it shoots out from under the vaulting and descends the cataract on the far side, and those who can do so grip any part of the boat within reach, but they all arrive safely in calmer waters, laughing with relief. We return to Temple Stairs with another boatman and thence, skirting the burnt City, on foot to Lincoln's Inn. A stiff breeze is blowing in from the west, stirring the plane trees. For the first time the air smells of grass and leaves and reminds us there is countryside beyond dirty London.

'So, was the visit worthwhile?' asks Aminta as we walk across the fields.

'Hubert knows that part of London. Even if he missed Lowman's pointing, I suspect that the party of sightseers may have given him a clue. As for the ship, he knows boats moor by the Tower. He knows there's a place called Sweden, though he thinks it's a town. That's all we've discovered. I'm sorry – you've had a wasted day.'

'I know that and you know that. But a jury hearing that he took us straight to the spot might think that indicated guilt.'

'Not if I was giving evidence. I'd say to them what I've just said to you. It proves very little.'

'But what if Lowman was telling them? He seemed very pleased with himself. He'll be keen to impress on a jury how clever he was to confirm Hubert's guilt – and how he discovered that Hubert lied about the boat from Sweden.'

'I'm sure he would. But they would hear my evidence too,' I say. 'Hubert is deluded. Not everything he says can be taken at face value. I'd make them see that.'

'If you are allowed to give evidence.'

'What could stop me?' I ask.

We have been back at Lincoln's Inn for some time when Will announces a visitor. It is Mr Smith and he looks worried.

'It's like this, sir,' he says. 'Mr Hubert told me something yesterday and swore me to secrecy. But then you were so kind to me . . . the money for the stockings . . . it's worried me ever since that I should have mentioned it to you . . . asked what you would advise me to do . . .' He looks at me pitifully.

'If you are asking whether you should betray your neighbour and tell us whatever you know, the answer is most certainly yes,' Aminta intervenes before I can answer.

This seems unnecessarily direct, but Smith seems strangely undeterred by any accusation of treachery. My gift of a pair of stockings outweighs any loyalty to neighbour Hubert.

'Very well,' Smith says. He takes out of his pocket a piece of paper, unfolds it and places it on the table in front of us. We are looking at a crudely drawn map. St Paul's is marked on one side. Streets are sketched in and there is a small cross close to the centre of the sheet.

'What are we supposed to make of this?' I ask.

'You see, sir, Mr Hubert told me yesterday that papers relating to Mr Peidloe's plot were hidden in the cellar of a house near St Paul's. They were going to the house when he was minded to shoot Mr Peidloe in the back. The papers are in a lead-lined box, buried for safety, and he thinks they will have survived the fire, even if the house hasn't. He fears that they will be found by the authorities and the names of the other conspirators revealed. So, he wanted me to retrieve the box and hide it for him until he is released, as he expects to be quite soon. He drew me this map so that I should find the house – he told me to look out for two strangely carved stone pillars in the shape of wild men. They stood by the front door, when there was a front door. Mr Hubert said that, inside the house, there would be stone steps leading down-wards to the cellar.'

'And you agreed to do what he asked?'

'No, sir. I thought about it and refused. I'm a law-abiding man, sir. Up until then I'd not been willing to believe much of what Mr Hubert said – killing Mr Peidloe and so forth. But this was proof of his wrongdoing. So, I said I'd have nothing to do with it. Mr Hubert replied that he would get somebody else to retrieve it tonight.'

'Who? He doesn't seem to have many friends.'

'Well, he did say he had one other, sir. So I took this with me anyway. If he's telling the truth, they'll be gone by the morning – the papers, sir. You'll need to act quickly.'

I look again at the strange map, the vaguely sketched outline of the City.

'But do you think Hubert *is* telling the truth?' I ask. 'Or is it his madness? And, if true, how does he know that the entrance to the cellar is not simply blocked by rubble or destroyed completely? The heat of the fire was very great: even a buried lead-lined box may not have survived.'

'Mr Hubert has no guile about him, sir. I think it is the truth, as far as he knows it, and no trick. I believe something was hidden there, though I could not say what or whether it will have survived the flames.'

'So, if I wish to recover the papers, you're saying I must come with you now?' I ask.

'With me? I hadn't thought, sir, but, yes, I could accompany you if you don't think you could find it yourself. It's just . . . I wouldn't want to stay . . . not in the ruins at night. And the sun will soon be down. But if you're happy to search for it yourself, I'll take you to the spot.'

Well, it's flattering to know he thinks I'm brave enough to stay and dig alone where he would fear to remain. But would

I be taking the risk for nothing? And outside, as Smith has pointed out, the sun is already setting.

'Do you wish me to accompany you, Mr Grey?' Will asks. 'I can stand guard while you dig – or vice versa if you prefer.'

Smith shakes his head. 'Too many of us, and we'll be spotted for sure. But Mr Grey and I might get through safe and unnoticed by the footpads.'

There's some sense in that, but there's an additional reason for Will not coming. 'Stay here, Will,' I say. 'If Mr Smith is right, and there is some danger, I may need you to organise a rescue party. If I don't return, get word to Lord Arlington in the morning. He'll need to look for me in a cellar near St Paul's – two wild men will show him the way – that's the best guidance you'll be able to give him.'

Will looks doubtful but nods. I don't think he trusts Smith. He'd rather be coming – even if I opt for watching, leaving him with the spade.

'Take me then,' says Aminta, who has remained unusually silent for a while. 'I'm smaller and less conspicuous than any of you men. And quieter. I won't draw attention to our party. I'm not offering to dig, but I could be one more pair of eyes to watch for danger.'

'Definitely not,' I say. For once I intend to be firm with her. 'Not at night. Will can see you home to Westminster. He won't need to go to Arlington until the morning.'

'I can get a coach,' she says. 'I won't trouble Will. It sounds as if he will have a busy day tomorrow. The poor man deserves some rest.'

I am pleased to see that she does not intend to argue with me. 'Good,' I say. 'That's settled then.'

*

It has taken longer than I thought to prepare. I have with me a lantern, a tinderbox and a small, neat shovel that Will has obtained from somewhere (I have not enquired too closely where) in Lincoln's Inn. Smith too has been provided with an old lantern for his return journey. I have my sword strapped to my waist. I have a length of rope in case the stairs have gone and I have to lower myself into the cellar. So far so good.

Smith has, however, grown more and more agitated with each delay. He reminds me several times that he does not wish to find himself in the ruins after dark. Now, as we finally make our way through the rubble, I am aware that the sun is already below the horizon – good for proceeding undetected but not so good for spotting any danger ahead. A dull, brick-red glow, scarcely strong enough to be called light, suffuses the ruins. It is a strange, horizontal landscape. Only the broken churches and lonely chimney stacks provide some vertical grace notes. Between the base heaps of blistered rubble are narrow, winding lanes, their courses defined by whether adjacent buildings collapsed inwards or outwards. The streets are full of traps for the unwary. If you take your eyes off the ground for a moment, you're almost certain to stumble. And, as the last of the light fades, I become more aware how many small fires yet burn here – cellars full of oil or neat stacks of timber that have been gently smouldering for days. Most of those cellars are now open to the sky – another pitfall for the hastening traveller.

Smith and I proceed largely in silence, not wishing to draw attention to ourselves. Smith, with the responsibility for finding the way, constantly glances from left to right, stops and checks his bearings. The vast hollow tooth of St Paul's provides us with a good landmark for the first part of our journey. From a distance, it still seems almost whole; the walls are standing, supported by their thick buttresses. Much of the window tracery is still in place. But the setting sun finds no glass to cast back its reflection. There is a chill emptiness to the roofless nave. The great doorway lies open to the world and there is only a Godless gloom within.

It is at St Paul's that we finally light our lanterns. They will help guide us, but may also guide others to us. We now have two small pools of light, but the darkness beyond them is all the more intense. There are many tales of travellers waylaid and robbed as they cross the ruins. Tonight we have seen nobody – no other lamps glow. And yet, after St Paul's, I increasingly feel we are being watched. Sometimes I turn and think I see a shadow move behind a wall, or I hear the sound of fallen masonry disturbed by a foot. London is far from silent. Stones heated by the fire continue to cool, contract and fracture. Walls that have been hanging for days on a flake of mortar finally crash into the street, sending up a cloud of dust. The damaged City is constantly moving, as if trying to find a more comfortable way to lie.

The map had implied that our destination was close to the cathedral, but Smith continues to advance with surprising confidence along the bleak, ashy streets. My instructions to Will that Arlington should search close to St Paul's will be of little assistance. Then, finally, he stops and points. At first I can find nothing, but then I realise I am hoping for too much – I am expecting to see two stone figures, erect and whole, when I should be looking for their fragmented remains. I cast my light to and fro, and there, half buried in a heap of bricks, I make out the shadowy head and upper torso of a man. His brows are garlanded with stone leaves and a rough stone club lies across his shoulder. The companion figure has vanished but I think we have found the house. We climb over the truncated outer wall and stand on what must once have been the stone floor of a substantial citizen's dwelling. I think nobody much has been this way since the fire. Pewter plates, well worth stealing, lie scattered on the blackened slabs. And, over to the right, is what seems to be the entrance to the cellar. A partly burnt beam lies across it. Nearby are a couple of enormous stones, smooth and flat. I try to work out where they can have fallen from, but amid so much destruction it is difficult to tell. It is fortunate that they did not fall across the stairway, because I don't think that the two of us could have moved them. The beam is an easier task, however. Together we grasp one end and are able to swing it round and away from the top of the steps. I crouch and hold up my lantern, then peer down into the cellar. The pale yellow beam shows me a steep flight of dusty stone stairs, leading into the black depths of an ancient arched chasm. A strong smell of wine rises to greet me. There are no footprints in the dust.

'That's as far as I'm going tonight,' says Smith, as he picks up his own lantern. 'I've brought you here. Now I want to get back to the world of the living as soon as I can.'

Though this is undoubtedly what we agreed, I am not sure I follow Smith's logic. We have got here safely together; it would be better for him to remain a short time rather than return alone – particularly if we have been observed.

'If you're worried about footpads, then stay while I search and we can go back together,' I say.

Smith shakes his head. 'It's not just footpads,' he says. 'There's something spooky about the ruins. You feel there are dead eyes on you the whole time.'

I must admit that I too had felt the same thing. But it is our imaginations playing tricks. I doubt the dead have much interest in us. I watch Smith go, the feeble light from his candle fading, then disappearing completely round a corner. From now on I must rely on my lantern alone. A cold breeze disturbs the ash, sending a cloud scudding almost invisibly across the stone floor, though I feel it against my skin.

I pull my scarf across my mouth and nose and turn my attention again to the staircase. Before descending, I stand as still as I can and look around me. If I were setting a trap, rather than possibly walking into one, what would I do? I might conceal myself at the bottom of the steps. Or, if I were more patient, there are plenty of low walls to hide behind and catch the unsuspecting searcher as he left the cellar with whatever he'd found. Either way, I could dispose of my victim quietly, underground, away from prying eyes.

I extinguish the lantern and remain there in the darkness for a full five minutes, listening for any sound within the cellar or above ground, watching for movement where there should be stillness. Once more I have a feeling – no more than that – that there is somebody out there observing me. But if the plan was for a band of men to follow and attack us, then they could have done it by now. Unless there's some part of their plan that I don't quite understand yet.

On the other hand, perhaps I have just worked for Arlington too long. Occasionally, I remind myself, you are given honest information with benign intent. Might it not be one of those rare instances of good faith that all agents encounter occasionally? I take out my tinderbox again and strike up a flame. With my lantern casting its wholly inadequate light on the worn stone steps below and on the vaulting above, I begin to descend into the gloom. One set of footsteps now marks the dust.

Chapter Thirteen

The air in the cellar is hot and unpleasant, but not unbearable. The conflagration does not seem to have reduced everything down here to ashes. This house was on the edge of the fire – unlucky enough for everything burnable above ground to have burnt, but not part of the vast, City-wide inferno that melted lead and glass. The smell I noticed earlier comes from some barrels of wine that have split in the heat, allowing their contents to cascade onto the earthen floor. Most of it has soaked or evaporated away, but there is a heady odour that, under different circumstances, might not have been disagreeable.

My hope was that the box had merely been hidden rather than buried; but there is nothing visible that meets Smith's description – there are some twisted staves and metal bands that were once barrels, a heap of small black wizened objects that may have been apples. No boxes, however, large or small. I check the floor carefully, looking for evidence of something buried in haste. But the hard-packed earth seems even and undisturbed. Has Smith taken me to the wrong cellar? I think not, because the wild man guided us here. Then, have others arrived before me? I can find no other way in. I do not think anyone has entered here for some time. Once more I look carefully up the stairs for any sign of movement. There is none.

Though the floor is earth, the walls and ceiling down here are one great stone arch, suggesting that a grand house once stood on the site. But at the far end, there is a barrier of rough planks – perhaps at some stage the original cellar was divided into two. I look to see whether the box might be hidden there. In one place the timbers seem damp and there is a smell that is not wine. I fear that a neighbour has built his privy slightly too close, but there is no trace there of a hiding place.

I begin to suspect not a cleverly set trap but a wild-goose chase. Hubert is undoubtedly mad. It is not surprising that he would have known this house by the strange figures at the door, and dreamt up this diversion without malice of any sort. Why did I think that a hastily drawn map gave any greater credence to the tale? Why did I listen to Smith, who has admitted that he does not know Hubert well? I think I should waste no more of my time here.

Then, finally, I do hear footsteps above – soft and careful, but unmistakable – and a rustling sound. Perhaps the trap is sprung, or perhaps, as Smith warned me, it is simply that others are in search of the same papers. Whoever they are, it is too late to extinguish my lantern again. They will have seen the light. And when they come, I may as well see who they are. I draw my sword as silently as I can and I wait at the bottom of the stairs.

The footsteps continue downwards. I watch to see how many pairs of feet appear, but all I see is a dusty skirt slowly descending, then a slim waist.

'Oh, it *is* you,' says Aminta, peering at me. 'That's a relief. I was almost beginning to wonder if I'd got the wrong cellar.'

'Yes,' Aminta admits. 'I did say I *could* get a coach back to Westminster. I just didn't say I was going to.'

'Did you follow me all the way here?'

'Of course not. Far too difficult. No cover anywhere except a few chimneys and church towers. I simply went straight to St Paul's, ahead of you, then waited there. Once the two of you stomped into view, I watched to see which way you went. Since you lit your lamps, that wasn't too difficult. I stayed back, in the darkness, until you reached the house with the two wild men guarding it – only one, as it turned out. I watched Smith scuttle away, coward that he is, but couldn't see you anywhere. Then, coming closer, I saw the light in the cellar.'

'That was very dangerous.'

'I'm sorry, but if it was dangerous for me, surely it was dangerous for you?'

'I'm armed,' I say. 'And I'm a man.'

'Yes, but I'm not rash to the point of stupidity,' she points out.

'So, why did you follow me?'

'Because at some point you were certain to need help. Did it not occur to you that Smith might attack you?'

'Yes,' I say. 'It was clear Will didn't trust him at all. That's why I kept him in front of me where I could see him.'

'If he didn't cut your throat as you travelled here, then you might still have been ambushed by somebody else after he left. I've been hiding up there watching to see if anyone followed you down the stairs. When nobody came, I thought I should join you. It's dark out there. I even prefer being here with you to being out there.'

'Thank you.'

'You're welcome. Anyway, for once Will was wrong: you haven't been attacked by Smith or anyone else. If it's a trap, it's a very inefficient one. Most disappointing. I hope you've at least found the letters.'

'Not a thing,' I say.

'You've looked properly?'

'What else do you imagine I've been doing? I've tried the floor. I searched all of the walls, including the one that's had a cesspit made too close to it.'

'In that case, the question is why we've been sent on such a fool's errand.'

'It's only me who's been sent,' I point out. 'You've gone voluntarily, in spite of not being stupid.'

'Well, at least Will won't have to go to Westminster tomorrow morning and report you missing,' says Aminta. 'Because it transpires you were in no danger at all.'

Then above us we hear the grating of stone on stone. I motion to Aminta to keep quiet and wait to see what happens next. But nobody comes down the stairs. The grating continues, then ceases. We look at each other.

'Wasn't there more light coming down the stairs before?' asks Aminta.

'The sun is long down . . .' I say.

'Even so, there was a little light from the moon,' says Aminta.

I advance up the stairs cautiously. Where I had expected to see the night sky, there is just the underside of a large slab of stone. I put the lantern down and, using both hands, try to push the obstacle to one side. It does not move at all. My hands slip against the smooth surface. I clearly spent too much time wondering if the beam across the entrance had been moved before and too little time wondering about those two giant slabs. Somebody has planned this and, now I finally know their purpose, I have to concede that they have not planned it badly. The trap has finally been sprung.

'Well, at least we know why we've been sent here,' says Aminta. 'It was to entomb us in a hot cellar. And the trick worked. I'm so glad I haven't had a completely wasted journey.'

'How right Will was not to trust Smith,' says Aminta.

'We can't be sure he deliberately led us into a trap,' I say.

'Can't we?'

'The question,' I say to Aminta, 'is how we get out. Any ideas? You said you were the clever one.'

'Yes, but I said nothing about physical labour. Moving large stones is men's work.'

'We'll just have to sit here until morning,' I say. 'Once Will has paid his visit to Arlington, somebody will come and find us. It may take an hour or two to locate the house, and two or three men to shift stones, but it can be done.'

'The house isn't at all where the map showed it,' says Aminta.

'You're right,' I say. 'Now I think upon it, I was surprised when Smith pressed on so confidently after we'd passed St Paul's. That's where Arlington will be looking but we're nowhere near it. It may take days for him to find us here. And, however much we yell, I doubt there will be anyone much up there to hear us, even when the sun rises.'

'Still, somebody knows exactly where we are.'

'Who?' I ask.

'Whoever trapped us down here. The question is why, and when they are coming back for us.'

We look at each other. I agree. A rescue some time in the next day or two may be too late.

'I can't shift the stone,' I say. 'Not by brute force or by cleverness. And the walls are all stone too. Except that one.'

'The cesspit one?'

'If shit can get through, so can we. It must be bare earth beyond the planks. If we can just dig two or three feet that way, we ought to be in the cesspit.'

'You *want* to be in the cesspit?'

'It's better than staying here to see what fate somebody had planned for us.'

'What a shame it's men's work, or I'd help you dig,' says Aminta.

But I am already levering off the wettest of the boards and testing the wall with my spade.

'Wait!' says Aminta.

'What?' I say.

'That may be where the shit is coming through, but the shaft must run all the way down that wall. Start higher up, where it's drier.'

I smash the spade into the wall as close to the top as I can, and begin mining inwards.

The soil is hard, but Will has fortunately stolen a good spade and the wall is even thinner and shoddier than I thought. After five minutes the blade breaks through and an appalling stench reaches our nostrils. I continue to hack away at the wall, enlarging the opening and pushing as much soil as I can down into the pit. Eventually I can get my head and shoulders through and look upwards. I am in a cesspit but I am looking at the stars. I'll need to climb seven or eight feet, my back against the wall and feet against the other side. It is slick and shiny, but I can see there are footholds. I explain this to Aminta.

'And you expect me to do the same?'

'It would be impractical in those skirts and petticoats. I shall climb up and then pull you out with this rope. The only danger is that I might slip and fall into the pit.'

'And if that happens?' asks Aminta.

I have often wondered how I might die. Drowning in a cesspit was not something I worried about before.

'It depends how much shit there is,' I say.

I keep hacking at the opening. The larger it is, the easier it will be to get Aminta out, but the longer I work, the more the danger that somebody will come back to finish us off. Eventually I take the rope and wrap it round my body. Then I squeeze through the hole until my back is firmly against the far wall. Slowly I work my way up, pushing with my boots, grasping anything I can with my hands, my back slipping and sliding against the slimy surface. Finally my head emerges into the night. I reach up and grasp the slimy edges of the hole with both hands and haul myself onto the dry ground, panting for breath. I have now covered my coat with ash, in addition to everything else, but I doubt I'd have wanted to wear it again anyway. For a moment I lie there with my eyes closed.

'Are you at the top yet?' asks Aminta from below.

'Yes,' I call back. 'Give me a moment and I'll lower the rope to you. I think we've saved Will the inconvenience of a visit to Arlington.'

Then, as I open my eyes, I notice a man standing over me. Like most travellers in the City, his face is half-covered with a scarf, but more unusually he has a large knife in his hand.

'Shall I bring your sword up with me?' Aminta calls from below. 'You left it on the floor.'

'My sword?' I say. 'Yes, now I think of it, that would have been helpful.'

Chapter Fourteen

'Who are you?' I ask, rising to a crouching position. 'Who sent you?'

The man in front of me says nothing. I suppose he doesn't need to. Maybe I haven't asked the right question yet.

That was one of the other things that Arlington's fencing master said to me. There's no harm in trying to get them to talk. They won't be able to persuade you that you want to die, but you may be able to persuade them that it would be a bad idea to kill you. There's really nothing to lose by it. This one doesn't seem open to persuasion. Still, I've now had time to rise fully to my feet and to grab a handful of gravel, hopefully unnoticed, from the dark floor as I do so.

'If you kill me,' I say, 'you'll hang for it.'

It's difficult to tell behind the mask, and with only moonlight to assist me, but he seems to be laughing. He definitely thinks he'll get away with it. To be fair, he probably will. He is slightly shorter than I am, but we possess only one weapon between us, and he has it. I doubt that his standards of fairness when fighting are any loftier than my own. I expect him to strike without warning.

'Are you going to throw that rope down?' Aminta calls. 'It's all right for you up there in the fresh air, but it's getting very smelly down here.'

'I've got a slight problem,' I call back.

'Can't you deal with it later?'

'Not really,' I say.

'Well, hurry up then.'

The man doesn't seem surprised that I'm having a conversation with a hole in the ground, so he presumably knows Aminta is down there. In which case he has probably had something to do with moving the stones – almost certainly with several friends to help him. Fortunately his friends seem to have decided that the job has been done for the moment. He's alone.

'I know who you are,' I say. He shakes his head sadly at this feeble ploy.

'Who are you talking to?' Aminta calls up to me. 'Even if you've met an old friend, you don't have time for idle chatter.'

Well, she's right about the idle chatter. Time to bring the discussion to a conclusion. I'm now upright and he's advanced as close to me as I think he's going to get before he strikes.

'Look,' I say to him. 'Let's see if we can find some shared advantage here. Whatever you're being paid to do this, I can pay you more. Let me explain how it's going ...'

A further piece of advice from the fencing master – hit them mid-sentence, preferably on a verb or a gerund. Grammatically it's the very last thing they'll expect.

Instinctively he puts up his hands to stop the shower of gravel striking his face and for a moment he closes his eyes. That gives me more than enough time to get my boot up and into his groin. That in turn allows me to close in on him with a rapid half-stride and smash my forehead into his nose, just as he lowers his hands to his breeches. He drops to the ground, with a surprised expression on the upper half of his face, and his knife bounces away into the darkness.

Make it easy for yourself, my fencing master always said. Don't try to do it all in a single blow. But, above all, finish the job. Don't think just because you've broken his right arm that he can't do something with his left arm. Stay alert until he's definitely dead or the whole thing may prove a great disappointment.

It is while I am contemplating this last point that I feel a hand curl round my leg. I try to pull away but it is too late – indeed my sudden movement actually assists my assailant. The world jolts alarmingly to the right and I come crashing down just short of the opening to the cesspit. A rich and pungent aroma rises to greet my nose. I can't see where he is, so I lash out wildly with my boot and am gratified to hear a muffled curse, the first words he has spoken. I sit up quickly so that I can evaluate how stupid I have been. Reasonably stupid seems to be the answer.

So, here's my position. I'm free, which is good. He's standing over me again, blood pouring from what is left of his nose, which is bad; but this time he is fortunately without the knife, which, I notice, has landed on the far side of the cesspit, with me between him and the weapon. That is very good indeed. Best of all, he is still alone and not calling for help. He knows his colleagues are already out of earshot.

He pauses, then makes a rush for the knife; but that means he has to take his eyes off me for a moment and watch what he is doing on the uneven ground. What with one thing and another, he's not as fast as he was. I kick out at his legs as he passes me and roll away again. This time I don't make contact – he must have seen it coming and sidestepped, though I hear his boots slip and slide alarmingly on the loose gravel. Now I fear I shall be facing a man with a knife again, but when I look up he has simply gone. How did he do that? Then I notice: clutching the very edge of the cesspit are approximately eight fingertips. He has lost his footing at just the wrong moment. I wait curiously to see what will happen. I remember that those edges are quite slimy. After a few moments there is a splash and Aminta screams.

'Are you all right?' I call down.

'I'm fine, but something has just fallen into the cesspit,' she calls back.

I look down to see if I can detect any movement. It is difficult to be sure. It's very dark down there. But even my fencing master would have to concede my assailant has probably run out of moves.

'Nothing of any importance,' I say. 'I'm lowering the rope to you now. Sorry about the delay.'

Will does not allow us to enter the chamber until we have removed and handed him our outer clothes.

'That was a perfectly good coat,' he mutters. 'I've no idea how to get it clean. As for those breeches . . . I'll send to your father, Lady Pole, for another dress. I think that one is spoilt for ever. I hope Mr Grey's best blanket will suffice in the meantime.'

'There are worse things that can befall a man,' I say. 'And I must apologise for losing your spade, Will. Our method of leaving the cellar precluded taking too much baggage.'

'We'll need to buy the gardener another one,' he says. 'Unless you think we can recover it.'

'I might be able to move the stone slabs with your help,' I say. 'I think it will require at least two men. Which points to my assailant having one or more helpers last night, though sadly they left him too soon.'

'And you found nothing, Mr Grey?'

'Nothing at all, Will. Either I've been very stupid and missed it, or I've been very stupid and fallen into a trap. Or both.'

'Smith ran off and left you?'

'Yes.'

'But who would want to imprison you there?'

'I don't know, but Smith was the only person who knew where I was going.'

'And he is the good friend of Mr Hubert's?'

'Exactly,' I say. 'That's who he is.'

Arlington's expression owes something to his contempt for my incompetence, but perhaps rather more to the residual odour of cesspit that has accompanied me to the Palace of Whitehall. I can't blame him either way.

'I didn't order you to go on your fool's errand,' says Arlington. 'There is no point in trying to claim the cost of a new suit of clothes.'

'I hadn't intended to,' I say. 'But I should certainly like to know who tried to kill me.'

'You think, Mr Grey, that I know the answer to that question?'

That had not been my meaning, but Arlington's sensitivity on the subject is interesting.

'It would not be the first time that I had got into difficulties because you had told me less than you might, my Lord.'

'It would not be the first time that you had displayed a regrettable lack of caution,' he snaps.

'It is easier to display the right amount of caution if you have all the facts at your disposal,' I say.

'You are told as much as I think you need to know, Mr Grey. If you don't like those terms then you don't have to work for me. I did not order you to seek out this Smith person. Had I known about this unlikely tale of letters in a lead box that might have survived the fire – a conflagration that melted the entire *lead* roof of St Paul's Cathedral – I might have advised you to wait until today and take an armed guard with you. I could have provided one. As it is, you were lured onwards by your own folly and arrogance.'

'You really have no idea who Smith is?'

'Why should I?'

'Because all manner of men come to you, as they did to Thurloe, with information to sell. Smith may have offered his services to you before selling them elsewhere.'

Arlington makes some pretence of considering this. 'You say he has a red birthmark on his face?'

'Yes.'

Arlington shakes his head. 'I don't think so, Mr Grey.'

'Hubert gave him the map,' I say. 'I can ask Hubert.'

'Hubert is mad. Nothing he says is to be trusted. I am not paying you to chase after shadows.'

'That is noted, my Lord,' I say. 'I shall do it for my own amusement. I assume you have no objection to my paying another visit to the White Lion Gaol? No charge to the King's Treasury – just part of the obligations of an English gentleman.'

Arlington scowls at me. I shouldn't have implied he knew

who had tried to kill me, especially if there's a good chance he may. Somebody clearly wants me dead. I'll need to watch my back a little more carefully in future.

'I know of no map,' says Hubert.

He has been brought up out of his cell and we are sitting in a small room with a view, through the bars, of the gaol's main courtyard. The sun is shining. A few of the more trusted prisoners are lounging in the dusty yard. This is not the least comfortable of prisons. Hubert could have fared worse. He could have been in the Tower.

'Your good friend Smith says you gave him the map,' I say.

'Did he?'

Hubert considers this for a very long time. I decide to jog his memory further. 'He told me you gave it to him because you had hidden some letters there. In a lead-lined box.'

Hubert suddenly seems very confused. 'Why did he say I would hide anything?'

'The letters contain some information that you wish to keep from the authorities. Perhaps they named your fellow conspirators?'

'I do not know their names.'

Well, he didn't need to think too long about that.

'So why would Smith inform me about the box?' I ask.

Hubert shakes his head. 'I think you are trying to trick me. He would not tell you that. There are no letters. And I have explained: it was me and Monsieur Peidloe and three others.'

'I thought it was twenty-three,' I say.

Hubert frowns as if trying to remember. 'No, he said three.'

'Who said three? It wasn't Peidloe, was it? Somebody else is sending you instructions.'

Hubert shakes his head and smiles as if he has finally seen through my deceit. 'I have told you everything, Mr Grey. I set the City ablaze. I placed the fireball through the window and not into the yard in the form of a triangle and full of dry wood for the oven. I killed Monsieur Peidloe. I shot him in the back, hard by St Paul's. I have told you this. You are lying about Mr Smith. Why would I hide anything in a cellar?'

Why indeed? 'How long have you known Smith?' I ask.

Hubert is resentful that my questions continue in this way. He feels he has dealt with this already. 'He said I had known him for some years.'

'He *said* that? What do you mean *he said that*?'

'I mean that is what he told me. That I think is clear enough.'

'And *did* you know him?'

'At first I thought not. Then he said I did. I was wrong.'

'When did he tell you this? You don't have to just repeat what he told you to say, Mr Hubert. If he's making you tell lies, he isn't your friend. Who does Smith work for?'

'I cannot tell you that,' he says. 'But I did kill Monsieur Peidloe, my master. I shot him in the back, hard by St Paul's. I set fire to the baker's shop. That is all you need to know, I think. And now I should like to go back to my cell.'

'I had hoped,' says Sir Felix, 'that you would have taken greater care of my daughter. Because of you she appears to have taken to walking the streets of London at night and abandoning perfectly good dresses in Lincoln's Inn. It is conduct that I would associate more with her mother.'

'On the contrary. By walking the streets of London at night, my dear father, I was merely following the example that *you* had set me. I scarcely remember my mother. And fortunately John has rescued both you and me from our respective follies.'

'I advised you not to work for Arlington, John,' says Sir Felix, ignoring Aminta's intervention. 'He will always put the King's interests before yours, and his own before the King's. Life as a lawyer may be dull, but you don't have to shovel shit in the dark.'

Actually shovelling shit in the dark is not a bad metaphor for a lot of what I do as a lawyer, but I usually do it in more comfort than I did last night. I remind myself that I still have to recover the shovel.

'I still have no idea what Arlington is covering up,' I say. 'But I'm certain that there's something he's not telling me.'

'You don't trust him?'

'He has never suggested that I should trust him, and he would know best. I can understand why he would wish to cover up a plot if that was in the King's interest, but I think that he is more closely concerned than that.'

'And you will endanger yourself and my daughter in your attempt to discover what that is?'

'Unless I find an easier way.'

Sir Felix pauses. 'Then perhaps I should tell you something, John. I wasn't sure whether it was right to betray a confidence but if it will save your getting trapped in another cellar . . . you'll remember Mr Graunt, the New River Director?'

'Yes, of course.'

'And whose appointment I recommended.'

'Because, presumably, you knew him well?'

'Well, no – not at all well, as it happens.'

'So why did you recommend him?'

'I was asked to do so by a distant kinsman of mine. Sir Thomas Clifford. I think you know him?'

'He is one of Arlington's creatures,' I say. 'Clever, obsequious and loyal to his master. When he was first elected an MP he came to Arlington for help. Now he is a Privy Councillor and one of the King's closest advisers. He is rumoured to be a Catholic, though he still attends Anglican services. Arlington will advance him further if he can – and protect him if he needs to.'

'Just so. I mean, it may signify nothing that Sir Thomas wanted Graunt in that position. Or that my Lord Arlington has made no mention to you of Sir Thomas's role in this, which I think he must be aware of. But I thought, under the circumstances, I should say something . . .'

'Thank you,' I say. 'Am I allowed to tell anyone else that?'

'Yes – if you need to and if you do not say that I told you. Sir Thomas *is* a kinsman, albeit a distant one. I should not wish him to think I was disloyal.'

'I shall not mention your name.'

Sir Felix nods. 'I have no doubt that Arlington would be pleased to advance you in the same way as he has Sir Thomas. He would value having you in a seat in the House of Commons. Or even the Lords if it could be arranged . . .'

'The price would be too high,' I say.

'Sorry,' says Sir Felix. 'The error is mine. I was forgetting that you were a stiff-necked Puritan.'

'It's the one thing he's really good at,' says Aminta.

'So,' says Lord Ashley, 'you think somebody tried to assassinate you?'

'Somebody certainly trapped me in a cellar and tried to prevent my leaving. I don't know what would have happened if we had remained. As I say, the man they had left to guard us certainly tried to kill me.'

'We?'

'Lady Pole accompanied me. Smith had gone – he stayed no longer than he had to. He did not come down into the cellar with me. I think he knew it was a trap.'

'And he deliberately led you into it?'

'Yes, through a clever bit of play-acting. He subtly made it clear that I would not find the house alone and ensured that I would ask for his help. He cunningly dissuaded me from taking my clerk. He is an accomplished liar.'

'You have changed your view of him.'

'Sometimes first impressions can be wrong, my Lord. Hubert said something very odd: that Smith had *told* him that they'd known each other for some time. Hubert is very suggestible and Smith has been making a lot of suggestions to him. The question is: on whose behalf?'

Ashley nods, then grimaces. Whatever pains him seems much as before, but I know that he would not welcome my interest or sympathy. He dislikes weakness in himself or others.

'We must track Smith down,' he says.

'I fully intend to. Hubert claims not to know who the real leader of this plot is. But I think Smith does and will reveal it under a little pressure. Hubert is clearly very loyal to somebody. But he had not been told about the map and the cellar – that confused him. Whoever the real leader is, he decided Hubert didn't need to know about that. So Hubert gave away more than was intended. His puppet-master made a mistake there, I think. That will help us.'

Ashley nods thoughtfully. 'And have you formed any view as to who that might be? It is strange, is it not, how everything leads back to my Lord Arlington? Sir Thomas Clifford, you say, requested the appointment of Graunt. And Clifford is undoubtedly Arlington's man. Graunt is still held under conditions that are not too trying for him – on Arlington's instructions. Arlington also delayed the recovery of Peidloe's body until it was too late to identify him or, without your expert advice, even to say how he died. Above all, Arlington has taken custody of Hubert, and is careful to ensure that he too is not uncomfortable and that only you question him – or at least he is anxious that I should not, in spite of my instructions from the King.'

'I am sure, my Lord, that Lord Arlington has no such wish . . .'

'Then I would suggest that you propose to him that I should question Hubert again – or Graunt. I don't much care which. If he acquiesces to either of those very reasonable suggestions, then I shall be forced to admit that I am wrong, at least on this occasion.'

'I shall be pleased to allay your fears, my Lord. On this occasion.'

'Because you think that Arlington isn't a devious pile of shit?'

Well, no, I rather think he is and that I have the scars to prove it. But I shake my head.

'Why not stop being Arlington's man for just a moment, Mr Grey? You can see as well as I can what's going on. For reasons neither of us understands, Arlington is covering somebody's trail as fast as he can. Sir Thomas Clifford's most likely. His own too quite possibly. There's a plot. He knows about it. He's hiding it. And you know I'm right.'

Again I say nothing.

'You are an intelligent man, Mr Grey,' Lord Ashley continues. 'Which of the two paths in front of you do you intend to take? Are you going to work for Arlington until, one way or another, he allows you to die in some obscure alleyway or country ditch? Or are you going to devote your life to drawing up wills and leases until you shrivel up and become like the dry parchment you write on?'

'I hadn't made a firm decision,' I say. 'Both sound good to me.'

Lord Ashley laughs. 'It will not surprise you that I was going to draw your attention to a third way,' he says. 'Look at Clifford. He was a nobody until Arlington took him up. Look at Joseph Williamson; just the same – a clergyman's son from the north, who thought he was lucky to be a Fellow of Queen's College. Then Arlington discovered him. Look at Samuel Pepys. His father's a tailor, but with the right connections he's now the confidant of the Duke of York. Lord Sandwich bought Pepys a clerkship at the Navy Office worth £350 a year, with God knows how much more in gifts and bribes from suppliers to the Navy. But Mr Pepys is not just rich – he has real power to do good or bad as he chooses. If he needs to talk to the King, he can talk to the King. If he wants to help somebody deserving, he can help them. You could have all that too. You just require somebody to find you a place, and you'll rise as fast as Pepys or Williamson. You don't need to skulk in muddy lanes in Devon to do it. You don't need to scuttle down dark corridors. And you certainly don't need to sit in your chamber being patronised by some Essex farmer with muddy boots who needs a copyhold endorsed.'

'And do you know of such a somebody, my Lord?'

'I think you know what I mean, Mr Grey.'

'Yes,' I say. 'I know what you mean.'

'I need good men around me,' says Ashley. 'Men I can trust to do what I need them to do.'

'I have a prior commitment,' I say.

'I think that Arlington has forfeited your loyalty.'

I nod. 'I'll need to think about it,' I say.

Chapter Fifteen

'Lord Ashley wishes to question Mr Hubert again,' I say.

'That will not be necessary,' snaps Arlington. 'I am satisfied that Hubert is blameless – mad, just as you report, but blameless for all that. It is scarcely surprising that he knew where the fire started. Everyone in London knows where the fire started – Pudding Lane. And, if he hadn't heard before, this Smith person will doubtless have informed him. The story of arriving by ship is patently invented. Why should Peidloe have taken him to Sweden anyway? What was his purpose? It does not lie on his route from Paris to London – not by a thousand miles. It is not even a Catholic country. Hubert cannot tell us what he did there. Why? Because he never went there. And Lowman proved that no such ship had docked. It's all a lie. A madman's lie. As for his claim that he is a murderer, we still have no good evidence that the body we have is even Peidloe's or, if it is, that he was murdered by Hubert. In the end we just have a handful of coins that anyone could have planted in his pocket before you arrived – the man you saw crouching over the body, for example. What was he doing if not that? Hubert can't even remember how many conspirators there were – three or twenty-three – and doesn't seem to think it matters very much. And he's right. It doesn't matter.'

'And Mr Graunt?' I say.

'I have your report. It was very clear. He forgot to return the key after inspecting the taps. Taps that, by oversight, had been left turned off. There is no need to delve further into that.'

We look at each other. I know that Sir Thomas Clifford had a role in appointing Graunt. I cannot reveal that now without also revealing the source of my information and Sir Felix's own indiscretion. But everything that Arlington says suggests he knows what happened as well as I do.

'Even so, perhaps I should speak to Mr Graunt again,' I say.

'Mr Grey, when I asked you to help me, my wish was that you should interview Mr Graunt and Mr Hubert. You have now done this. As I say, your reports are quite clear, to me at least – there is no good reason to suspect either man of treason. I am grateful to you and shall ensure that the King sees them and that you are paid for your time. But I do not need you to speak to Mr Graunt again – he has told us all he can. I do not need you to speak to Mr Hubert again – I do not need to know that the number of conspirators is now thirteen or thirty-three or that he reached Sweden via Virginia or Constantinople. I do not need you to chase after Mr Smith. Above all, I do not need you to accuse me of withholding information from you. Your role in this matter is over. Thank you for your assistance. There is nothing more for you to do. I bid you good day, sir.'

'Fifty Pounds received from Lord Arlington,' says Will. 'That's rapid payment.'

'It's too much,' I say. 'He's paying me not only for what I've done but for what I'm not going to do.'

'A bribe to stay out of his affairs?'

'Yes.'

'A bribe not to assist his rival Lord Ashley?'

'Possibly.'

'That's kind of him then, Mr Grey. He only needed to order you to stop. You've nothing to gain by prying into matters that don't concern us, sir. If Lord Arlington does not wish you to speak further to Mr Graunt, then I would not speak to Mr Graunt. He'll hear about it if you do, sooner or later. He always does.'

'I still intend to discover the truth, Will. I shan't let Hubert hang if he is innocent and I shan't let Arlington bring down the only honest minister the King has. I'll speak to Sir Thomas Clifford.'

'Oh, I wouldn't do that, sir! Not if I were you. Lord Arlington would certainly come to hear of it. Anyway, I doubt Sir Thomas will speak to you.'

I smile. 'It depends on how I ask him,' I say.

'Yes, of course, I can tell you where to find Sir Thomas,' says Sir Felix. 'But if Arlington has ordered you not to investigate further, then I wouldn't do it. After all, you can hardly expect Sir Thomas not to mention your visit, at least in passing. And you'll get nothing from my kinsman, because Sir Thomas has probably already consulted Arlington on what to do and has been told to say nothing – especially to you.'

'But he would speak to me,' says Aminta, looking up from her sewing. 'And Arlington can scarcely forbid me to visit my own family.'

'Distant family,' says Sir Felix thoughtfully.

'But still my family rather than Arlington's.'

'Does Sir Thomas know you?' Sir Felix asks me. 'Would he recognise your face?'

'No,' I say. 'I doubt if he knows I exist.'

'Then you might accompany Aminta *incognito*,' says Sir Felix.

'But in what capacity?' I ask.

'As my serving man,' says Aminta. 'Nobody could doubt the need for a lady to be accompanied by one of her servants through these dangerous streets. And he would take less care what he said in front of my footman than if I introduced you as a cousin or neighbour.'

'I'm not dressed as a servant,' I say.

'In those black clothes you might be almost anything – an impoverished clergyman, a scrivener, an out-of-work plague doctor. If you hoped your dress would excite comment anywhere at all, then sadly I must disappoint you. The scar on your cheek may invite interest, however. I shall have to say that you were in a drunken brawl, which is not far from the truth, and that I had to rescue you from the White Lion Gaol, which is not far from the truth either.'

'Could I not have acquired the wound in some more creditable way?'

'No, I don't think so. A wound like that always more or less condemns a man as disreputable. Anyway, I doubt if Sir Thomas will ask. It's not as if you will be somebody of any importance.'

Sir Thomas Clifford is ill at ease. He eyes us suspiciously. Sir Felix is right. Arlington will have already warned him to take care.

Sir Thomas's face is framed by a large blond wig, elaborately curled. His blond moustache is small and neatly trimmed, as the fashion now is. His nose is too small and slightly upturned. There is more than a little of the pig about that nose. A pig that has been interrupted burrowing into some yellow straw. It is a face that could easily descend into petulance and may do so very soon.

'Your man could wait for you in the kitchens,' he says. 'I am sure he will find it tedious remaining here, listening to things he does not understand. My cook could draw him a tankard of small beer.'

'He'd probably like that,' says Aminta, 'but it would be quite wrong to indulge him, in case he expects such treatment every day. I shall not be long here and he will not trouble us sitting at the back of the room as he is. He will pay no attention to what we say – he is, as you have already noted, somewhat feeble-minded. Nor is he decorative. We employ him very much out of charity.'

'How did he injure his face?'

'He was attacked during the fire. A mob thought he was a Catholic.'

'Ah,' says Sir Thomas. He looks on me in a more kindly manner.

'But he isn't,' says Aminta, wishing it to be clear how much sympathy I am entitled to. 'If anything I'd say he was something of a Puritan. You need not pity him in any way. All of his misfortunes – and they are more than you could imagine – are entirely his own fault.'

Clifford looks me up and down with a certain amount of contempt, then turns away.

'Very well, how can I help you, Lady Pole?'

'I come on my father's behalf. At your request, Sir Thomas, he recommended Mr John Graunt to be a Director of the New River Company. Mr Graunt has since been arrested, as you know, on suspicion of having cut off the water supply to the City at a critical time. My father is naturally concerned.'

Clifford glances at me before speaking. 'He need not be, Lady Pole. I have spoken to . . . some people. I understand that Mr Graunt will be cleared of any blame. The other Directors will not be implicated.'

'Who told you that?'

'I really cannot say.'

'Was it Lord Arlington?'

Sir Thomas smiles uneasily.

'I see,' says Aminta sweetly. 'Well, I must respect that confidence, Sir Thomas. My father was curious, however, to know why you had wished Mr Graunt to be placed in that role.'

'I have known Mr Graunt for some time,' he says. 'I had promised to assist him when I could. The position arose – I asked your father to put his name forward. I explained that to your father at the time. I am sorry that he has been inconvenienced in this way.'

'It was kind of you to assist Mr Graunt. Mr Graunt is perhaps a family member?'

'No. Merely an acquaintance. That is the way things work at court, as you are aware. He would, in due course, have assisted me in return. *Manus manum lavat.* And I should of course have been indebted to your father. As I still am, naturally. If there's anything I can do—'

'You have no other connection to Graunt? No other reason for putting his name forward?'

Sir Thomas looks aghast. 'No,' he says quickly. 'Has Graunt suggested that I do?'

'I have never met Mr Graunt,' says Aminta. 'But your connection to him seems slight. As you say, such favours are part of the currency of the court. Is it possible that somebody else had asked you to place him there if you could?'

'Who had you in mind?'

'You must owe Lord Arlington a favour or two.'

'My Lord Arlington again?' Sir Thomas attempts to laugh but does not quite succeed. 'Lord Arlington would have no interest in such a minor appointment . . . Are you sure that we should be speaking in front of your servant, Lady Pole? He seems to be listening to us very intently.'

'I had a spaniel once who did the same thing. It was almost as if he understood every word. He was not the most obedient of dogs – always getting stuck in holes or sticking his nose into something foul. Not a dog you could rely on. I suppose it's just that he wasn't that well bred.'

I cough pointedly, but neither of them seems to notice.

'I am surprised that you kept such an animal,' says Sir Thomas.

'Oh, he could be useful sometimes. Do you know a Mr Smith, Sir Thomas?'

'No,' says Sir Thomas. 'Not at all.'

'A man with a strawberry birthmark,' says Aminta.

'I know nobody named Smith. Are you saying he has something to do with Mr Graunt?'

'We're unsure,' says Aminta.

'We?'

'My father and I.'

Sir Thomas looks rather unhappy. He swallows hard.

'Of course,' says Sir Thomas. He takes out his gold pocket watch and consults it. 'You and your father. Indeed. I am sorry, Lady Pole, that I cannot help you. I now realise that I have duties elsewhere of a pressing nature that I had clean forgot. I must ask you to leave. Now. Please give Sir Felix my best wishes.'

'So,' says Aminta, as we return to Westminster, 'what did you learn from that?'

'That you think I resemble your spaniel?' I say.

'Oh no, not a bit. He was much nicer than I claimed. I rather liked him, in fact. No, I meant how Sir Thomas was like to be-shit himself at the mere mention of his master, Arlington. Also his abrupt denial that he knew Mr Smith.'

'Perhaps he doesn't?'

'Everyone knows a Mr Smith,' says Aminta. 'You may not know him well, but you'd at least pause and consider. You'd ask *which* Mr Smith, wouldn't you? Not just deny that you'd ever known anyone of that name.'

'Yes,' I agree.

'So I'd say Arlington has already discussed this affair with Sir Thomas and mentioned Smith amongst other characters in play. Sir Thomas has been warned to deny knowing anything, even to the extent of forgetting every Mr Smith he has ever known. Perhaps he's wise to. Somebody tried to kill us. And somebody was shot in the back . . .'

' . . . *hard by St Paul's*,' I say.

'Indeed,' says Aminta. 'I know that. He was shot near the cathedral.'

'No,' I say, 'he was shot *hard by St Paul's*. Every time I spoke to Hubert, he used precisely those words. He always used exactly the same phrase, as if he'd learned it by rote. It's the same with starting the fire – he always says he "set London ablaze". He always describes the yard at Pudding Lane as being "in the form of a triangle and full of dry wood". Most of his English is quite simple – almost stilted – but every now and then he comes up with a phrase that doesn't sound like him at all. And he repeats it over and over again, fearing to make any variation in case it's wrong.'

'So somebody has told him exactly what to say? Word for word?'

'Precisely. Most of the time he repeats the same words verbatim. But when he has time to think for himself he comes up with all sorts of nonsense. Whoever is feeding him this information knows they can't trust him to lie for himself – so they've given him a script. He's fine when he sticks to it, but he's a loose cannon when he doesn't – either because he's forgotten or because he was never told how to answer a particular question.'

'And you think Smith is his tutor? So who is feeding the information to Smith? They've told him things very few people would know.'

'Lord Ashley is convinced it's Arlington behind it all,' I say. 'Everything Arlington's done suggests it. And there are too many things Hubert knows that must have come from Arlington's office.'

'Could it be Williamson rather than Arlington?'

'No, I doubt that.'

'So, it's Arlington himself then?'

I pause. Arlington has never hesitated to send me into fights ill-informed and badly prepared. He has been content for me to languish in captivity when a word from him could have freed me. But he has never gone to the trouble of actually trying to kill me. Why should he?

'Or Sir Thomas Clifford,' I say. 'He'd have contacts inside Arlington's office. I need to find Smith urgently and question him again. Arlington thinks he will have fled London, having tried to have me killed, but Smith may think I am dead and that he has nothing to fear. The real problem is that Smith no longer has a house in which we can find him.'

'What do we know about him? A red birthmark. A widower who had recently lost a wife and children to the Plague. Now homeless because of the fire.'

'It's not a great deal to go on,' I say.

'It may be enough,' says Aminta. 'Those displaced by the fire are living in the fields all round London. Let's start with Moor Fields.'

The weather is fortunately still warm and dry. Most of these temporary structures, here in Moor Fields, would not stand even a light shower of rain. Whole families are encamped under a tarpaulin or in a makeshift hut of rough planks salvaged from the wreckage. Children play in the dust in the warm September sunshine. Nobody I speak to complains of their loss – everyone is convinced that others have suffered worse than they have. The panic of the first night of the fire, and the horror as dawn revealed the extent of the destruction, has been followed by a quiet, dull resignation. Things will get better. But in the meantime, the tents and the shacks fill the open space, as if it were a fair with very little to sell. Smoke rises languidly from cooking pots. People begin to get to know their new neighbours. There is a low buzz of earnest conversation everywhere. But I hear no laughter.

We make enquiries for a man named Smith, with a prominent red birthmark, living somewhere in the City. I also enquire after Monsieur Peidloe. There are plenty of reports of Frenchmen living in London, in spite of the fact that we are at war with France. But I can find nobody who knew Peidloe and nobody named Smith with a red birthmark on his face.

'Of course,' says Aminta, 'it is unlikely that either gave his real name. Being called "Smith" is as close as you can get to having no name at all. I am not even sure the name "Peidloe" exists.'

We watch the encampment begin to prepare for the evening. There is a bustle about the place. Signs of cooking increase.

'Nobody complained of their ill-luck,' I say. 'Everyone told me that there were plenty worse off than themselves. And nobody was begging for money.'

'That's Londoners for you,' says Will, who has never lived anywhere else. 'Finest people on earth.'

'It is a shame that they did not show their better qualities on the night that the fire broke out,' I say.

We tour the fields for another hour without finding anyone who knew Monsieur Peidloe or who has seen a man with a bright red birthmark, though many waste my time by reciting a long list of Frenchmen that they have known at one time or another. As we finally give up for the day, we pass somebody that I must have spoken to earlier.

'Did you find him, sir, your friend with the birthmark?'

I turn to the man, who has just looked up from his cooking pot, a plump man with a careworn face and a much-stained coat, straining at its seams – probably the only suit of clothes he now possesses. What did he say his name was? Sparrow,

I think, though anyone less like that small nimble bird is difficult to imagine.

'No, Mr Sparrow,' I say. 'Nor the Frenchman we were seeking.'

'What was the Frenchman's name again?'

'Peidloe,' I say.

'I think I've heard of somebody with a similar name,' he says.

I nod without enthusiasm. I've lost count of the number of times I've been told that today. I decide to waste no more time.

'If you do remember, you can find me at Lincoln's Inn,' I say.

'Well, I wish you good luck for tomorrow, Mr Grey. I think there are some camped over by Clerkenwell. Your friend might perchance be there.'

I give him five Shillings – all I have left in my pocket. He'll need it. They'll all need it.

When we get back to Aminta's lodgings there is no sign of her father. But a young woman is waiting on the doorstep.

'I'm sorry to trouble you, my Lady,' she says, 'but my husband has vanished. I don't know who else to turn to.'

I am introduced to her. She is Abigail Farley, an actress formerly employed by Aminta's company. Her husband, Richard Farley, is an actor.

'Well, he was an actor, sir,' she says to me. 'Until the theatres closed because of the Plague. He's been working where he can since then. He never earned much from his acting – he didn't have the looks for it, you might say – but most what he's had since the Plague has been poor work. Then he found something paying well, but he'd never tell me what it was – clerking, he said, but that's not really his line. I was worried whether it was as legal as I'd like, but we have no more savings, sir, so I kept quiet and took the Guineas when he brought them home. Then, the night before last, he left saying he'd be away for a couple of hours. But he never returned.'

I exchange glances with Aminta. There would seem to be several very simple explanations.

'Does your husband frequent taverns?' I ask.

'No, sir, he most certainly docs not. Nor does he have another woman, if you're about to ask me that. I'd not worry, sir, except they're seizing men for the Navy, sir. I wondered if they might have taken him. Or, if he went into the City, he may have been attacked by robbers.'

'He won't have been pressed into service unless he looked like a seaman,' I say. 'It is true that the City is a dangerous place, but why would he have ventured there?'

'I don't know,' she says. 'But I don't know who he's working for.'

'I have some contacts,' I say. 'There's a Mr Pepys who may have a list of those impressed by the Navy. And I can make enquiries at Lord Arlington's office. I can promise nothing, but somebody may have news of him.'

She looks at me oddly when I mention Arlington.

'I don't want to trouble you, sir,' she says.

She's right if she thinks I won't have much success. Arlington doesn't collect information on every husband who has stayed out too long. Still, it would seem that she's heard of Arlington.

'It would be no trouble,' I say.

She shakes her head. 'Thank you, sir,' she says primly, 'but that won't be necessary. I didn't know where to turn and so came to my Lady for advice. But if you have heard nothing, my Lady, there are still other friends of his who I can speak to.'

'I thought she wanted help,' I say to Aminta after Abigail has left. 'She seemed to change her mind when I mentioned Arlington.'

'I think she'd just realised she'd rather not know,' says Aminta. 'She suspects her husband has lied to her and fears that he is dead. But she prefers the fear to the certainty. She knows who Arlington is and knows his reputation. She probably thinks there's a very good chance Arlington *will* know what's happened to her husband, if he's caught up in espionage or anything like it. It's like having a letter in front of you that you think contains bad news and not being willing to open it, because it can't hurt you until you do.'

Had I been killed in Devon rather than merely injured, I doubt that anyone would have known where I was buried. But I do not say that. Perhaps Aminta thinks it, however, because for a while we wait in silence for Sir Felix to return. It gets dark. Aminta goes and lights some candles.

'What time did your father leave?' I ask.

'I don't know,' she says.

She checks his room again and finds nothing missing. It seems unlikely that he can have planned to go far when he left the house.

'It is not only actors who vanish mysteriously in this City,' I say.

'Do not joke, John. Where could he have gone to?'

'Perhaps he has found out where his mistress is now lodged?'

'Perhaps,' she says.

We wait together for another hour, talking but not really listening to each other's replies. Every now and then Aminta rises and walks over to the window and glances out into the night. Then there is a banging at the door below. I go down and a boy hands me a letter – a single sheet of paper, sealed with a quickly applied blob of red wax and addressed to Aminta. I give the boy a coin and take the letter back up to her.

'It's my father's writing,' she says. She quickly breaks open the seal and reads, her face falling with every word.

'What is it?' I ask.

'I begin to think that nobody I know is safe,' she says. 'My father's been arrested. On Arlington's orders. He's in the Tower.'

Chapter Sixteen

I think that Arlington is not going to see me. I am kept standing for an hour in an anteroom. I ask if I can talk to Joseph Williamson instead. I am told that he too is busy. But eventually I am summoned in. I do not think that Arlington has been doing very much in the meantime, other than read today's postbag. He carefully turns a pile of letters face down as I enter the room.

'Why didn't you tell me that Sir Felix Clifford was involved in this business?' he demands, before I can say anything. 'You undertake highly sensitive work for me and fail to tell me that a near relative of yours may have been complicit in the very treason that you are investigating.'

'Sir Felix is no relative of mine,' I say.

'Really?' he asks.

We lived in the same village. My father ran off with his wife. But that does not make him kin. You might say it presented me with a conflict of interest of sorts, but in no way does it make him kin. Not legally.

'Yes, really,' I say. 'We've known each other a long time, but we are not related in any way.'

'You were, as I understand it, to marry his daughter?' asks Arlington.

'I have never been betrothed to her.'

Arlington raises a sceptical eyebrow. But again he is wrong for all that. Twice I have failed to propose to Aminta in the most negligent fashion, once before she married the obnoxious Roger Pole and once after he died. But I have made no offer and she has accepted none. There is no contract.

'She accompanied you, however, when you took Hubert to view the ruins?' asks Arlington, turning over a paper at the top of the pile and glancing at it briefly.

I should have known that would get back to him.

'Yes,' I say.

'Why?'

'I thought her advice would be helpful. It has been helpful in the past. You yourself have profited by it before now.'

'In this case it was extremely foolish. Almost as foolish as if you had taken Sir Felix himself. What in God's name were you thinking of, Grey? Can you keep nothing secret?'

'You can trust them both,' I say.

'And you know instinctively who to trust?' Arlington sneers.

Again I finger the scar on my right cheek. Perhaps it would not be a good idea to claim that my judgement is infallible. 'Sir Felix has always been loyal to His Majesty and to the last King. They also are kin to Sir Thomas Clifford. One of the King's ministers.'

I wait to see if there is any reaction from Arlington. If he knows of his protégé's role in all this, he is hiding it very well.

'I believe they are very distantly related,' says Arlington. 'But even if Sir Felix were Sir Thomas's brother, it would not mean that he can be trusted.'

Of course, it might mean neither could be trusted.

'And so you've sent Sir Felix to the Tower?' I ask.

'For the time being.'

'That is where traitors are sent. He is no traitor.'

Arlington smiles. 'If he is indeed innocent, he has nothing to fear. Where was he on the night of the fire? I merely ask out of curiosity.'

Shall I say what I know? Would Sir Felix wish me to reveal the nature of his alibi? Would Aminta?

'You'll have to ask him,' I say. 'You know where to find him.'

'We shall ask him. And let us hope that he confirms that you have no way of knowing where he was. Like you, I do not enjoy being told less than the truth.'

Is it too late to say that I believe his evening was spent in innocent fornication? Probably.

'And Mr Graunt?' I ask.

'He also remains in custody,' says Arlington.

'May I know where?'

'No, you may not. I have already made it clear that you have no further role in this investigation.'

Well, that seems to be that. Then it occurs to me to make an enquiry. 'Are you employing a Mr Farley?' I ask.

Arlington looks blank. 'What relevance does that have?'

Well, none, I suppose. It had occurred to me, as it had to his wife, that Richard Farley might be working for Arlington – he does employ out-of-work actors on account of their skills at dissembling. But I do not think Arlington knows him. I have done what I can, which has proved to be very little. I stand up and place my hat back on my head.

'Is Lady Pole permitted to visit her father?' I ask.

'Not at present.'

'May she write to him?'

'She should leave any letter to him unsealed so that it may be checked by the Keeper of the Tower.'

'I had never assumed it would not be checked,' I say.

'I fear that you are much out of favour with Arlington,' says Lord Ashley. 'And I fear too that it is my fault. I am not, however, wholly without influence. We can have your father-in-law out of the Tower before too long.'

'He is not my father-in-law,' I say.

'I shall nevertheless do my best for you. Sir Felix was ill-advised to recommend Graunt, but Arlington would scarcely risk bringing down his ally, Sir Thomas, by prosecuting Lady Pole's father. I think Sir Felix has nothing to fear.' Ashley pauses. 'Unless he's guilty, of course. Has that occurred to you? Where was he on the night of the fire?'

'He was in the City,' I say. 'But not fire-raising.'

'You are certain of that? You know where he was all night?'

I know where he says he was. But Sir Felix has no reason to plot against the King.

'He is innocent,' I say. 'But he would still rather not remain in the Tower.'

'Then, on that assurance from a man I trust, I shall ensure that he does not remain there. I should like to see him out as much as you would. In the meantime, you will return to your legal work?'

'Arlington has no further use for me,' I say. 'So, I may as well do that.'

'Have you considered my offer?'

'I thought our discussion was merely hypothetical.'

'I don't think so, Mr Grey. I meant it when I said that I

could find you a profitable place at court, and you know that I meant it. Let me be specific, if it helps: the post of Clerk of the Exchequer is within my gift.'

'Is it vacant?'

'It could be made so. The present holder could be bought out. I think he might wish to retire to the country. Or you might choose to employ him as your deputy, if you did not wish to spend too much time in the office. It would still be very profitable for you. Think about it.'

'And what would you want in return, my Lord?'

'Your complete loyalty. I do not think you would find that difficult. It is in your nature. It is helpful to me to have people I can rely on in certain places. I know who I can trust, and I trust you, Mr Grey.'

'I have no desire for a sinecure,' I say.

'Don't worry,' says Ashley. 'I would find plenty of things for you to do.'

I consider this. I know what Pepys would reply, and he is one of the cleverest men in the King's service. And it would be an honour to work for Lord Ashley on any terms. Why then do I hesitate?

'I'm going to see Hubert again,' I say. 'There has to be some way of making him tell us what he knows.'

'I think we've already done that,' says Ashley impatiently. 'He has confessed. The rest must be for a judge and jury to decide. To return to our discussion—'

'I still don't believe his confession,' I say. 'He was being controlled, through Smith, by others. I think Arlington at least knows who those others are. If he won't tell me, then perhaps Smith will. And if I can't find Smith, I'll have to find a way of beating the truth out of Hubert.'

Lord Ashley shakes his head. 'I would not advise it.'

'Why?' I ask.

'You should never make enemies unnecessarily. Especially not at your age. Trust me. You've done all you can. You must let this go.'

'Even at the risk of allowing an innocent man to hang?'

'Yes,' he says. 'If it's a man of no value to you.'

We look at each other. There is a streak of ruthlessness in Lord Ashley that, I realise, I have still to acquire myself. I doubt if Lord Ashley would have hesitated long enough in Devon to acquire the scar that I have on my cheek.

'Perhaps, my Lord, you might not find me as reliable as you need me to be,' I say.

'No,' he says. 'Perhaps I wouldn't.'

The prow of the boat grates against the stone stairs. In the brief instant in which vessel and shore are in harmony, I jump onto dry land and throw the boatman his sixpence. He pockets it and has pushed away into the stream before I have reached the top of the steps. I in turn set off through the streets of Southwark.

'Good afternoon, Mr Grey,' says Lowman cheerfully. 'Do you need to speak to Mr Hubert again so soon?'

'Lord Arlington had one or two more questions,' I say. 'He has asked me to visit him.'

I wait to see if Lowman will show any surprise at this, but he just nods. 'I thought we'd established his guilt very nicely, but no doubt he can condemn himself further. He'll still hang just the once, but we wouldn't wish him to escape the noose because of some cheap lawyer's trick. Sorry, Mr Grey, you're a lawyer yourself, of course.'

'But not a cheap one.'

'Indeed. Well, best to have his confession nailed down tightly anyway. I'll take you to his cell now. I can't bring him up here any more – Lord Arlington has ordered that I guard him more closely in future. And he hasn't had a visitor for a while. He'll probably be pleased to see somebody down there. Not that he ever seems to get lonely. He doesn't need company the way the rest of us do.'

Hubert looks up, mildly interested, as Lowman unlocks the door and lets me in. When you are a prisoner you get little choice as to your visitors, but there are few other diversions.

'Will you need me, Mr Grey?' Lowman asks, jangling his keys. He seems disappointed to learn that his low cunning will not be required today, and departs, not troubling to close the door after him. He trusts me not to run off with his prisoner.

'Look,' I say. 'This may be the last time I can see you, Mr Hubert. If there is anything more you can tell me, I need to know now.'

He nods. 'I have told you everything.'

'I don't think so,' I say. 'You realise that you can – indeed almost certainly will – hang if you continue to say that you started the fire and killed Mr Peidloe?'

He smiles. 'Not if I tell the truth.'

'No, Mr Hubert, it doesn't work like that. If you insist you set fire to the City, you will hang; and the others, your masters, are going to escape scot-free.'

He shakes his head.

'Do you want to die, Mr Hubert?' I ask.

He considers carefully. 'We all have to die,' he says. 'It is not a matter over which we have any choice. You too will die, I think.'

'I shall not die as painfully as you will.'

He shrugs again. 'You do not know that.'

That may be true. However bad a death Hubert has at the hands of the hangman, mine may yet be worse.

'But you don't need to die now,' I say. 'I don't think that you started the fire. I don't think that you have killed anyone. I think you are being . . . persuaded to tell me things that never happened. If you tell me the truth – the real truth, not the lies you are being fed – I can help you.'

He looks at me with his milky blue eyes. 'I have already promised I shall tell the truth,' he says, as if explaining something any idiot could understand. 'I killed Monsieur Peidloe hard by St Paul's.'

'That's what you keep saying. Who told you to use those words? Was it Mr Smith?'

'I have promised to tell the truth.'

'Very well. You say you shot Mr Peidloe in the back. How did that happen? Tell me exactly.'

'He said he would not pay me. I shot him.'

'So, why did he turn his back to you?'

Hubert closes his eyes for a moment, then shakes his head.

'Perhaps they didn't tell you what to say in answer to that question?' I ask.

'I shot him in the back, hard by St Paul's.'

I want to slap his face and keep slapping it until I get an answer that isn't something he's learned by rote.

'Where did you get the gun?' I ask.

'It was my father's. I brought it over with me from France with sufficient powder and shot.'

'With sufficient powder and shot?' I ask. 'Are you sure those are the right words?'

He frowns again, as if worried that he has got this wrong. 'I brought it over from France,' he says slowly, '*with sufficient powder and shot*. Yes, that is correct.'

'What did you do with the gun? Where is it now?'

'I do not know the answer to that question.'

'You mean they didn't tell you what to say. They've abandoned you, Mr Hubert. You are going to have to make up your own lies from now on.'

'I do not know the answer to that question,' he repeats determinedly.

'Did you leave the gun there, where you shot him?'

Again he screws up his eyes. 'No, he took it.'

'*He* took it. Who took it? You said it was just you and Peidloe there.'

'Yes, that is right.'

'Well, Peidloe couldn't have taken it as he was dead. There was another man there with you, wasn't there?'

'No.'

I think of the man I saw with the gun, shorter than Hubert, his half-covered face in the shadows and his red birthmark invisible to me. 'It was Smith, wasn't it? He was with you that night.'

'I do not know the answer to that question.'

'Did Smith give you the gun? Or did he shoot Peidloe himself? That's it, isn't it? Smith killed him and told you to say you had. Why are you doing this?'

'It was my father's gun. I brought it over with me from France with sufficient powder and shot. I shot Monsieur Peidloe hard by St Paul's. I set the City ablaze.'

I walk across the room to where he is sitting, then I bring the back of my hand down sharply across his face. He looks up at me, surprised but unafraid. I might as well strike my cooking pot to make it boil faster. Fortunately my cooking pot does not face the same dangers that Robert Hubert does.

'Listen,' I say quietly, my face very close to his. 'I know that somebody is telling you what answers to give me. And they are the *wrong answers*. These people, whoever they are, are not your friends. They didn't tell you about the map or the hidden letters. They just left you to sweat when I asked you about them. You are going to hang and they won't care, because I think it will suit them very well if you do hang. I know a lot of powerful people, Mr Hubert. Some think you are guilty and some think you are innocent, but none of them will stir a finger to save you. I am all you have. So, who is the leader of this plot? Is it Sir Thomas Clifford?'

Hubert shakes his head.

'Is it Lord Arlington?'

'I do not know the answer to that question.'

'Is it Joseph Williamson?'

'I do not know the answer to that question.'

I pause, not knowing if I want the answer to my final question.

'Is it Sir Felix Clifford?'

He shakes his head.

'Then, Mr Hubert, for the love of God, just tell me *who it is*.'

'I do not know the answer to that question.'

This time Hubert doesn't even look up when I strike him with the full force of my hand. He stares at the clean rushes on the stone floor.

'You should not have done that,' he says. 'I am pleased I will not have to see you again.'

*

'How was he today?' Lowman asks.

'Much as usual,' I say, rubbing my hand. 'You haven't seen Mr Smith again?'

'Hubert asks for him all the time, but he hasn't been here. A lot of people who have been burnt out of their houses are heading off into the country to stay with friends or family. Maybe that's where he's gone. After the fire . . . some people have just vanished.'

'Yes, maybe he has,' I say. Whoever is masterminding the plot, I have little doubt that Smith is as expendable as Hubert.

I walk back through Southwark in a pensive mood. My promise that I would break Hubert has proved a vain one. My army of questions has charged his redoubt and been thrown back. But I am sure of one thing that I did not know before – Hubert was not alone that night, and I think it was Smith that I saw crouching over the body. But that small fact may not help anyone. I doubt that I shall get a further opportunity to question Hubert. It can only be a matter of time before Arlington notifies the gaoler that I am not to be admitted or the gaoler tells Arlington that I have assaulted his prisoner.

I am fortunate that, when I reach the stairs, a boat is waiting there, empty of passengers. The boatman waves at me. He is a tall man in a close-fitting cap, under which he seems to be bald. His face is weather-beaten. He has suffered an injury somewhere, and wears a patch where his left eye should be. He fixes me with his remaining one.

'Mr Grey?' he asks.

'Yes,' I reply.

'Lord Arlington sends his compliments. He asked me to look out for you, sir, and take you to him as soon as I could find you.'

Arlington is worryingly well informed. He has discovered my illicit trip to Southwark almost before I knew I was going there. If I fail to obey this summons, there will no doubt be another that is less polite. I'd wanted to report back to Ashley first, but he'll understand why I cannot refuse this invitation from my paymaster.

'Very well,' I say.

I board the boat and the man pushes out into the stream. We are a little above London Bridge and the tide is running swiftly towards the sea, making a great roar as it sweeps through the arches. At first I think we will head upstream, close to the bank where the flow is slackest, then cross to the safety of the far side and Whitehall Stairs; but the man heads straight out into the fastest current, bringing the boat round in mid-stream so that we are suddenly facing the bridge and starting to drift towards it.

'We can't stop here,' I say, 'or we'll be swept under the arches and down river.'

'That's exactly where we're going, sir. Under the bridge. My instructions are to take you to the Tower by the fastest route.'

Chapter Seventeen

We are starting to move more quickly now, picking up speed all the time. Sitting in the stern, facing the boatman, I can see the bridge over his shoulder, the jumble of houses, the stone arches and the great wooden starlings that stretch out into the river, protecting the piers. The boatman does not need to take another stroke in order for us to reach our destination – the tide will do that – but he will need all his skill in steering to ensure that we pass cleanly through an arch rather than fetch up against the starlings or the stone-work and overturn. The arches were always narrow and are made more hazardous still by the debris that has been floating here since the fire. The boatman smiles, head tilted on one side.

'You seem nervous, sir? You'll have shot the arches before?' he asks.

I think of the crowd of apprentices we saw clinging to the sides of their boat.

'The bridge is for wise men to pass over and fools to pass under,' I say.

'That is indeed the old saying, but unfortunately your destination lies on the far side and my instructions are to waste no time.'

'I'd have got a boat from that side of the bridge, had I known where we were bound,' I say. 'Why did Arlington ask you to wait there?'

'Because that's where he told me you'd be. I thought you wouldn't be afraid, sir. A little trip under the bridge. You surprise me.'

I find I too have an overwhelming desire to grip the sides of the boat. Well, there will be plenty of time to do that when we reach the bridge. I am perplexed that Arlington, in most ways a cautious man, has given these instructions. Why does he need me so urgently? And, if he needs me at all, why risk drowning me before I can get to him?

'Just row,' I say. 'And watch where you're going.'

'Perhaps you're not a good swimmer, sir?' the waterman asks, still leaning on his oars. 'Might that be the reason for your concern?'

'That too is none of your business,' I say.

He smiles again, as if having a joke at my expense. It is clear he thinks that I am a coward and fear drowning. He also thinks I can't swim. Then let him. I have no intention of giving him any information that he doesn't need. I swim well enough, though I would not care to have to reach the bank that way in this filthy, fast-moving water. And, if I go in, at the very least he's coming with me. So, let's hope he can swim too.

'You need to steer to the right,' I say. 'Keep to the centre of the main arch. We may just get through unscathed.'

He shakes his head. 'I know this river better than you, sir. You leave me to decide which arch is the right one.'

He looks over his shoulder and pulls hard with his left-hand blade. We are now being swept towards not the centre arch but a narrower one much closer to the bank. As we pass under the bridge we shall drop about six feet in a tumultuous rush of billowing white water. I have in fact done it before, but never sober. Based on my previous experiences, I think the time has finally come to grip the sides of the boat very firmly indeed and hope that he is as adept as he believes. The great structure rushes towards us. Then we are in deep, cold shadow, with the roar of the water echoing off the slime-green sides of the arch.

It is at this moment that my waterman decides to abandon his oars. He has, it would seem, more important things to do. With my eyes still adjusting to the light, all I see is him reaching under his seat and producing some kind of club. I raise my hands just a little too late. The blow glances off my arm and strikes the side of my head. I fall forward, clinging desperately to his leather jerkin and throwing him back onto his seat. He is still struggling to rise as the boat shoots out on the far side into the bright sunlight. Just for a moment, we seem to hang at the top of the waterfall. Then the bow tips forwards and so do we. The boat is sucked down into the vortex. I cannot stop myself rising helplessly into the air as the craft falls and falls and falls. I lose my grip on my assailant. Then I am under the cold, swirling, green water, kicking hard to get to the surface again.

As my head emerges, I see the boatman already striking out for the bank, believing his work is done. But our transport is only a few feet away, now overturned but still floating. My head is throbbing and my arm feels useless but I kick out again with my legs and my good hand makes contact with the hull.

I can no longer see my assailant and he can no longer see me. That is satisfactory from every point of view. I do not wish for a further struggle in the water that I will certainly lose. With me clutching its slippery side, the boat and I drift some way together before I see another vessel approaching. The man rowing it waves and calls for me to hang on. That was always my plan. A hand reaches down to me and I am pulled, with gallons of water streaming from my clothes, into the awaiting skiff.

'We saw you come through the arch, sir. Did you lose your oars as you entered it? It's easily done if you brush against the starlings as the stream carries you through. That's a nasty knock you've taken as you fell from the boat. Was it just you in the boat?'

'Yes,' I say. It seems the simplest answer.

'It's not an advisable thing to do, sir – coming under the bridge when the tide is flowing so strong – not unless you know the river. I've been a waterman for twenty years, and I never shoot the bridge when the tide is running unless I have to. You can always scull through later at slack water without danger, if that's what you need to do. We'll tow your boat to the shore, but with no oars, this is as far as you'll be going today, sir.'

The boatman leaves me – I still dripping, he half a Guinea better off – and I wring out my clothes bit by bit on the dark brown, rubbish-covered mudflats below the Tower. I have lost my hat, but I have at least saved my sword, my purse, and indeed my life. I have no reason to believe that Arlington is really waiting for me at the Tower, but if he is I have no plans to see him as I am, muddy and stinking of Thames water. I wouldn't wish to be accused of treason without the advantage of clean linen.

I leave the boat where it is and trudge the short distance across the glistening ooze to the nearest moss-covered stairs, then up them, muddy footprint by muddy footprint. Once firmly on cobblestones again, I take a route that prudently skirts the burnt City, back to Lincoln's Inn. I shall not trouble you with Will's comments on my return, other than to say that for the second time this week he disposes of one of my suits of clothes with much shaking of his head.

'Arlington tried to have you killed?' asks Aminta.

'That is what I believe. His boatman thought I could not swim.'

'So he gave you that blow to the head to make sure you wouldn't?'

'With the blow to my head and my arm, I would have drowned if the overturned boat had not been so close. I'm sure his instructions were that I was not to reach the Tower alive.'

'Well, at least your arm is only bruised, and the wound to your head is nothing compared to the scar you already have. You've been very lucky twice now.'

'Buried alive, almost stabbed to death and almost drowned? Yes, you could call that good fortune, I suppose.'

'I had lost my count. Thrice fortunate. Would you recognise the boatman again?'

'I think so. Tall. Bald. One eye. If he is a London waterman, then it should be possible to find him and question him. He doubtless thinks I'm dead so he won't be expecting me to reappear.'

'The dead rarely do.'

Aminta and I look at each other. She finally voices the words that had occurred to us both the other night. 'So, John, do you think that this is how your career will end: drowned in the Thames or buried in a cesspit after an inglorious scuffle, with your family none the wiser?'

'Only if I continue to work for Arlington,' I say, 'and, if he wants me dead as much as it would seem, that seems unlikely at present.'

Lord Ashley opens his eyes in surprise when he sees me. My immersion in the river has not improved my appearance, it would seem, and the bruise on my head has acquired some interesting colour over night. I briefly explain why I may not be looking my best.

'And this waterman was sent by Arlington?'

'So the man said. It must have been somebody who knew I would be in Southwark. Not many people have the army of spies that Arlington possesses.'

'Precisely. And Arlington also had the knowledge and the resources to trap you and Lady Pole in the cellar. I think Arlington is pulling Smith's strings, and Hubert's and maybe Peidloe's too. It explains why Arlington has kept Hubert and Graunt safely locked away, but charged neither of them with any offence. And detained Sir Felix so that he can disclose nothing of what he knows. The nature of the plot that Arlington has been hiding starts to reveal itself, does it not? A confederacy of Frenchmen and English Catholics, intent on burning down the City: Arlington at the best knows about it and protects them; at the worst he is the poisonous spider at the very centre of the web. It would certainly explain why he has been so anxious to deny any plot – and why he has gulled the King into saying this publicly. It might also explain Hubert's conviction that no harm can come to him, no matter what he says to us. My Lord Arlington will look after him, so long as he draws all suspicion away from the guilty men.'

'He said the Lord would protect him,' I say. 'I thought he was placing his trust in God.'

'I suspect, Mr Grey, that Hubert has just been laughing at us.'

'Not that,' I say. 'I don't think I've ever seen him laugh.'

'Still, if Arlington suspects that you know this . . . that your investigations were getting close to exposing him . . . that would give him more than enough cause to imprison you in the cellar or to drown you.'

'The waterman thought I couldn't swim and would drown – that was his mistake. I think I should be able to get him to talk, once I find him. If nothing else, I'll get him to confirm who paid him.'

Ashley looks concerned. 'You might. However, he will still recognise you as soon as you approach him. I can order some of my servants to search the river. There are places where the watermen congregate. My men can bring him in and you can question him. You have given us a good description . . . unless he has fled the City, I think we'll find him.'

'If Arlington is protecting him then he may feel safe to remain.'

'That will be his second mistake then,' says Ashley.

Joseph Williamson takes a sip of the wine that Will has poured for him and nods appreciatively.

'Did Lord Arlington send you?' I ask. 'Perhaps to check whether I was still alive?'

'He doesn't know I've come to Lincoln's Inn. Not for the moment. As for your still being alive, he felt, to be perfectly honest, that your fears for your safety were excessive. I see, however, that you have acquired a new blow to the head, so perhaps he was mistaken.'

'Lord Arlington would probably feel it was of no account.'

'Would he? Then I shall report that I found you well. I came, however, to give you some advice.'

'You work for Arlington. Why should I trust any advice you give me?'

'I have to say, John, that your insistence that my Lord does not wish you well puzzles me greatly.'

'He's tried to kill me twice – once by sending me on a wild-goose chase to the ruins, then by providing me with a boatman who thought it would be a good idea to drown me as we passed under the bridge.'

Williamson laughs. 'He wouldn't do that. My Lord can be ... single-minded in his approach, shall we say? But he would not endanger your life in that way.'

'You think not? I have both scars and bruises to suggest otherwise.'

'Oh, I'm not saying that one day you won't die on some harebrained scheme of our master's. But he would scarcely try to kill you. It would be a waste of a useful asset. You have annoyed him greatly by not telling him of your dealings with Sir Felix Clifford. I fear that Sir Felix is suffering some inconvenience as a result – he's in the Tower when he might have just been under house arrest. But that omission is your only fault. It doesn't mean that my Lord wants you dead. If he wanted you dead, then you would be dead by now.'

'So what *does* my Lord want?' I ask.

'He wants you to go back to your legal practice and not to meddle further with Hubert,' says Williamson. 'Leave it to us.'

'I'm not being ordered back to my kennel,' I say. 'I'm not Arlington's dog and I'll meddle with Hubert if I want to.'

'We're both his dogs and you'll listen to me carefully. You'll stay in Lincoln's Inn and attend to your clients. Don't think that my Lord does not know that you were in Southwark today.'

'Since he sent his assassin to meet me there, I'm sure he does know.'

Williamson puts down his wine and shakes his head. 'Enough of this, John. You were . . . *are* . . . Arlington's most trusted agent,' he says. 'In this case you have a conflict of interest that you should have told him about. That has angered him, because he is a proud man and quick to anger. But when my Lord next needs you, he will conveniently forget all that, because he must. In the meantime *you* must forget Hubert. It's no longer your business whether he is innocent or guilty. It is no longer your concern if he hangs. And you must forget any imagined hurt you have suffered. Let Lord Arlington deal with this matter as he wishes.'

'If Hubert were an innocent man, a mere dupe who had somehow been made to say that he started the fire, would that be a relevant consideration?' I demand.

'No. It would not be relevant in any way. The security of the State is more important than the safety of any individual citizen. If that were not true, we could never send a single soldier into battle.'

I look at Williamson. I don't think he would deceive me, but that doesn't mean that he knows the truth.

'I intend to find out if Hubert started the fire. And I won't be bullied or bribed,' I say. 'You can tell my Lord that.'

Williamson laughs. 'Well, there's no chance of your being bribed,' he says. 'Not by Lord Arlington.'

*

When I arrive back at Lincoln's Inn I find a message waiting for me. My Lord Ashley has information for me. Indeed, he rather thinks he has my boatman.

Chapter Eighteen

'Is this the fellow?' asks Lord Ashley.

The man who stands before me, held firmly and not too kindly by two of Ashley's servants, certainly looks like my boatman. He is tall and bald. He is dressed in the leather jerkin and coarse woollen breeches of the watermen. But it would have helped if Lord Ashley's men had been more gentle with him. His face is streaked with grime and there is blood across his forehead and running down his cheek. He no longer has the confident smile that I saw in the boat. He moves with difficulty, as if it hurts him to do so.

'Yes, I rather think it is,' I say.

'I am afraid that he was reluctant to come with my men at first,' says Lord Ashley. 'But they were able to persuade him. He's called Ebenezer Jones, by the way – or he claims to be.'

'They had no right . . .' says the boatman. He glares at Lord Ashley, which is brave in view of the treatment he has had.

'I had more right to arrest you than you did to assault Mr Grey,' says Lord Ashley.

Ebenezer Jones says nothing. I think he complains not of the arrest itself, but of the blows that followed it.

'Does he admit it then?' I ask. 'Was he ordered to kill me?'

'Answer Mr Grey,' says Lord Ashley. 'Do you admit it?'

Jones nods. Possibly he does not wish for another beating.

'And tell him who instructed you to do it.'

'Lord Arlington,' he says bitterly. 'I've done work for him before, but not like that. He said to wait by the stairs at Southwark for a gentleman called John Grey – solemn looking and dressed in dark clothes like a Puritan. I was to pick him up and say we were bound for the Tower, then, when we were out of sight under the bridge, I was to pitch him out of the boat into the water and let him drown – it was to look like an accident. When I surfaced and didn't see you . . . I was sure that you had drowned, sir. I'm very sorry, sir, for what I did. I lost everything in the fire and I needed the money Lord Arlington offered.'

'Did he offer you a lot?' I ask.

He laughs. 'You know Lord Arlington, sir. He offered no more than he had to. Not a penny more, I promise you that. And I lost a good set of oars that he won't be paying me for.'

'Did he say why he wanted me dead?' I ask.

'No, sir. Not exactly,' Jones says. 'He just told me that you were a traitor and a danger to the State. You had to die but in a way that would not inconvenience the King. I am sorry, sir. I didn't want to do it, but times are hard and it is every man for himself.'

'And it was just Lord Arlington you spoke to?' I ask.

'Yes, Mr Grey, sir.'

'Did you speak to a man named Joseph Williamson?'

The boatman looks at Ashley, alarmed.

'Just tell the truth,' says Lord Ashley. 'Just say truly whether you've ever met Joseph Williamson or not. There's no need to lie. Unless you want another beating.'

'No, sir,' Jones says, swallowing hard. 'I saw Arlington alone in his rooms at the Palace. I didn't meet anyone called Williamson.'

'If you are lying, I'll have you flogged until some time after you remember the truth,' says Lord Ashley. 'You know I can do that.'

'That is the truth, my Lord, so help me. I only saw Lord Arlington, sir. Nobody else.'

'Take him away,' says Lord Ashley. 'Take him back down to the cellars and chain him up again.'

'But, my Lord—' says the boatman.

Lord Ashley nods to the two men and Jones-the-boatman is dragged away before he can protest further.

'Don't feel sorry for him,' says Lord Ashley. 'He's lucky we didn't just drown him once he'd confessed.'

'I do feel sorry for him,' I say. 'It would seem that he was forced into it by poverty, just as Smith probably was. He appears contrite. What will you do with him? Arlington will hardly let him stand trial in a court of law. Either he'll spirit him away somewhere or he'll arrange to have his throat cut. I'm beginning to fear that may have been Smith's fate.'

Lord Ashley looks at me for a moment then nods his agreement. 'You are right that we can scarcely expect Arlington to have recourse to conventional justice. We may need to keep the man under lock and key for another few days or weeks in case he has any more to tell us. Then we can take him to the City magistrates – though, as Arlington planned for you, we can also arrange for him to be dropped quietly into the river.

Which would you prefer? It is entirely your choice. You don't seem a squeamish man, Mr Grey.'

Again I see the streak of ruthlessness in Ashley that I lack myself. His body may be weaker than most, but his resolve is like iron.

'I've never killed anyone unless I had to,' I say. 'It's a rule I have and that I'd prefer to stick to. I'd have killed him on the river if it had been his life or mine, but that is no longer the case. There is no need to ill-treat him further. I think he has told us all he can.'

Lord Ashley looks doubtful. 'It may still be safer to detain him a while longer. But you should take it as a compliment that Arlington is so anxious to have you put out of the way. He clearly thinks that you and only you can expose his schemes. That is high praise.'

'Praise I'd be happy to forgo,' I say. 'Well, we've found one of my attackers and got him to confess. We just need to locate Smith before it's too late and get him to confirm Arlington's role in that other little charade.'

The following day we do indeed find Smith, but he has little to tell us. Will returns from an errand I have sent him on with some news. A body has been dragged out of the river. A man, so it is reported, with a red birthmark on his face. His body is being held in the crypt of St Katharine's.

'If you hurry, sir, you may get there before they bury him,' says Will.

I am ferried eastwards once again, but this time we pass under the bridge at low tide, when the current has slowed to a trickle. We scull through slowly, the steady splash of the blades echoing under the great vault. At St Katharine's, the church-warden allows me to view the dead man.

'They found him on a mud bank yesterday afternoon,' he says. 'His body must have floated under the bridge and fetched up here. But he didn't drown.'

He pulls back an old, ochre-coloured sheet that has been covering the body. There is no doubt. Whoever Smith was working for, somebody has caught up with him. There is a stab wound in his back. There was no need to drown him. None at all.

'His name is Peter Smith,' I say. 'I know him.'

The churchwarden shakes his head. 'No, sir. You're wrong there. He's already been identified by his wife. He was an actor. His name's Richard Farley.'

'I should have realised the man calling himself Smith was an actor,' I say. 'I must applaud the performance that he gave when luring me into the burnt-out City. But Will saw through him – he thought Farley's act of piety was a little overdone.'

Aminta nods. 'It should have occurred to me, when Abigail reported him missing, that something like this might have happened. I've only seen him once or twice on stage, with plenty of greasepaint on. I had no idea he had a birthmark. Abigail said something about his not having the looks for acting. I understand what she meant. Still, it sounds as if you should have listened more carefully to your clerk. There's more to Will Atkins than meets the eye.'

'True,' I say.

'If this Smith or Farley was in Arlington's pay, then is Abigail part of it too? She certainly recognised Arlington's name when you mentioned it. And she stopped asking questions very quickly.'

'It might be wise to assume she is,' I say. 'Though I wouldn't mind seeing her again. We're running out of witnesses, Aminta. This is a dangerous business for anyone who gets involved in it. Peidloe has been shot and Farley has been stabbed and dumped in the Thames. My head and arm still ache from the last attempt on my own life. Hubert has, I think, told me all he dares or wishes to tell. I need another source of information.'

'There's a gentleman waiting for you,' says Will on my return to Lincoln's Inn. 'A Mr Jonathan Sparrow. We met him in Moor Fields, he says.'

I have to think for a moment who Mr Sparrow is, then I remember – the fat man with the cooking pot and troubled face. 'Very well,' I say. 'Let's see what he has to say for himself.'

'It was when I was giving evidence to the Parliamentary Commission,' Sparrow says. 'I was telling them about a near neighbour of mine – a Frenchman. I thought he was called Boileau. Then I remembered you'd spoken of a Mr Peidloe. So, I thought: Peidloe, Boileau. They're not that different really, are they sir? All these French names are much of a muchness.'

'Have you seen this person since the fire?'

'No, sir, not at all. He's vanished, but then a lot of people have.'

'What did he look like?'

'Tall. Spare.'

'Did he possess a rusty red suit and yellow stockings?'

'Yellow hose, certainly. I do remember that. And a red doublet, I think.'

Well, that sounds like our man.

'What else can you tell me about him?' I ask.

'Such as, sir?'

'Did he do or say anything that suggested he was plotting to burn down London?'

In court that might be regarded as leading the witness, but Sparrow looks as if he could do with a little leading. His manner is slow and ponderous.

'He certainly had a lot of visitors, sir; proper meetings with half a dozen men or more – some sort of philosophical society, he said. I'd see them coming and going, and sometimes one of them might come to my shop asking for directions, if they hadn't been before.'

He looks at me, slightly out of breath from informing on his neighbour.

'And there was nobody named Smith who visited him?' I ask. 'The other man I was searching for. He may have also called himself Richard Farley. Red birthmark on his face.'

'Yes, you mentioned him before. I remember. No, I saw nobody with a red birthmark, but then I doubt I saw everyone who went there – especially if they didn't want to be seen.'

'Mr Hubert?' I ask. 'Robert Hubert?'

'Yes, there was a man named Robert. But I only saw him once or twice. I did speak to him once though, when he was leaving with Mr Peidloe.'

'What was he like?'

'He was a distracted sort of fellow – you could never quite follow his conversation, if you see what I mean. Mr Peidloe didn't treat him well, in my opinion, sir. Snapped at him all the time and Robert never answered him back at all.'

'So, Peidloe was very much in charge of things?'

'Of the two of them? Yes, I'd have said so.'

'Did a Mr Graunt ever visit your neighbour?'

Sparrow laughs. 'Like I say, I had no cause to ask for names.

I'd remember their faces though, those that I saw. There was one gentleman I saw arrive in his carriage a couple of times, but he always descended in the next road and walked the final few yards. Didn't want to draw too much attention to himself. He wore a fine periwig and had a small, neat moustache. Yes, I saw him very well.'

That's interesting. 'Might he have been called Clifford?' I ask.

Sparrow laughs again and shakes his head again. 'He wasn't the sort to talk to the likes of me. Far too high and mighty. He didn't behave as if he wanted to tell people his name.'

'If I took you to Mr Graunt,' I ask, 'could you tell me if he'd been to one of Peidloe's meetings?'

'I could try, sir. I could see if I could identify the gentleman with the carriage too, if you showed me this Mr Clifford. And if you made it worth my while.'

'Thank you,' I say, handing Sparrow a couple of gold coins. 'You have been very helpful, Mr Sparrow. Where can I find you?'

'I'm still camping where you saw me last on the edge of the fields. I'll be there for a while. Me and my family – we've nowhere else to go. Not since the French bastards set fire to London. It would be good if we can send one or two of them to the hangman, wouldn't it?'

'Now I've spoken to Sparrow, I think I'm beginning to understand it all,' I say.

Lord Ashley pours me another glass of Canary. We are ensconced in his rooms in the Palace. It is a warm evening. Candlelight plays on the dark oak panelling. A breeze blows through an open window, stirring the curtains and bringing the first scent of autumn. We might be a hundred miles from the dusty ruins.

'Go on, Mr Grey,' he says.

'The plotters clearly met at Peidloe's house. The group included Hubert and Graunt. But they had a leader, and my best guess is that it was Sir Thomas Clifford. At some point, I think Arlington learned of the group through his spy network, and sent Farley, under the name of Smith, to join it.'

'To what end?'

'To discover more, I imagine. That's what his agents do. If Smith had uncovered anything useful, then he would have arranged to arrest Peidloe and the rest, unless they could lead Arlington to somebody more important.'

'And then?'

'They did lead him to somebody more important. And, to his horror, Arlington discovered that person was Sir Thomas – a sympathiser at least and, as I say, quite possibly the leader. Arlington could not bring them all to justice without implicating his closest ally.'

'Why do you suspect Sir Thomas so strongly?'

'He's a known Catholic sympathiser. He had access, via Arlington's office, to the information that was passed to Hubert. He initiated Graunt's appointment. He was very uncomfortable when questioned on the matter. And I think I shall shortly have absolute proof.'

'How?'

'I'll come to that.'

'Very well, Mr Grey. So, what happened next?'

'Arlington dithered, in a way that Thurloe would never have done. While he did so, the group proceeded with its plans anyway. But they were better prepared than he imagined. On the first of September the leader, without warning, put his plan into operation. Graunt, whom Clifford had placed at the New River Company, was sent to turn off the water. Then Peidloe set off into the City, taking Hubert with him. Peidloe should not have succeeded, but the wind was high and the City was like tinder. His small fire spread. Smith was also with them – or at least was with them at St Paul's. He realised it had all gone out of control – this wasn't yet another hopeless plot, but a group who actually were capable of destroying London. In desperation, Smith shot Peidloe, but much too late. Hubert got away—'

Ashley holds up a hand. 'You say *Peidloe* started the fire. You still hold Hubert blameless?'

'Sparrow said that Hubert never dared to answer back. I think he was always under Peidloe's complete control. Whatever he did – and I think it was very little – I don't think he can be held responsible for the fire or the murder.'

'Very well. Go on.'

'When Arlington first heard of the fire, he thought little of it, because fires are not uncommon. Then a smoke-blackened Smith reported back to him and suddenly he realised that this had happened because of his lethargy and because of the treasonous actions of Sir Thomas Clifford. So Arlington had to cover up any possibility of a plot. When Hubert was arrested, he quickly dispatched Smith to tell him exactly what to say, reassuring him that he would come to no harm if he did as he was told – and perhaps that he faced immediate execution if he failed to comply. He then sent me to question Hubert, thinking I'd either report that he was mad or at the very worst that the only plotters were Peidloe and Hubert. But there were loose ends for Arlington to tie up. When he discovered

Sir Felix's very minor part in the proceedings, Sir Felix too had to be arrested and kept safely out of the way, in case he revealed Sir Thomas's connection. When Arlington knew I was close to discovering the truth, he stood me down; then, when I continued, contrary to his orders, he twice attempted to kill me. The alternative to my death was that his foolishness and Sir Thomas's treachery would be revealed. It would have been the end of both of them.'

'And Smith?'

'I fear that he also knew too much. Perhaps he even tried to blackmail Arlington with what he had.'

For a long time Lord Ashley remains silent. 'Well done, Mr Grey,' he says eventually. 'I think that is it exactly. Can you prove any of this, though?'

'That was the most interesting thing about Sparrow's story. As I say, before he was burnt out of his house, he lived close to Peidloe. He saw many of the conspirators and thought he could identify Graunt. He also spoke of a man who arrived in a carriage and left it in the next street to avoid attention. Sparrow was sure he'd know him too.'

Well, now I have twice impressed Lord Ashley. 'Sparrow was *certain* he could?' he asks.

'He said he'd seen him more than once. He didn't know the man's name. But from what Sparrow told me, I'm sure it's Clifford. Anyway, it will be easy to confirm.'

Lord Ashley nods thoughtfully. 'Mr Grey, you have my admiration. This is remarkable work. Are you sure you can find Sparrow again?'

'He is camped out in Moor Fields. I can arrange for him to see Sir Thomas and identify him,' I say. 'I could bring Sparrow to you and you could interview him first if you wish.'

Lord Ashley shakes his head. 'That will not be necessary. I'm sure you have already got as much out of Sparrow as you can. I agree it would be helpful if he could see Sir Thomas Clifford in person. Tomorrow, perhaps, or the day after.'

'I may be able to arrange it today.'

'I'd like to make some enquiries first. You say Sparrow came to you. You should always beware of anyone too eager to inform on their neighbours. We know little about the man, or who he might be working for. We can't be certain that he isn't in Arlington's pay. He seems to have played down Hubert's role, which makes me suspicious ... Let me make enquiries before we decide to trust him.'

'I think Sparrow is genuine,' I say. 'But I can wait a day or so. Should we question your waterman again?'

'Question him?' asks Lord Ashley. 'I released him, since that seemed to be what you wished. It went contrary to my judgement, but he had offended against you rather than against me. I hope, Mr Grey, that that was wise.'

Did I suggest that? I thought I had merely said not to drown him.

'I hope so too,' I say.

It is raining. This is what was needed on the first night of the fire – then we might all have slept in peace and awoken to old London as it was. My cloak has already been soaked through during my trip across the river, the boat bouncing through the wind-whipped waves, spray and rain indistinguishable. Now the water works through to my other clothes as I trudge the mud of Southwark, half blinded by the stinging rain. I clutch my hat to prevent it spinning away and back to the river. The streets are awash; water cascades from the eaves of the houses.

Having considered the matter further, perhaps I shall try to discover what Hubert has to say about these various gentlemen that Sparrow has described. Ashley may be right that I will get nothing from him, but it is worth the trip across the river.

I arrive at the prison and huddle for a moment in the shelter of the great arch, pressed against the door. I knock on the ancient, gnarled wood and a panel slides open.

'I've come to see Mr Hubert,' I say.

'And who are you exactly?' asks a man I do not recognise.

'John Grey,' I say.

The man behind the grille shakes his head. 'He's gone,' he says.

'Where?' I ask.

'I said, he's gone. Why should I care where?'

'Because I'd be happy to pay in order to know.'

'I'd be happy to take your money, but I still can't tell you.'

'Can I speak to Mr Lowman?'

'He's not at home.'

'Can I speak to anyone else?'

'No. Not you, Mr Grey. You can't speak to anyone at all.'

The panel slides shut abruptly. I don't think it would reopen if I knocked again. Arlington has taken Hubert somewhere where I cannot speak to him. Lowman has been told not to see me. A new porter, less amenable to doing my bidding, has been put in place. I must at least have been asking the right questions.

I splash back towards Lincoln's Inn. Aminta's presence in my chamber is no longer a matter for surprise, but the fresh bruise on her face is.

'A man came to my father's lodgings,' she says. 'He informed me that if I spoke to you again then I would not be safe in London and my father would most certainly be executed. He gave me this in case I doubted his word on either matter.'

'Who sent him?'

'He didn't say, but he was a tall bald man with one eye.'

I remember my fencing master's advice not to take my eye off my opponent until he is undoubtedly dead. I have released my enemy, spitting poison, back into the City.

'The waterman who tried to kill me ...' I say. 'This is my fault, Aminta. Ashley released him, thinking that was my wish. He's one of Arlington's men, and he has clearly gone straight back to his master for further instructions. Arlington knows you visited Sir Thomas. This is his warning not to meddle again.'

'A brief letter would have sufficed,' she says.

'You can stay here until we put this creature out of the way, as we should have done before. You will be safe with me and Will.'

'On the contrary. I think that my remaining here might endanger all three of us,' says Aminta. 'You cannot watch your own back and mine. Will has already gone to seek other lodgings for me – he thinks that I might stay with his former employer, your old landlady. Arlington is not likely to think of coming for me there, unless he knows your past history very well indeed.'

'I am sorry that you should have had this trouble because of me,' I say.

Aminta shakes her head. 'Who can say exactly what Arlington is afraid of, or which of us is to blame. I agree it seems likely that Sir Thomas has told him of my visit. I hadn't expected him to approve, but I didn't think that Arlington would resort to sending some ruffian to assault a lady. It would seem nobody is safe.'

'Hopefully he has no idea about Sparrow,' I say. 'Though he says he gave evidence to the Commission, so it may be that he has already drawn himself to Arlington's attention. I'll warn him to change his place of residence for the moment, then I'll come and find him again when Lord Ashley is ready. But I'll stay here with you until Will returns.'

Aminta shakes her head. 'No, go now. I think we're all in danger and the sooner Mr Sparrow knows that the better.'

The rain continues to fall. Fortunately many of those who were camping in the fields have already gone – taken in by kinsmen or by neighbours whose houses have survived the fire. The open space is half empty. It is not difficult to find Sparrow. He is kneeling, the rain streaming off his back, his family and his possessions around him, dismantling their tent.

'I'm glad I have found you,' I say.

He looks up at me with contempt. He is not pleased in any way.

'I can't talk to you,' he mutters, gathering in the sheet of wet canvas as fast as he can.

'You are moving? Hopefully you have somewhere dry to go to?'

He stops his work and stands for a moment, hands on hips, breathing heavily from the exertion of taking down his home. Water drips from his lank hair and runs down his pink face. 'I can tell you nothing, Mr Grey. Nothing at all. Who is it that you work for?'

'Nobody,' I say.

He shakes his head. 'You might have told me that you had been dismissed from your post by Lord Arlington.'

'I have no post,' I say.

'No, not since you committed treason.'

'I have also committed no treason,' I say. 'I have merely tried to uncover one. Who has been talking to you? They have been lying, I swear that.'

Sparrow gives a dismissive shake of his head. 'This isn't a matter for the likes of me – I was a fool ever to give evidence to the Commission, let alone speak to you. Once they don't need us any more, the great ones are content to let us make our own way to Hell. You too are in danger, Mr Grey. And so, I think, is everyone who is stupid enough to associate with you. Do you know a bald, one-eyed man – dresses in a leather jerkin and waistcoat like a waterman?'

'Yes,' I say.

'I thought you might. Then perhaps I've already told you all you need to know.'

'Has he been here today?'

'Well, I've just described him to you, but I haven't had a chance to pack my tent yet, so what do you think? At least my wife and children weren't here when he called. He could only threaten *me*. I'm not planning they should be here if he comes back. You have an enemy there and I think you have an even greater enemy in Lord Arlington.' He looks around as he says this, but I see no sign of the waterman or anyone else who might be listening to us. 'I've been told that if I speak to you again it will be the worse for me and for my family. It may be that he's lying, as you say, but I don't think I'll stay around and call his bluff. He may not kill my wife and children, but then again he might. I've lost everything, Mr Grey, except them. So, thank you for your Guineas, but we are going somewhere where we'll be safer. I'm not telling you where and we're going there today.'

'Lord Ashley can protect you,' I say.

'That's good to hear. So, where was he this afternoon then? I don't think he's anything like as powerful as you seem to think. I'm sorry, Mr Grey. I'm no traitor and I'm no fool. If you say you're no traitor either, then good luck to you. But you won't be meeting me again, and I'd be grateful if you'd leave now before anyone sees us together.'

'The man in the carriage,' I say. 'Could you at least tell me—?'

Sparrow laughs bitterly. 'You won't get another word from me on any of it. And don't try to give me any money. If you really want to kill me and my family, then make sure that somebody sees you paying me for my services.'

I take my hand out of my pocket, where I had indeed started to retrieve my purse.

'I'm sorry that I have caused you to lose even this home,' I say.

'So am I,' he says. 'Very sorry indeed. Now I'm going to a safer place, and my advice to you is that you should do the same. Whatever it is you're up to, somebody out there is very determined to stop you. And he's very well informed. I see from the scar on your cheek and the bruise on your brow that you've been in fights before, but whoever is after you this time can track a man down and slit his throat before he even knows he's being followed.'

*

'I warned the porter at the gate on Lincoln's Inn Fields not to admit any one-eyed men,' says Will, checking the courtyard below then closing the shutters.

'Good,' I say. 'I won't be taken by surprise this time.'

'That's easily said, Mr Grey. We can't be on our guard twenty-four hours a day. He has to catch us napping only once. And we have no idea where he is now.'

'I know where Lord Arlington is though,' I say.

'Are you certain he's behind it, sir?'

'Who else?' I say.

'I'm not sure I'd trust any of them, sir.'

'Well, I certainly don't trust Arlington, and the time has come to make my views clear to him.'

'That wouldn't be a good idea, sir,' says Will.

'Yes,' I say. 'I know that.'

Chapter Nineteen

'I would advise against it, John,' says Williamson. 'I have already explained to you . . .'

'Arlington wishes to try to kill me to stop me exposing his conspiracy—'

'And I have already pointed out that he does not.'

'So what did Lord Arlington say when you told him that I knew exactly what he was doing?'

'I was not so foolish as to tell him any such thing. Nor should you. You would have been better staying at home until this rain ceased.'

I shake my head. My wet hair sends a shower of droplets in Williamson's direction, but he stands his ground. 'Then I'll have to tell him now,' I say. 'His attempts to stop me are an accolade of a kind. But when he endangers the lives of others around me, I feel I have the right to state my objections and state them clearly.'

'He has done nothing of the sort . . .'

'Would he tell you if he had?'

Williamson purses his lips. He is aware that Arlington tells him only what he wishes him to know. I think that Williamson occasionally returns the compliment.

'I still think it inadvisable for you to say the sort of things to Arlington that I think you plan to say.'

'Just tell him I'm here. After that I absolve you from further responsibility.'

'Very well,' says Williamson. 'I've done my best to save you. If you really are intent on your own destruction, then there's nothing more I can do. Wait here, John. Don't move even an inch from that spot. And, if he's happy to see you, I would suggest that you are polite. That at least won't kill you.'

Arlington is not at all happy to see me. I think he may have been made even less happy by Williamson's insistence that he admits me, for Williamson is, I think, still my friend.

'I thought, Mr Grey, that I had made it clear that you need not concern yourself further with this matter?'

'You are making that quite difficult for me to do, my Lord,' I say.

'In what way, pray?'

Arlington is at his most pompous when annoyed. He glares at me over his glossy black nose patch and his neatly trimmed moustache. His face is framed by the luxuriant locks of his freshly brushed wig. My own long wet hair and unshaved chin will not impress him much. A curled wig might be a useful acquisition for me. If I live long enough to wear it.

'Twice this week somebody has tried to kill me,' I say. 'I do not necessarily object to that, but I do object strongly to the ill-treatment of Lady Pole and the continuing imprisonment of her father. I must insist that you cease your harassment of both of them.'

'And you believe that I have the faintest notion of what you are talking about?'

'I would respectfully suggest, my Lord, that you sanctioned the attempts on my life and the harassment of Lady Pole.'

For some reason this does not surprise him.

'Go on,' he says. 'Suggest it. I still have no idea what you mean.'

'First Mr Smith lures me to a cellar in the City where he tries to kill me. Then a waterman conveys me, on your instructions, out onto the river, claiming that you needed to meet me at the Tower and takes it upon himself to drown me.'

'I have given no such instructions. Why would I wish to see you at the Tower, when I could see you here?'

'The man has already admitted that you did.'

'And you believe him, I suppose?'

'Why should I not?'

'Because it goes against all logic. Under what circumstances did he make this extraordinary claim?'

'Lord Ashley tracked the man down and questioned him.'

'Ah! Lord *Ashley*. Did it occur to you, after the attack that you claim happened on the Thames, to ask *me* to find this waterman for you and question him? I could have done that.'

'I saw no point in asking you to interrogate your own man, my Lord. You then sent the same person to intimidate both Lady Pole and a fat and pink-faced witness named Sparrow, who had previously given evidence to the Parliamentary Commission. Sparrow told me that he could identify all of the conspirators, including a gentleman who arrived at their meetings in a fine coach.'

I watch Arlington's face but he gives nothing away.

'And this gentleman in a fine coach is supposed to be who? Me?'

'No, but I think it is somebody you know well. Sparrow would have been able to confirm it, but you have ensured that he has fled.'

'This Sparrow: you say he gave evidence to the Commission?'

'Yes.'

'Mr Grey, most of the evidence to the Commission has been unbelievable nonsense. Mr Sparrow's, if your summary of it is correct, is neither the most nor the least preposterous. If I credited even half of what I have heard, then London should already be in the control of both the French and the Dutch through the machinations of everyone's next-door neighbour. Did Mr Sparrow offer any proof at all for his accusations?'

'He will,' I say. 'He will lay the whole plot open to view.'

Arlington smiles. 'Ah, the *plot*! So, Mr Grey, explain how you and Lord Ashley think this plot was to work, because I am still unclear about that.'

'I think you know far more about that than I do, my Lord. I'm sure your Mr Farley has been keeping you well informed. Though since he is now dead, that will no longer be possible.'

'Farley? Farley? I've never even heard of Farley.'

'Oh, I rather think you have; I mentioned him once before – the man who called himself Smith? And you probably know who killed him.'

'Smith's dead?'

'Yes.'

'Well I never met him dead or alive. But – forgive me if I am being a little slow here – you think I'd be interested to know he was really called Farley?'

'Richard Farley,' I say. 'As you know well.'

'And I know this because I apparently employed him?'

'Yes.'

'And Mr Graunt? Do I employ him too? My payroll is bigger than I ever imagined. I shall need to ask His Majesty for more money.'

I ignore this attempt at irony from a man with a black nose patch.

'Sparrow could have confirmed this but, yes, I believe he may have been one of the plotters.'

'And my colleague, Sir Thomas Clifford?'

'I've said nothing about him.'

'That is true. But he has already contacted me about a strange visit he received from Lady Pole. I assume that you were the scarred serving man who accompanied her? I see from your face that that is the case. If you suspected a Clifford, then you might have spent your time more wisely investigating Sir Felix Clifford, who had plenty of opportunity. Yes, Mr Grey, I am now aware he was in the City when the fire broke out – and that you knew that and didn't tell me. And yet you accuse *me* of withholding information from *you*. I dearly wish that I had the knowledge that you believe I have. I cannot be certain there was no Catholic plot, but I am certain that the State has not been overthrown and that a witch-hunt now would be unprofitable for everyone. I have no idea who has tried to have you killed – less still who has killed *your* Mr Farley – but it isn't me.'

'Perhaps I should have told you that I saw Sir Felix in the City,' I say. 'But he has done nothing to deserve his imprisonment.'

'He is there for his own safety, Mr Grey,' says Arlington. 'I am aware that Lord Ashley too would like to see him released. That would be inadvisable. Sir Felix may still be in some danger. You must learn to trust me. On this and other matters.'

I have done nothing in the end except let Arlington know that I am aware of his treasons but am powerless to prevent them. That may not have been wise. Not for the first time I have to concede that Will gave me good counsel. As did Joseph Williamson.

I place my soaking-wet hat on my head and adjust it to an angle that pleases me. Then I leave Arlington to his schemes. Whatever they are.

'I hope you had a profitable meeting?' asks Williamson, as I pass him in the corridor.

'I was extremely polite,' I say. 'I'm grateful to you for your advice.'

The rain is falling again as I leave the Palace. Low, menacing clouds hang over London. Aware I am now dripping water from my hat, hair and coat, I walk up to Fleet Street and across the untidy fields to Lincoln's Inn. Even here everything is still covered with a thin layer of ash, which the rain has not yet been able to shift. The roofs, the ground, the trees are still streaked with it. Leaves are turning brown almost unseen. Another storm or two and perhaps these western suburbs at least will begin to look as they did.

I nod to the porter as I pass through the great red-brick gates.

'A lady was asking after you, sir. Quite pretty.' He winks at me.

'Did she give her name?'

'No sir, but she seemed to know where she would find you.'

It sounds as if Aminta is paying me a visit. Though I do not know why, my heart suddenly feels lighter and I quicken my pace. As I approach my staircase, a figure steps out right in front of me. I am about to greet her warmly, then I stop dead. It is not Aminta. It is Abigail Farley. And she is clutching a heavy pistol, already cocked.

'You killed my husband,' she says.

'I think we should talk about this inside,' I say, 'and without that gun.'

'You'd like that, wouldn't you?'

'Yes,' I say. 'That's why I suggested it.'

'Bastard!' she yells.

She raises the gun, holding it in both hands, so that it is about three feet away and pointing at my head. You normally don't miss at that range. Even if you're not used to handling guns, as I suspect she isn't.

Then she pulls the trigger.

Chapter Twenty

Abigail swears and looks accusingly at the gun in her hands. 'It's what happens if you allow the powder to get wet,' I say. 'For example, if you stand around in the rain with the pistol cocked and ready to fire.'

'You knew it would misfire?'

'Pistols often do, even if you take great care. On a day like this, it was almost a certainty.'

I take the gun from her. She does not attempt to keep it. It is heavy in my hand and would have had some kick to it if it had fired. She might have missed, even if the powder had been dry.

'Why don't you come inside,' I say. 'Let's continue the conversation there. You're soaking wet and I also need to dry out a bit.'

Will is mildly surprised to see me, clutching a pistol and escorting a strange lady up to my rooms. It's not Aminta but she seems respectable, so he still makes tea. My bill for groceries will be quite large this month. He also sets about lighting a fire in my chamber while it brews. None of us is very dry.

'Jones told me,' Abigail says, still standing. 'He told me that you'd killed my husband.'

Will looks up, mildly curious. At least he now knows who is visiting.

'You mean Ebenezer Jones?' I ask. 'Tall, one eye – does dirty work for Arlington?'

'Well, you seem to know him better than I do. I take it he was telling the truth then?'

'Not exactly, Mrs Farley. Your husband tried to kill me,' I say, 'on Arlington's orders. First he helped trap me and Lady Pole in a ruined cellar. Then one of his friends tried to stab me when I dug my way out. I've been attempting to find him ever since. But somebody else caught up with him first.'

She looks at me uncertainly. She has a wife's natural suspicion that it must be her husband's fault in some way, but quite reasonably also retains doubts about me.

'He'd never try to kill you,' she says.

'I was there. I think I'd know. So was Lady Pole.'

'And Lady Pole will swear to that?'

'Yes. I'm sorry your husband is dead, but I think it's Lord Arlington you need to complain to. It's not particularly safe being one of his agents, as I know to my cost. Arlington may well have ordered your husband's death.'

Abigail still regards me with cautious mistrust. But she knows her late husband and, it would seem, knows Arlington. 'I knew Richard was an idiot to work for him,' she says suddenly. 'I told him not to.'

'Did your husband tell you exactly what he was doing?' I ask.

'No, not a thing. I'd worked out who his master must be for myself – I know one or two other actors who'd acted as

Arlington's agents. I think Richard was frightened, but he was more afraid of telling me than he was of doing it.'

'Did he mention the names of anyone else he was working with?'

She shakes her head.

'Do you need money?' I ask.

She laughs. 'No, he was being well rewarded for what he did. It would seem Arlington always paid handsomely.'

Not in my experience.

'Then what he was doing must have been very important indeed,' I say.

The rain has finally eased off. It is a cool night, and the moon gives a silver tinge to the scudding clouds. Though Will has offered to cook supper, I am on my way to see Aminta, in a dry coat and my third-best hat. For some reason, the one thing that Arlington said that I believe is that her father is in the Tower for his own safety. Though I do not understand why, I shall convey to her this small reassurance. She is lodged with my former landlady, whose current house has escaped the fire. I am greeted at the door as a long-lost son and as a suitable match for her still-unmarried daughter.

'We have missed you, Mr Grey,' says Mistress Reynolds. 'You are always welcome here, as is your friend, Lady Pole.' Mistress Reynolds's tongue lovingly caresses the title.

'Is Lady Pole within?' I ask.

'She most certainly is,' she says playfully. 'And I think she has a surprise for you.'

'Really?' I ask.

Mistress Reynolds looks coy and then says: 'I am sworn to secrecy, but you'll never guess who has come to stay with her.'

She is right. I won't guess because I have no time to play this game.

'So, who is that?' I ask.

'Sir Felix,' says Mistress Reynolds. 'Lady Pole's father. But for some reason, he's wearing petticoats.'

'I don't know why you are scowling like that, John,' says Aminta. 'You had made no effort to get my father released, so I had to. It was a simple matter to gain access to him in the Tower, disguise him in an old dress . . .'

'Simple?'

'I obtained the assistance of Sir Thomas Clifford.'

'Which he gave willingly?'

'It was as willing as it needed to be. I think he feels badly about his role in my father's imprisonment. He understands that he owes him a favour. He also fears that, knowing what I do, I may make trouble for him. He fears that quite a lot. He wrote a letter requesting that the guards admitted me and two other ladies.'

'Who were these other ladies?'

'Two of the actresses from my company came with me.'

'And you claimed that they were what exactly? Your sisters?'

'One played the part of my maid – she specialises in playing pert young serving women – and one was my father's illegitimate daughter, conceived shortly before the Battle of Naseby.'

'Naseby? A nice touch.'

'Thank you. I thought so too. Anyone who knows our family well would have no difficulty in crediting it. The illegitimate daughter wore two dresses, my maid and I wore extra petticoats. We hid the rouge in the basket, under the food and the brandy we were taking to my poor father. Over the food was a cloth that we used to cover his hair – there was no time to cut and curl it as a lady of quality would have done, and it is becoming rather thin. In the end, it all worked very well.'

'Did it? You seem, however, to be missing out some stages in the escape.'

'Well, perhaps a few, just to prevent your being an accessory after the fact.'

'That is too kind.'

'Yes, thinking about it, it probably is. Very well, here's what we did. The three of us entered, my maid weeping and wailing at kind Sir Felix's imprisonment.'

'I noticed that you didn't,' said Sir Felix. 'You neither wept nor wailed.'

'She didn't really mean it,' said Aminta. 'It was only play-acting.'

'No, I suppose she didn't,' said Sir Felix. 'A charming girl.'

'But not available. On any terms.'

'A pity.'

'But true for all that. Once the guard's attention was elsewhere—'

'Why was it elsewhere?' I ask.

'We'd given the guard the bottle of brandy from the basket when we arrived. He decided to consume it quickly before his colleague came on duty. A sensible precaution. While he was thus engaged, my father shaved off his moustache . . .'

'It will grow again,' says Sir Felix, rubbing his upper lip.

'Then I divested myself of my surplus petticoats, as did my maid, and my father put them on over his breeches. His illegitimate daughter, hussy that she is, had already removed the additional dress, which, with the headscarf, completed my father's *toilette*. He applied a smudge of rouge to both cheeks.

We then proceeded to act out a little play. My maid left and came back. The bastard girl did the same shortly after. My maid left and did not come back. The bastard left again and did. How many women are there now in the cell?'

'I've no idea,' I say.

'Nor did the guard. After a while two more ladies departed, while I remained having a conversation with an empty cell. Then I left too, sobbing a little.'

'That's something at least,' says Sir Felix.

'I had intended to engage the guard in conversation,' Aminta continues, 'in order to give my father longer to make his exit, but the man was already snoring in his chair, the almost empty bottle on the table beside him. I caught up with my father and his charming bastard, and the three of us exited together and onto Tower Green.

'Actually,' says Sir Felix, 'I think the brandy might have achieved our ends without the necessity for dressing up. Not that it wasn't enjoyable flirting with the gatekeeper as we left. It's good to know that I could still obtain a husband whenever I wished.'

'We proceeded directly to this house, where you find me and my father now.' Aminta pauses in her narration. 'You still don't look happy, John. That sour expression is spoiling the evening air. Maybe you should just congratulate me on the success of my plan and go home on your own and sup on cold mutton and small beer.'

'Lord Arlington,' I say, 'has told me, only this afternoon, that Sir Felix was in the Tower for his own safety. Outside, according to my Lord, he would be at the greatest risk.'

'At risk from whom?'

'He didn't say.'

'Should you not have asked?'

'I didn't know that you were planning to arrange for your father to escape from the Tower. It was a foolish thing to do, in any case.'

'I didn't know either,' says Sir Felix. 'Had I been consulted, I too would have advised against it, but once presented with these petticoats it seemed a pity not to try. Escapes from the Tower are rare. I haven't had an adventure like it since I was obliged to flee Fairfax's cavalry after the Battle of Naseby.'

'The question is what to do now,' I say. 'We can scarcely expect your escape to go unnoticed.'

'I could, I suppose, break back into the Tower,' says Sir Felix. 'I doubt that the guard will yet be sober.'

'That would be an unusual course of action,' I say.

'And advisable only if we choose to believe anything Arlington says,' observes Aminta.

'I think you are wrong to assume that Arlington would lie to you,' says Sir Felix. 'He might not tell you the truth, but I do not think he would lie.'

'You must both stay here,' I say. 'As soon as we can, we'll get Sir Felix back to Essex. I doubt that anyone will look for him there.'

'I find it difficult to believe anyone will look for me anywhere,' says Sir Felix. 'Arlington must know that, uniquely amongst my family, I'm no danger to him at all.'

'I doubt that Lord Arlington will now see it that way. Our best hope – our only hope – is to persuade or force Sparrow to give evidence, however little he wishes to do so. Ashley felt we should investigate him further, but there's no time for that now. We need to discover urgently who the real ringleader is, before you are re-arrested. I'm going to find Sparrow.'

'But you've no idea where he's gone,' Sir Felix points out.

'My guess is that he's still in London. He's got a young family and no money. It won't be that easy for them to travel far on foot. I'll start by asking at Moor Fields in case he told anyone what his plans were.'

'I'll come with you,' says Aminta. 'There's no point in protesting. There are few people you can call on who know what Sparrow looks like. Just me and Will.'

Chapter Twenty-One

Will, Aminta and I survey the unkempt expanse of grass in front of us. The army of homeless Londoners who were here only a few days ago has gone. In front of me is a neat square of bricks filled with ashes and partly burnt sticks – an abandoned campfire or an allegory of a lost London, as you prefer. Beyond, almost as far as the eye can see, lie scattered poles, sheets of canvas, boards and planks – all now unneeded – that once made up a small town. Here and there a hovel remains – people who either have no relatives to go to or who prefer this to their charity. We make enquiries where we can, but nobody knows or cares where Sparrow might have gone.

The ash – deposited during the fire, dampened down by the rain, and dried again by the autumn sunshine – is now once again blowing around the almost deserted camp in small dust clouds. Nobody would stay here if they had anywhere to go.

As we trudge back through the ruined City, however, we see that new dwellings have mushroomed overnight. Huts made of rough-hewn planks have been erected within ruined walls. Cellars have been boarded over and made watertight, with new wooden steps leading down to them. Citizens are staking out their ground and reclaiming their property before somebody else does. Twisting paths have been cleared from each reoccupied dwelling to the larger streets. The smoke that now rises is from cooking fires, and the smell of roasting meat wafts through the air.

'What if Sparrow has moved back too?' asks Aminta.

'He lived near Hubert's house,' I say. 'It would have been somewhere near St Paul's. We might as well try there.'

We make our enquiries, going from shack to shack. All three of us are tired by the time I knock on the door of a well-constructed lean-to, made up of a surviving brick wall on one side and three passable partitions of pine planking, with a flap of heavy canvas for a door. At our approach the flap is pulled back in a most untrusting manner and then quickly dropped again. But Will nods to me. We have spotted our man.

Will stands firmly in the path, in case Sparrow decides to run for it. But our man has little fight left in him.

'I've told you,' says Sparrow sullenly, 'I want nothing more to do with you.'

'Then you should have fled further,' I say.

'This is my home,' he says. 'Or it will be once I can rebuild.'

'It can be expensive building a house,' I say. 'And, with a family like yours – well, the sooner it can be done, the better, I'd say.'

He looks at Aminta and then at me. He can probably tell what I'm thinking, but then I'm not thinking anything terribly subtle or original.

'How much will you pay me?' he asks.

'I won't pay you anything,' I say, 'but I know somebody who will. The man I want you to identify is a dangerous traitor.

Information like that is always worth a few Guineas to somebody. Obviously, if you have other more pressing matters to attend to ...'

Sparrow looks frightened, but he's probably run out of places to hide.

'What do you need me to do?' he asks.

'Nothing very dangerous,' I say. 'I'll hire a carriage. You and I can sit in it and watch some fine gentlemen coming and going from the Palace. When you see one that you know – I mean one who attended the meetings at Mr Peidloe's house – you can tell me. I'll then do my best to arrange payment.'

'What if they see us?'

'I honestly couldn't say. You'd probably be in much the same sort of danger that you are now, but slightly richer.'

'And nobody will know?'

'Just me and Lord Ashley for the moment. Later we may need you to give evidence in court, but for the moment we just need you to identify somebody.'

He doesn't like the idea of giving evidence, but he can see he has little choice.

'When?' he asks.

'Tomorrow morning. Meet me at Lincoln's Inn at eight.'

As we walk away, I look back at Sparrow's hovel. The flap is open a crack. He's keeping a watch for further intruders. Well, he has to hold out only until tomorrow. Hopefully he won't run again before then.

The carriage I have hired for the day is neither very new nor very smart. The seats are leather, cracked and once perhaps yellow. The paint is also cracked but dark grey – not I think its original colour, but almost certainly its final one. The wheels bear witness to many knocks and scuffs; they are as round as they need to be. The horse looks, to give him his due, experienced at this sort of work. He is patient and placid. He will not be unhappy, at his time of life, to spend a day stationary in Westminster or anywhere else. Our equipage is, in short, as near perfect as possible for the task I have in mind.

Sparrow is nervous – more nervous than I had expected – and very much regretting his decision to accept an undefined sum of money from an undisclosed source, merely to feed his starving family. He wears a cloak, as much for covering the lower half of his face as anything else, and a hat, which adequately covers the upper half. Rarely have I seen anyone try harder to look like a spy. He climbs on board slowly, as if that may offer him some protection. He is sweating, though whether from fear or too much clothing is unclear. I make a quick signal to the driver that our party is complete, and we are on our way before Sparrow can jump out again.

We station ourselves in Whitehall, in the open, as honest men might choose to do, but not inviting attention. The driver descends casually and inspects the wheels and axles with great care, as if there might be some fault with them. Then he feeds the horse. We sit back in the cracked and once yellow seats in the gloomy interior of the coach and watch.

The streets are crowded. I recognise a lawyer who has chambers close to mine and wonder what business brings him this way. A royal footman passes by on an equally unknown errand. Sparrow shows mild interest when I point out Lady Castlemaine climbing into her carriage, with a deafening rustle of brocaded silk at five Pounds a yard. A maid meticulously arranges my Lady's skirts before carefully joining her on the opposite seat, but she still earns a cross word for some fault in this delicate procedure. Then Joseph Williamson comes into view. I hope that the interior of the coach is as dark as I believe it to be. Fortunately Williamson does not even glance in our direction, but walks straight past the sentry and into the Palace. I look enquiringly at Sparrow, but he shakes his head. For all his bluff northern honesty, I would have wagered a small amount on the mysterious gentleman we are here to identify being Arlington's deputy.

Many others pass by. Once the coachman looks in to enquire if I really wish to remain here at five Shillings an hour, but I assure him that I do. He shrugs and goes to sit on his box and await further orders. The horse shakes itself.

A coach arrives and, at last, I see Sir Thomas Clifford descend. He obligingly stands beside his transport for half a minute, talking to the coachman.

'Is that the man?' I whisper to Sparrow.

'No,' comes the muffled reply from behind the cloak.

Clifford enters the Palace and is gone. It is another half an hour before a second suspect arrives in his own newly painted carriage and four. I know the vehicle well. I have occasionally been allowed to travel in it. A footman leaps down and opens the door. Arlington gets out.

'Do you recognise him?' I ask.

Sparrow pauses for a moment then says: 'Yes, that's the one. I'd know him anywhere.'

Well, now I finally know the truth.

'Are you certain?'

'Of course. He came to Mr Peidloe's house several times. I'd forgotten that nose patch, but now I've seen him again, I've no doubt at all. So, now you know who your traitor is, how do I get paid?'

'I shall arrange that,' I say. 'I think you will find your reward is not ungenerous.'

Lord Ashley would probably have preferred to have completed his own enquiries into Sparrow's trustworthiness, but he is not displeased with the results I have obtained.

'So, neither Sir Thomas Clifford nor Mr Williamson, but Arlington himself?' he asks. His normally pinched face bears a broad smile.

'Yes, Sparrow identified him as the gentleman who visited Peidloe. The nose patch was the final clue.'

'And you think Sparrow will say the same to the King?'

'I think he'll give evidence if we pay him and offer him sufficient protection. Once Arlington is in the Tower awaiting trial, he can be no danger to Sparrow anyway.'

'What do you propose to do now then?' he asks.

'First I must go to Essex,' I say. 'Sir Felix has succeeded in breaking free of Arlington's grasp. He escaped from the Tower with the aid of Lady Pole. But Arlington implied that he was held only for his own safety. I do not understand what this danger was. The attacks on me and Lady Pole have come from Arlington himself. But I think it is better that I get him and Lady Pole safely away to Essex for a while.'

'Which part of Essex?' Ashley asks.

'Clavershall West,' I say. 'It is where I grew up and my mother and stepfather still live there.'

'But you do not intend to stay there for ever?'

'I think not,' I say.

'You have done well, Mr Grey,' says Ashley. 'You have done very well indeed. So, now your former master has been ex-posed for what he is, will you finally accept my offer of a place?

There can now be no possible reason for a refusal, since your old master faces disgrace and exile. The clerkship remains open. And it will lead to greater and more profitable things.'

'No, my Lord,' I say. 'I shall return to writing wills and drawing up contracts.'

'The duties I am proposing are not great. You would not find them burdensome. I admire your skills, Mr Grey. I would rather have you by my side than think of you rotting in Lincoln's Inn.'

'Thank you, but I must decline,' I say.

'Surely you do not remain loyal to Arlington after all he has done?'

I shake my head. It has little to do with Arlington and more to do with my having seen enough of the court to know that I have no wish to be a courtier. Pepys enjoys it. I wouldn't.

Lord Ashley purses his lips. He is not happy. He would not, in his youth, have turned down such a chance. It puzzles him that I do. 'Very well,' he says. 'I have made you an offer that few men would refuse and that I think you may yet regret declining. But God speed for Essex, if that is your choice.'

'But will Sparrow really testify against Arlington?' asks Sir Felix.

'I think he will. Once Arlington is safely in the Tower,' I say. 'In the meantime, there is danger for everyone whom Arlington suspects may know his secret – not only Sparrow, but also you, me and Aminta. Sparrow is hiding out amongst the ruins, but I don't recommend it if you have anywhere else to go. You and Aminta would be better off back in Essex for a few days at least. Legally, Sir Felix, you are a wanted man, and will remain so as long as Arlington is Secretary of State. That will not be for long, but it is a relevant consideration.'

'We'll need to hire a carriage,' says Aminta.

'I have one outside,' I say. 'It is generally sound, possesses at least three good wheels and has one well-rested horse to pull it. It should take us to Islington, though I fear not much further. But from there we can find another coach tomorrow to take us into Essex.'

The Angel Inn is a large building with a fashionable classical facade, hiding an older galleried courtyard behind. Its location outside London gives us some sense of security – it is unlikely that this will be the first place that Arlington will search for us and we shall not be here long. We have no difficulty in obtaining rooms for the night and seats on a coach that will convey us as far as Saffron Walden. We have supped well and both Sir Felix and I have drunk perhaps a little more than is good for us. Aminta has proceeded to her chamber and left us to our wine.

'It is kind of you to escort us,' says Sir Felix. 'But will you not remain in Essex yourself for a few days? Your mother will welcome a visit, I'm sure.'

'If I do not return swiftly to London,' I say, 'then Arlington may not be brought to justice. I shall need to reassure Sparrow he can safely give evidence.'

'You are a brave man, John. Many would have taken Arlington's gold and looked the other way. Your father would have done.'

I look at Sir Felix. He does not often speak of my father, though he must occasionally think about the man who stole his wife.

'I cannot excuse everything that my father did . . .' I say.

Sir Felix pours some more wine. 'It was not straightforward. There were . . . wrongs on both sides.'

We drink for a while in silence.

'My father died penniless in Flanders,' I say.

'I know,' he says. 'I almost died penniless in Flanders my-self. It was a common mistake to make – some who fled Cromwell's rule died only weeks before the King was restored. In the end, far fewer Cavaliers returned from exile than went into it. That means there are not so many of us to prick the King's conscience now, of course. I'm sure he's grateful to those who had the good grace to die elsewhere and not plague him with demands for places at court or for the restitution of their lost estates – not that I begrudge your mother and stepfather owning my former house.'

'She didn't marry my stepfather just to gain control of the manor,' I say.

'You think not?' says Sir Felix. 'Well, it was a happy chance then.'

'Yes,' I say.

'I had always hoped – as your mother had – that you and Aminta might mend matters. I mean, your family distantly owned the manor before us. Now your mother has contrived to wrest it back. But a marriage between the two of you – forgive me for speaking so bluntly – would have ensured that descendants of both families would have had firm title to the place for ever. Now that Roger Pole is sadly no longer with us, there could be no impediment that I can think of . . .'

Can he not? I pick up my glass and drain it. Then I place it firmly on the table.

'Sir Felix,' I say, 'I cannot marry your daughter because I have the strongest suspicion that you are in fact my father.'

'I am certain of it,' he says, 'or I would scarcely have sug-gested that you marry Aminta.'

Drunk though we both undoubtedly are, I can see the flaw in his logic.

'You are suggesting I knowingly enter into an incestuous relationship with my own sister?' I ask.

Sir Felix shakes his head. 'I need to make myself absolutely clear,' he says. 'Legally – and that is what will carry weight with the Church – you are the son of Matthew Grey, late surgeon to His Majesty's Army and abductor of my wife. Similarly, the baptismal records of the church in Clavershall West will show beyond any reasonable doubt that Aminta is the daughter of Sir Felix and Lady Clifford, lord and lady of that same manor. But your own conception took place – if I may use such words in your presence – when your purported father was elsewhere. I have always had every good reason to suspect you were my son, but it was when you visited us in Brussels and I noticed the resemblance to your late half-brother Marius that I was really certain of it. Aminta's birth, conversely, occurred after I in my turn had been absent on a campaign of some length, but when Matthew Grey had been present. In case that is not plain enough for you, then let me conclude by saying that you should properly bear the surname of Clifford and be heir to a baronetcy. Aminta should conversely possess the surname Grey in her own right. I am not proposing that you should change your name, but I see no legal or moral reason why Aminta should not legally become Mistress Grey if she has no objection on any other grounds. I had assumed that you had worked all of this out for yourself, though judging by the strange oaths that you are now uttering, I take it that you did not. Your language does at least reassure me that you are no Puritan, which was my only reservation on the matter.'

'So, I can marry Aminta?' I say.

'If you are asking for her hand, then I am happy to grant it, though in a sense I suppose that was her late father's responsibility. If you are merely enquiring whether in principle anyone might know just cause or impediment why you should not be joined in matrimony, then the answer is that it is unlikely, unless they know something that I do not. There is really only one person still alive who might do so, and I doubt your mother will wish to raise objections at the ceremony if nobody else does. She has always enjoyed weddings.'

I stare for some time into my wine. I had thought it was pale yellow but, on reflection, I see that it is pure gold. My reveries are disturbed only when Sir Felix starts snoring. I rise with some difficulty, and stagger up the stairs to our chamber, leaving my father to sleep it off as best he can.

Chapter Twenty-Two

I am back where I was conceived – or within a few hundred
yards of it. During the long coach ride to Saffron Walden,
I have not elicited from Sir Felix any further details of my early
history. Occasionally, during the bumpy ride, he looked at me
as if he was aware that he had once said something to me that
he should not have done, but that he was not entirely certain
what. On the shorter and even less comfortable journey from
Saffron Walden to the village, he slept soundly.

As we roll into Clavershall West, I notice how small the
place has grown. No sooner have we reached beginning of the
long brick wall that encloses the grounds of the manor house
than we are at the crossroads, at the very centre of the village.
Surely the road was once much longer than it is now? Surely the
walls were once twice the height they are? From here, just by
turning your head, you can see almost everything Clavershall
has to offer – the ancient, half-timbered houses straggle away
in four directions, at first in solid rows with overlapping and
competing roofs of dirty thatch – then they peter out in pairs
and single dwellings, amid tidy gardens and fruitful orchards.

In the middle distance, above the trees, rises the stumpy spire of our parish church, where Aminta's mendacious baptismal records and mine sit side by side in silent complicity.

Autumn seems further advanced here. The giant trees that bound the manor park are already a riot of dark green, red and brown, all tinged by the sun with glistening gold. Some leaves have fallen and sit in soft, dry heaps where the wind has swept them. A few men, none of whom I recognise, lean back on the benches outside the inn, enjoying the late sunshine. But there is a chill in the air for all that. A raw, rain-lashed Essex winter is waiting somewhere beyond the low, rounded hills.

It is towards the main gate of the manor – or the Big House, as it is known locally – that I make my way, leaving Aminta and Sir Felix to proceed at their own pace to the New House, which they rent, I am not sure on what terms, from my mother. The Park gate is closed – my stepfather always left it open for the villagers to wander through as they wished, but my mother does not share things in that manner. I unlatch it and pass through.

My mother is strangely unsurprised at my arrival after many months away. It is as if I had been to the market in Saffron Walden for the day and returned a little later than planned and unaccountably sober.

'What on earth have you done to your face?' she says, as I enter the parlour.

'I was in a fight,' I say.

'Working for Lord Arlington?'

'Yes.'

'I hoped you'd grown up a little since you became a lawyer.'

'It was a grown-up fight.'

She shakes her head. She knows there is no such thing. 'And

your clothes are covered in dust,' she adds, lightly brushing my shoulders with her hand. Her hand searches for her kerchief to wipe some spot from my face. She licks a lace-embroidered corner, then fortunately recalls I am a lawyer of several years' standing.

'The coach dropped us in Saffron Walden,' I say, watching her tuck the slightly damp square of linen back in her sleeve. 'All we could find to bring us the last few miles was a carter's waggon that was heading for Royston. Sir Felix and Aminta have gone to the New House, but I have no doubt that they will come and pay their respects tomorrow.'

'They should have warned me that they were coming. I could have got Martha to warm the beds for them. I fear the mattresses will be damp after so long away, even with the fine summer we've had. It doesn't pay to leave these things. I think that all the damp in England drains into Essex. I do understand that Aminta may find the village dull, but I think that Sir Felix should take more care of his property – that is to say, my property. I cannot for the life of me see why he needs to go to London at his age. What can he possibly do there? I am several years younger than he is and I am perfectly content to live in the country.'

I nod. I have no doubt that, unchecked, she will spend much time explaining to me how Sir Felix might mend his behaviour. I suspect she is as aware as I am of the attractions London holds for Sir Felix, and once would have held for her. Sadly she was born too soon to be one of the courtesans who flit from bed to bed at Whitehall. She'd have liked that.

'How is the Colonel?' I ask.

'Your stepfather imagines he is ill,' she says of her second and present husband. 'He has taken to his bed, leaving me to run the estate. Not that he ever really knew how to run it. Not properly. You cannot understand your rights and your duties unless you are born to it – merely being rich is not enough. I have had to spend more than a little of the Colonel's money, occasionally with his knowledge, ensuring that he keeps up the more important traditions – if you are going to feast the tenants, there is no point at all in doing it in the niggardly way he did before he married me. Can you believe that he actually served them beef broth one year? Sir Felix would never have done that, for all his other faults. That you cannot afford to pay the butcher's bill does not mean that the village should be deprived of its roast ox.'

I think of the string of unpaid bills that Sir Felix has happily left all over England, France and the Spanish Netherlands. I agree that it takes many generations of breeding to do that with a completely untroubled conscience. I doubt that Sir Felix pays rent to my mother for the New House any more than he paid it to the Colonel in the old days for living at the Lodge.

'Of course,' my mother adds, 'the Colonel does not go whoring in London, as Sir Felix enjoys doing, but the village would scarcely regard that as compensation for having to consume beef broth.'

'Possibly not,' I say.

I look around the room. The harsh simplicity that I remember from my visits here when the Colonel lived an inexpensive bachelor existence has long since been softened. Light still streams through the tall windows with their yellowish diamond panes, but the simple elm chairs have been forced to give way to well-upholstered replacements, and the creamy oak panelling now hides coyly behind bright new tapestries.

The table is draped with a soft red, blue and moss-green Turkey carpet. I wonder if my stepfather will be able to pay his butcher's bill if my mother continues to spend his money as it really ought to be spent.

'Mother,' I say, 'I'm thinking of asking Aminta to marry me.'

'Well, John, don't expect me to congratulate you on your sagacity. You should have asked her years ago. I might have had half a dozen grandchildren by now if you had. But better late than never, I suppose. I can't think why you have delayed so long, other than her marriage to a Viscount. I rather liked Roger Pole – he had qualities that you lack. I always found him charming and full of lavish and well-deserved compliments. But on balance I suppose it's better for everyone that he's dead. It doesn't pay to be too sentimental where one's own interests are concerned.'

'I think you are well aware why I have held back,' I say.

'Your natural gaucheness and lack of tact?'

'No, mother, my parentage.'

'I concede that your father's ancestors amounted to very little, but my own were lords of the manor here in Henry the First's time. You have nothing to be ashamed of.'

'I concede that in all respects. That wasn't what I meant.'

'No?'

'My concern, as you are well aware, was that Sir Felix was my real father.'

'I thought we had discussed that and I'd said that nobody could possibly know?'

'You actually said that he wasn't my father.'

'Did I? Well, it's much the same thing when you think about it.'

'He says that he *is* my father.'

'That was very forward of him, I must say. Still, as long as he doesn't tell anyone else, I don't see much harm in your knowing.'

'He also says that Aminta is really my father's – your first husband's – child.'

'I suppose that's no real surprise to me, but what a disappointment for her. Does she know?'

'I couldn't say. She may have guessed. She is no fool.'

'True. She isn't. And she is very good-looking. Is Sir Felix *sure* she's Matthew's daughter? She is most unlike my late husband in so many ways. Of course, I am not at all like my own mother, a fussy and interfering old lady who had the annoying conviction she was always right. Fortunately not all parental traits are passed on to the children. Still, I can see that this news is useful from your point of view if you really had any scruples. It is not entirely unknown here for people to marry their sisters. I am told that in Norfolk it is impolite not to.'

'You approve, then, of my intentions?'

'Of course I approve.' My mother kisses me absent-mindedly, as if she were making some minor adjustment to a vase of flowers she'd just brought in from the garden. 'My only concern is that your maladroitness in these matters may still stand in your way. There is so much you can still get wrong. Perhaps it would be better if I spoke to her?'

'I can propose to a lady without your help,' I say.

My mother looks doubtful but nods. 'Then don't leave it too long. All you need to do is—'

'I know what to do and what to say.'

'Very well, if you think so, dear. Now we should go and visit your stepfather, who I'm sure is most anxious to see you.

But Lord, you do have a lot of fathers at the moment, even if one is dead and another most unreasonably believes he is dying.'

The fine autumn weather has continued. It is a bright, cold morning and I am proceeding from the manor to the New House. My suit of clothes is newly brushed by Martha and I am wearing my stepfather's new beaver hat, with my mother's consent, at least. My stockings also belong, in the strictest legal sense, to another; but my own have been rejected as unbefitting for the suitor of a Viscountess. I am graciously permitted to wear my own shoes and carry my own sword. I decline the loan of a lace cravat and a brocaded sash. If my stepfather were only two or three inches taller, my mother would have forced me to wear his entire wardrobe.

The road is firm beneath my feet; last week's rains have not yet turned it into the quagmire that it will soon become and that it will remain for the duration of a rain-lashed Essex winter. There are a few late roses blooming in the gardens of the cottages that I pass. I reach the ford and skip lightly over the smooth grey stepping stones, as I have done many times before. My heart is beating hard as I cover the final few yards and open the gate to the New House. Nathaniel, formerly one of my mother's servants, is in the garden, pruning some bushes.

'Welcome home, Mr John,' he says. 'It's good to see you back again. Were you looking to visit Sir Felix and my Lady? I'm afraid they're called away to Royston. A message awaited them that one of Sir Felix's kinsmen had died and they must go and pay their respects and stay for the funeral. They'll be back in two or three days, they said.'

'I should have come earlier,' I say. 'I thought they'd be tired after their journey yesterday and sleep late.'

'I'm sure they mean no harm by having a dead cousin, Mr John. But you'll see them soon enough, sir.'

'Yes,' I say. 'I'll see them soon enough.'

My mother is unimpressed. 'I told you that I should do it for you,' she says.

'Did you know that Sir Felix's cousin in Royston had died?'

'No, but such things are always a possibility. Hertfordshire is not a healthy county.'

'I'll visit them on their return,' I say. 'A day or two can make no difference.'

'Let us hope not,' she says. 'I am sure that Aminta's head is not easily turned, but all sorts of young men attend funerals nowadays.'

The morning passes slowly. My mother is kept busy tending to the imaginary sufferings, as she classes them, of my stepfather. I go out into the Park and then, when the attractions of counting the deer have palled, to the village inn. Ben Bowman serves me with almost as much beer as I have paid him for. He is a little plumper, a little more red-faced than before, but otherwise not much seems to have changed.

'Are you back for long, Master John?' he asks.

'A few days,' I say.

'Not long enough to make me rich then?'

At first I think that the accusation that I drink too much must come by some strange route from my clerk. Then I realise that Ben is referring to incidents in my distant past. Whenever you come home, you step back several years, and are obliged to become a person that you scarcely now remember. If I told

Ben that I had killed two men since I last saw him, and had almost been killed myself three times, would he even believe me? I don't think so.

'In view of how much you charge, Ben, one pint makes you rich enough,' I say.

'Best beer, that is,' he says. 'You'll not get as good as that in London.'

I take another sip. He's right. It's better than London beer and, though I shall not admit it to him, much cheaper than in a London hostelry.

'And Lady Aminta's back too?' he says.

Ben's well informed.

'Yes,' I say.

'And Sir Felix?'

There are, it seems, few secrets in a village this size.

'Yes,' I say.

'Just like old times.'

'Almost,' I say.

'How did you come by that scar, by the way?'

'What scar?' I ask.

'The one on your face,' he says.

'I hadn't noticed one,' I say. 'I'll trouble you for another seven-eighths of a pint, Ben Bowman, then I'd better go home for dinner.'

I think that the afternoon will also be quiet, but at about two o'clock I see a cloud of dust above the Park wall, first moving up the London Road, then entering the wide-open gates. The rider dismounts. My mother, as mistress of the house, receives the letter and reluctantly hands over a Shilling.

'It seems to be for you, John,' she says, even more reluctant to part with this interesting document when the contents are still unknown to her.

'I may have failed to propose but I can open my own letters,' I say.

'I suppose so,' she says, handing it to me, but she remains unconvinced that, having read it, I will tell her what it says.

I break the seal very slowly, while my mother taps her finger on the table, and I open the folded sheet.

'It's from Mr Sparrow,' I say, frowning. 'He says that he may be in danger.'

'Does he say why?'

I show my mother the letter.

'He is very vague,' she says. 'I think he might have been more discursive. I find it very annoying to know only half the story.'

'Perhaps he didn't want to commit whatever it is to writing,' I say. 'The letter might have been intercepted. I agree it would have been helpful . . . to me . . . to know more. But it's clear he wants me to return to London.'

'To London? I cannot conceive you have any special responsibility for Mr Sparrow. I think you should at least delay your departure until the Cliffords have buried such members of the family as they feel would be better for it and have returned from Royston.'

I consider this.

'He is the only witness I have who can testify that Arlington is plotting against the State. But I can ride to London, see Sparrow, and return before the Cliffords are back,' I say.

'Does it really matter if Arlington is plotting against the State?' asks my mother. 'I used to plot against the State myself and, on reflection, it really made very little difference to anything. I don't know why I bothered. Gentlemen wear a little more lace now, and I must say that I feel the cold more than I did under Cromwell, but otherwise almost nothing has changed with the return of the King. I think you should stay and propose to Aminta and then, if all is well in that respect, go and prevent Arlington's treason. Your father – I mean my first husband rather than the other choices available to you – was much the same as you in that respect. Always off somewhere, trying to prevent King Charles being evicted from his throne. Of course, in one sense it mattered a great deal whether the King was deposed – one should maintain traditions wherever possible – but in many other ways it didn't. It certainly wasn't worth going off to war and leaving me to the mercies of Sir Felix. Or not from his point of view, anyway.'

'Aminta is unlikely to change her mind in two or three days, whoever she meets at the funeral.'

'You are assuming that she wishes to marry you at the moment, which may or may not be true. Wives are not just to be summoned with a snap of your fingers. We like to feel that you men have gone to some effort to persuade us, even when we plan to leave you no choice in the matter.'

I look at her. Didn't Aminta say much the same to me?

'I shall be back,' I say, 'before Aminta even knows I've been away.'

My mother looks doubtful, but I know I am right.

The sun is scarcely up and I am galloping on a horse supplied by Ben Bowman and warranted to get me to London by this evening. He is not as fast as Ben claimed, for which I think I shall soon be very grateful. It is some time since I spent a whole day in the saddle, and my muscles are already starting to ache. But I plan to make as few stops as I can. Tomorrow the horse can rest before the return journey, which is more than I shall be able to do.

I put my head down and the countryside flashes past me.

The light is fading as I ride slowly into Lincoln's Inn. I take my horse to the stables and leave him to be unsaddled, rubbed down and fed. I mount the stairs with some difficulty. Will is surprised to see me back so soon, but then it is my turn to be puzzled.

'No, sir, I haven't seen Mr Sparrow,' he says.

'He didn't come looking for me?'

'No, sir.'

'But, in that case, who told him where I was?'

'I have no idea, sir. Not me.'

'He says he is in danger.'

'Then I'm sure he is. In which case he would be best advised to leave London for the time being. He can scarcely expect you to mount guard over him all day and night.'

The same thought had occurred to me as I thundered along the Essex highways. I might or might not be able to help him, but flight would have been his best plan and remaining where he was the worst.

'I'll find out tonight,' I say.

'Take care, sir. That one-eyed man . . . I've seen him around the Inn, watching.'

'Let him watch then. I'll keep my wits about me. But if I don't return, then alert Lord Ashley. And send a message to my mother – she'll know what needs doing in Essex if I am detained.'

Will looks doubtful. 'Not Lord Arlington, sir? Or Mr Williamson?'

'I've told you. Sparrow identified Arlington as the gentleman in the coach.'

'Yes, sir. He did. That's what he said. Well, at least I'd go well armed if I were you. The ruins have become even more dangerous in the last few days. Men go in and don't come out again.'

'I have my sword,' I say.

'I would take a pistol too,' says Will. 'Even a whole regiment of cavalry may not be too much at the moment, if you could lay your hands on one.'

The light from my lamp casts strange shadows on the crumbling stone walls – shadows that move silently, always changing shape, growing and shrinking. Nothing is quite what it seems to be. Several times I stop and listen. The sound that I noticed before of the City cooling – the slow cracking of stones and the music of falling mortar – has gone. In its place is a deep silence. Only in the far distance can I hear the blurred sounds of voices and carts in unburnt Westminster and the quarterly succession of Westminster and Clerkenwell church bells, calling out plaintively to the cold, stair-less towers of the City. From cellars and between the boards of the newly built shacks, I see flickering candlelight. Once or twice a dark face appears unexpectedly from behind a makeshift door, then vanishes as fast. I have no doubt that a pistol or musket sits close at hand in each dwelling. How else would anyone stay?

There is enough moonlight that I can see St Paul's looming mass from a distance. I make my way towards it, threading through the maze of cleared paths. I lose myself several times before I finally find myself in the remains of the street that once held Sparrow's house. There is his shack. I am about to approach it, when I see the door-flap open and a figure comes into view. I quickly extinguish my own lamp and wait and watch from behind a wall. The figure looks in my direction, as if he had seen the light. He starts towards me, but it is too dark to locate me. For a while he too is in shadow, then the moonlight catches his face. Our one-eyed friend has not followed – he has preceded me. And he has got to Sparrow first. He is now very close, close enough for me to hear his breathing, but I am secure where I am behind my wall. And whatever he came to do, he has done. I wait until he has passed and his footsteps have receded, then I walk quickly in the moonlight towards the streak of light from Sparrow's door. I burst in, fearing to find him and his family dead, or at least huddled together in terror, but they all are sitting comfortably round a table made from rough planks, and on the table are gold coins neatly stacked in several piles of ten each. The room is lit by a single candle, but that is enough to make the coins sparkle invitingly. Gold retains its purity, however grubby its source.

Sparrow leaps up as I enter. He looks from me to the gold and from the gold to me and then swallows hard. Does he know that I saw Arlington's man leaving?

'Well, well, Mr Sparrow,' I say. 'It would seem that your fortune has changed, and very much for the better. I congratulate you, sir.'

Sparrow swallows hard again. 'Mr Grey . . .' he begins, but he does not seem to know how the sentence is to finish.

I carefully remove from my pocket the pistol that Will so wisely advised me to take. 'Sit down, Mr Sparrow,' I say. 'Make yourself comfortable. Then please explain to me why you are taking gold from Lord Arlington and, more to the point, why you have summoned me back when you seem to be in no danger of any kind at all.'

Chapter Twenty-Three

'I have a right to the money,' says Sparrow. 'Where it comes from is no business of yours. I've done all you asked me to do. I've told you who was in the coach. I didn't invite you here, Mr Grey, whatever you may think. And I'd be grateful if you would leave now.'

'Not until I know what Arlington is paying you for,' I say. 'Is that payment for *not* testifying against him?'

Mrs Sparrow has been looking from me to Sparrow and back again. She decides it's time to clarify matters. 'You don't have to be concerned, Mr Grey,' she interjects helpfully. 'It's not from Lord Arlington.'

'Keep quiet, woman!' says Sparrow with a sudden urgency.

Mrs Sparrow looks surprised and indignant. She glares at Sparrow.

'So who *is* the money from, Mrs Sparrow?' I say.

'It's not your concern, Mr Grey,' says Sparrow.

'I'm asking your wife,' I say. 'It would seem that you may not have told her the full story. She never met Ebenezer Jones on his first visit to you, did she? She seems unaware of how much danger you have put her and your children in.'

'What danger?' she asks.

'Don't listen to him,' says Sparrow. 'Can't you see what he's doing? There's no danger, you stupid woman.'

'You seemed worried enough when I came through the door,' I say.

Mrs Sparrow, standing with her hands on both hips, has had enough. 'It's from Lord Ashley,' she says. 'What's wrong with that?'

Sparrow is on his feet and facing his wife. 'I said . . .'

'He told *me*,' says Mrs Sparrow, 'that there was no harm in taking Lord Ashley's money. He said you'd promised him that Lord Ashley would pay.'

'Yes,' I say. 'I did.'

'There!' says Sparrow triumphantly, but nobody is listening to him.

'And it was brought to you by the man with one eye?' I ask her.

'Yes. That's right. By Lord Ashley's man,' says Mrs Sparrow. 'I don't understand what's going on, but that money is not from Lord Arlington.'

'But I do understand,' I say. 'Finally, I do understand.'

Because, if Jones is Ashley's man, then it was Ashley, not Arlington, who tried to have me killed on the Thames. It was Ashley who arranged the little charade in which Jones 'confessed' to working for Arlington. It is about Ashley's plot, not Arlington's, that I know more than I should. Whatever this plot is, and whoever killed Peidloe, it is Ashley behind it. If I am going to be killed by anyone in the next four and twenty hours, it will be by Ashley. He did his best to bribe me with a comfortable position, but I opted to be murdered instead. Sparrow is so much cleverer than I am.

'Did Ashley tell you to go with me in the coach and identify Arlington?' I ask.

Sparrow says nothing. I cock the pistol and I point it at his head.

'I've never killed a man in front of his wife and children,' I say, 'so this will be a new experience for me.'

'You wouldn't,' sneers Sparrow.

'You're right,' I say. 'Once you're dead you're not much use to me. Perhaps I'll just shoot you through the leg. You'll probably find, after I've done it, that you prefer to talk than have me shoot you through the other one as well. At this range the ball will shatter the bone, but if your wife can get you to a surgeon quickly, he may be able to amputate what's left of the limb before you bleed to death. I'd like to give you that chance, Mr Sparrow. I'm not an unreasonable man. But, if I were you, I'd start relating everything you know now. I can't promise this gun won't go off by accident while you make up your mind.'

I've seen Sparrow sweat before, but now silver drops pour down his face in the candlelight. 'All right,' he says. 'Ashley found me here before you did. He told me that I should agree to help and wait with you until I saw a man with a black patch on his nose. Then I should tell you he was the one I saw go to Peidloe's house. He's paid me what we agreed. There it is on the table. It's mine and I deserve every penny. Is that enough for you?'

'Not remotely enough,' I say. 'Who did you really see at Peidloe's house? Ashley?'

Sparrow nods. 'I recognised him as soon as he pulled back the door-flap.'

'Did you also write a letter to me, asking me to come back to London?' I ask.

'Letter? I don't even know where you were.'

'So, that also was Ashley,' I say. I told him I would get Sir Felix to Essex. He asked which bit of Essex and I told him that too. I couldn't have done more to help him find us. How safe are Aminta and Sir Felix now? At least they were in Royston when Ashley's messenger came.

'I'm sorry,' says Sparrow. 'He didn't leave me any choice.'

'Can we keep the money?' asks Mrs Sparrow.

I lower the gun with a sense of relief – it's quite heavy to hold it ready for so long.

'If I were you,' I say, 'I'd take it and run for the country. Lord Ashley cares very little about what happens to his friends, once he no longer has a use for them. And you know a great deal more than you should. You must have forty Guineas there. That will last for six months at least – maybe a year if you are frugal.'

'And then?' asks Sparrow.

'Do you imagine I care?' I ask.

I uncock the pistol and place it back in my pocket. I take up my unlit lantern and pull back the canvas door. Outside everything is still. But I shall make my way by moonlight until I am clear of this spot. Ashley may have men watching. After all, he summoned me back here.

I step outside and let the flap close. I look at the tower of St Paul's to get my bearings. Ten minutes to St Paul's then, if all goes well, another ten to the City gates and safety. Then tomorrow I shall pay an early visit to Lord Arlington. I hear a footstep behind me. Has Sparrow remembered something else to tell me?

Suddenly I am thrown forward. The ground comes up to meet me and the darkness closes in.

Chapter Twenty-Four

The world is swaying gently beneath me, first one way, then the other. My face is pressed against damp boards. The sour smell of stagnant water is overwhelming. I feel sick. My head aches. My arms ache too and it takes a moment to realise that this is because they are tied behind me. I try to move my legs and discover that they are bound too at the ankles. It is dark where I am, but it may not be night. I think there are no windows in this place. I strain my neck and raise my head but, for all my efforts, I just have another view of nothing.

The swaying continues. I become aware of a rhythmic splashing sound that is not, after all, as I had first thought, in my head. I must be on board a ship at anchor. And, unless I have been unconscious for much longer than I think, then we must be on the Thames – there is no other river nearby that would take a vessel of any size.

For a while all that happens is the continuing throbbing of my head, then there is a grating noise and a sudden painful flood of light. Above me somebody has opened a hatch and is climbing down a ladder. I hear approaching boot-steps on the damp boards – the slow tread of a man who has come from the daylight outside to the half-light here and whose eyes have yet to adjust. I, conversely, accustomed to darkness, would have no difficulty in seeing him if I were not face downwards. Will that serve to my advantage? Not tied up here as I am. I decide to remain still until I know more. Then a toe makes contact with my side. The pain, compared with that in my head, is nothing at all.

'He's still out cold,' somebody calls to a companion beyond the hatch. 'What do you want me to do with him?'

'Is he dead?' asks a more distant voice.

A smell of sweat and tar descends towards me. A face approaches mine, bringing with it the additional odour of stale beer. 'He's breathing,' says the man.

'Then wait for his Lordship,' comes the reply. 'No point in doing anything with him until then.'

'If he wants him thrown overboard, it'll be better done further down river.'

'And after dark.'

'True enough. Too many people watching here anyway.'

I hear somebody get to their feet with a grunt, then footsteps again, first on the damp boards then on the ladder. I risk rolling over, as quietly as I can. The man ascending the ladder with his back to me is Jones, Ashley's waterman. I watch his hat, then his neck, then his leather coat, then his boots vanish. I roll back again. At least nobody will be kicking me again for a while.

Somewhere above me the hatch is closed and the light goes out.

*

Time passes slowly to the rhythm of the boat wallowing at anchor. I hear a church bell striking nine o'clock and, less distinctly, the noises of the river – the calls of boatmen, the cracking of sails as a boat tacks up or down and, I think, the roar of the water passing under London Bridge. We must be somewhere below the bridge, but not too far off – perhaps just downstream of the Tower. I have been out cold for several hours if it is now nine in the morning. Somewhere, a long way away in Essex, Aminta will be sitting, looking out at her sunlit garden, pen in hand, paper on her table. Where I am, time passes slowly. She must have written a whole scene by now. I wonder if I shall ever see it acted? Perhaps not. Eventually I hear the sound of a wherry approaching, the splash of the oars, then the side of the smaller boat grinding and rubbing against ours, and indistinct voices.

The hatch opens again and feet descend, the first carefully and awkwardly. I lie still again, but I do not need to see in order to identify the first speaker.

'You must have struck him very hard,' says Ashley. It doesn't sound as much like a reprimand as I would have wished.

'It's difficult, my Lord, to judge these things precisely,' says Jones apologetically. 'He's here and he's not dead. Wasn't that what you wanted?'

'Yes, that's all I asked for,' says Ashley. 'Let's wake him up and see what he has to say for himself.'

A hand rather than a boot is employed to shake me. I decide it would be better to regain consciousness before other methods are tried. I roll over slowly, and I blink at the light radiating down through the hatch behind Ashley's head. For a moment, I think he has a halo, but only for a moment.

'Good morning, Mr Grey,' says Ashley. He is leaning on his

stick looking down at me. He must have found the steps down into the hold difficult, but doubtless the pleasure of seeing me tied up compensates for that.

'Where am I?' I ask.

'On a boat,' says Ashley. 'But with your forensic skills, you'd probably worked that out.'

'A boat moored near St Katharine's by the Tower,' I say.

'Well done, Mr Grey. Lord Arlington was not mistaken in his high regard for your intellect. It is a pity that that information can be of no possible use to you.'

'And why have you brought me here?'

'I think you know that. I had offered you the chance to work with us. Turning the post down suggested that your loyalty to me was less than I had hoped for. Running off to Essex with one of my key witnesses against Arlington suggested even more. I need complete loyalty from my people – complete trust. However, I shall offer you one last chance. Come over to me. Help me put together the evidence that will show clearly that Arlington conspired with Peidloe and instructed Hubert to burn the City down. It can be done. You had pretty much constructed it already. You will be our star witness at Arlington's trial – one of his own creatures, reluctantly revealing his master's treachery. We'll tell you exactly what to say – word for word. When Hubert has been hanged, as he will be, and Arlington is either in the Tower or in exile, then we can see how much further we can advance you. I know you have reservations, but it has to be better than this, surely?'

'How can I work for you now I know the truth?'

'You know only some of the truth,' he says. 'What you know shouldn't be enough to prevent you.'

'Then perhaps you'd like to tell me the rest? Or do we need

to sail immediately so that I can be drowned in the right place at the right time?'

Ashley nods. 'I have no objection to your knowing why you are going to die, if you insist on doing so. I still can't persuade you . . . ? Very well, then. What do you think you know?'

'I think Arlington isn't guilty,' I say. 'You are.'

'Is that what you really believe?'

'I'm certain of it. Jones works for you. Sparrow told me so, and Jones is here now by your side if I had any cause to doubt it. Once I knew that, everything else fell into place. And Hubert does not deserve to hang. Did he even start the fire?'

'Hubert?' says Ashley. 'I wouldn't trust him to polish my watch, let alone play with fireballs. Farynor was careless with his oven. Williamson, who interviewed him, is certain of it. So am I.'

'So what did happen?'

'I think you've worked that out, Mr Grey. You gave me a very good summary of events.'

'Except that it wasn't Arlington who discovered Peidloe's plot – it was you. And you decided that it suited your ends very well that the plot should be allowed to proceed up to a point where you could disclose it as a Catholic threat to the State.'

'Again, I congratulate you, Mr Grey. I must correct you only on one point. It wasn't Peidloe's plot. Peidloe was almost as mad as Hubert. It would have got nowhere with Peidloe leading it. Graunt was always the real leader – cold, calculating, and very assured. He'd had a small group of Catholic sympathisers around him for some time, but he could see he'd have to wait for the right moment. He'd seen too many plots – Royalist, Republican, Fifth Monarchist – fail because they lacked patience.'

'It was Thurloe's standard method,' I say. 'The only difference is that he was looking for Royalist plots on Cromwell's behalf. Infiltrate a group. Give them the rope to hang themselves. If necessary show them how to tie the knot. Use them as an object lesson to deter others.'

'Precisely. And why not? In this case, the wrongdoers would meet a painful end, the people of London would learn a salutary lesson about their Catholic neighbours, the Catholic party at court would be discredited. The King might even be persuaded to exclude his brother from the succession, or at least to break off with his Catholic whore. Chances like this come all too rarely.'

'So you persuaded Graunt that the time was right? How?'

'Smith, or Farley as you now know him, was employed by me.'

'Yes, I should have worked that out before. His wife said he was being paid well. That couldn't have been Lord Arlington.'

Ashley smiles. 'Actors make good agents – they're used to playing at being other people, at showing emotions that they don't actually feel or concealing those that they do. He was one of the best. I had him reporting to me on the activities of Papists. He discovered the group and, on my instructions, he joined them and persuaded them that French troops were ready to land and take control in the name of the Duke of York – we merely needed something to divert the authorities on the night they landed. A large fire, say. Peidloe, already a member of the group, was for immediate action. Graunt took some persuading, but he had, purely by chance, just been appointed a Director of the New River Company. That suggested a possible plan if, as Director, he was able to gain access to taps controlling the water supply to the City. I had no idea that Sir Thomas Clifford had proposed him for the office – that was certainly a bonus.'

'And Hubert?'

'A Protestant, as you know, who hated Catholics. One of his forebears was killed on St Bartholomew's night. He had a score to settle. Smith – let's continue to call him that because that's what he called himself – felt he needed help managing the project. He found Hubert by chance, persuaded him that they knew each other from way back, and signed him up. Hubert had few friends and was willing enough to discover he had such a good one whom he'd somehow forgotten. The advantage of having a madman as an agent is that, if they are captured, then they can be dismissed as just that – mad. Nothing they say will necessarily be believed. Unless they are properly briefed, of course.'

'And you too were involved. Sparrow saw you attending at least one of the meetings.'

'He was mistaken. As the Commission is discovering, people remember all sorts of strange things after the event. I would not have been so foolish as to meet the plotters. But I did meet with Smith and Hubert at Hubert's house, quite close to Peidloe's, taking the precaution of leaving my carriage in another street. Smith had allocated to Hubert a key role – accompanying Peidloe on the night and then giving evidence against him. But Hubert needed convincing it would be free of risk for him – he was mad, but not mad enough to want to hang. So Smith got me to give Hubert the necessary assurance that, if he did what we asked and stuck to his story, he would be safe. I was helped by the fact that he'd heard of me. He saw me as the leader of the Protestants in England – perhaps even of the Protestants in Europe. His leader. And I think he also saw me as a father figure. His relationship with his own father had not been good. I was the father he had never had. The one who didn't find him odd in any way.'

'And so he'll willingly go to his death for you?'

'No, I explained that – he thinks I'll save him. And he'll think that right up to the moment they tighten the noose round his neck.'

'But he didn't start the fire?'

'On the night in question, Graunt set off to Clerkenwell to cut off the water supply. Smith, Hubert and Peidloe went to start a small fire somewhere. But the baker's shop was burning before they even left Hubert's house. Peidloe insisted they go west and start another fire near the Palace. Smith's account was confused, but it's clear that, near St Paul's, Hubert started arguing with Peidloe about his fee for the job. Hubert never could work out when to keep his mouth shut. Peidloe, who in one sense was no fool, countered that he'd suspected Hubert was a double agent all along. He wasn't going to pay him a penny. It was beginning to look nasty. That was the point when Smith took the opportunity to shoot Peidloe in the back – a very good decision under the circumstances. We had no possible further use for him. Hubert ran off, but you showed up just as Smith was trying to work out what to do with the body.'

'So, you'd lost your witness?'

'Exactly. For a day or so it looked as if it had all been a waste of time. Graunt had clearly tampered with the water supply, but since the fire had started accidentally at Farynor's bakery, that didn't take us anywhere much. Graunt, who'd expected to see French troops on the streets the following morning, probably felt a bit of a fool; but he knew he wasn't going to hang, because it all looked like an unfortunate error.'

'Then Hubert came back.'

'Arrested at Romford. Yes, that was a stroke of luck. Suddenly we had our witness again. Smith found him at the gaol, terrified about what would happen to him. Smith calmed him down, coached him in what he must tell people. As I say, left to his own devices he'd have said whatever nonsense came into his head. So Smith gave him the exact words, got him to repeat them, and told him not to deviate from them at all. If he did that, he was in no danger.'

'So Hubert said it all to save his skin?'

'I'd like to think he did it out of loyalty to me. I value loyalty, Mr Grey, as you know.'

'And almost none of what he said was true?'

'We didn't need him to say what was true. We just needed him to say it was a Catholic plot.'

'What about his visits to Paris and Sweden?'

'Yes, when he departed from the script, we ended up with some very strange evidence indeed. That's why we discouraged his thinking for himself. But for the most part he did as we asked, and he's said more than enough to hang. He did well for me. I have no complaints.'

'Well done, my Lord.'

'Thank you, Mr Grey. But Arlington's no fool. He's talked to Graunt. He got you to talk to Hubert. Above all, he's talked to the King and the Duke of York. He knows perfectly well there's no Catholic uprising worth the name. And for the King's sake he doesn't want phantom plots emerging from nowhere. He'd have also picked up early on that his protégé

Sir Thomas Clifford had got some mud on his hands. That was going to make him doubly cautious.'

'Arlington said nothing to me about Sir Thomas.'

'You didn't need to know. And no doubt he saw the two of us as allies. And so we could have been allies, John. But you persisted in wanting to know the truth – to prove that Hubert was innocent, as if that mattered. So you either had to be bought or disposed of. I really did my best to buy you. Few other men would have had the patience that I did. You have to admit that.'

'So, when I said no, you got Smith to try to kill me?'

'Smith was supposed to leave you there in the cellar. Had all gone according to plan, my men would have rescued you from Arlington's trap the following morning. You'd have been very grateful and much less loyal to your old master. But Smith instructed one of his companions to remain and ensure that you did not get away. That was a mistake.'

'Then you tried to have me drowned but, when the second attempt failed, Jones swore it was Arlington. That was very clever. I believed it. And you had him beaten so that it would appear true.'

Ashley turns and looks at Jones, who smiles.

'He was paid well for that piece of acting. And a little pig's blood goes a long way. Others I did not need to pay. They were willing to kill you free of charge.'

'You mean you informed Mistress Farley that I had killed her husband?'

'Yes. I mean, in a way, you had. He died because of what you knew. It wasn't safe to leave him to sell his story to you or Arlington.'

'Your love of loyalty does not extend to giving it to others.'

'I never said it did.'

'I should kill you here and now.'

'Unfortunately you are tied up with very strong ropes and we have your sword and pistol. And posterity may not agree with you – if any of this were ever to come to light. Did you study history at school? Were you taught about the reign of Mary Tudor? If the Catholics gain control, that is what we shall have again, Mr Grey. Bonfires in Smithfield that will never be put out. Cardinals issuing instructions to the King. The Inquisition plying its trade in Lambeth Palace. I do genuinely regret your coming death, but think of the thousands of other deaths if we ever have a Papist monarch. Now we shall be spared that, because of the terrible warning provided by this Catholic plot. Unlike most courtiers, I do go amongst the citizens of London, Mr Grey. I know what they think. And they think that James Duke of York must never succeed to the throne of these kingdoms. If the King does not produce a legitimate heir, then the bastard Duke of Monmouth must rule after him. William the Conqueror was a bastard – it is no impediment. The French Papist Hubert will shortly be hanged, because he will insist on it. Your own death will be less public, but as you vanish beneath the waters of the Thames, you will have the comfort of knowing that you have not died in vain.'

'But won't people know it was Farynor who started the fire?'

'They'll believe what they want to believe, and at the moment the citizens of London want to believe that they've lost all they have because of a well-planned French plot to seize the City – not because of a very avoidable accident in a baker's shop. I think we should let them have that, don't you? We'll have a plaque put up somewhere, saying that, by the permission of heaven, Protestant London was destroyed by the scheming Papists. Or something of the sort. And that's what history will record.'

'Thank you,' I say. 'Well, that's very clear. I'm grateful to you for explaining it all to me. Perhaps on second thoughts that clerkship of yours would be of interest after all.'

'To save your skin you're happy to see your master Arlington exiled?'

'Yes,' I say.

'And you will give evidence that will help hang Hubert, even though he is innocent?'

'Yes,' I say.

'And against Sir Felix Clifford?'

'Why is that necessary?' I ask. 'Did he play any part in the plot?'

Ashley smiles. 'If I said yes, would you believe me? He has nothing to thank the King for. He might wish to depose him and see if his brother is more grateful to ancient Cavaliers.'

'He has the sort of loyalty you would never begin to understand,' I say.

'Perhaps I don't need to understand it. Anyway, what do you say? I may as well bring down one of Arlington's allies if I can, and Sir Felix's conviction should do that. Why should you care? You've said: Sir Felix is no kin to you of any sort.'

'I have known him all my life.'

'That doesn't exempt him from justice – and there is no doubt that he recommended Graunt, and Graunt turned off the water supply. And he was in the City on the first night of the fire – you told me yourself that you saw him there. It must have crossed your mind that there was more to his presence there than simply visiting his mistress? It will be very easy to have him found guilty. I would require you only to confirm you saw him there. That should be enough for any reasonable Protestant jury. What do you say?'

'Very well,' I say. 'I'll swear to that too.'

'To save your own skin, you'll see Sir Felix hanged, drawn and quartered as a traitor?'

'Yes. Just untie me and set me free. When you need me to do so, I'll give evidence.'

Ashley laughs. 'Do you really think I'm that stupid?' he says. 'That you would give evidence against Arlington and Hubert, yes, perhaps. But not Sir Felix. Do you imagine I'm going to free you, on the basis of a vague promise, so you can run off to Arlington and tell him what you know? It was a good effort on your part, but sadly you've just over-egged the pudding. Well, don't worry, I can probably manage without your help. Unless ... here's an idea that might suit both of us. Would you like to sign a statement now saying that Sir Felix is a traitor? We'd untie one hand so you could do it. Once I had that in my possession, I think I could actually trust you to behave. If you did, I might not even need to use it. I might just keep it, locked away in a cabinet of curiosities that I possess. It could be our own secret. Nobody would need to know about it. Not the court. Not the King. Not Sir Felix. Not even Lady Pole ... Unless you went back on your word, of course, and failed to testify against Arlington. Then they might all find out what sort of loyalty you have to your friends. So, give me a signature now and we'll untie the ropes and let you go wherever you wish ... Would that be convenient for you?'

'Go to hell,' I say.

'No food for the prisoner and no water,' says Ashley to Jones. 'Let's give him time to think. I'll be back later to dictate his confession. Or to tell you where to drop him.'

Uneven footsteps cross the deck and mount the ladder. The hatch closes. I am in darkness again.

'Given the choice between doing what they expect and what they don't expect, give them a surprise.' That was another thing my fencing master told me, in between showing me how to insert a blade neatly between somebody's ribs and how to beg for mercy in Spanish, Catalan and Portuguese: all useful skills. Tied up as I am, doing the unexpected is not easy. 'If there's a reason for them keeping you alive, don't try to argue against it.' That too was sound advice from the same source. In practice, I'd done my best to persuade Ashley that I was a danger to him, mocked him and convinced him that the only way out was to drop me in the river. I could see now that that might have been a mistake. I lie with my face against the musty decking. I have two hours, perhaps three, to find a way of getting out of here before Ashley realises I won't sign his document and decides precisely how he wants me killed. There must be a way out. It has to be possible.

Judging by the church bells, two hours have gone by, and I have no more idea how to escape than I had before. I use my arms to push myself into a sitting position, but with my ankles tied I cannot easily stand. I certainly cannot climb a ladder, bound as I am, even if I could reach it. I have been left no convenient sharp piece of metal to cut through my ropes – or, at least, I can no more see such a tool than I can see anything else. Then I hear the splash of oars approaching. Ashley is returning sooner than expected. Perhaps I should beg for mercy in Catalan. It has the advantage that it will be the very last thing he'll be expecting.

I hear shouts from our ship to the rowing boat and back again. Somebody sounds annoyed and somebody very insistent. Then there is a shot. This could be very good or very bad. In a moment I think that I shall find out which.

There are footsteps on the deck above me, and more voices. Then the hatch is dragged back again. A red-coated soldier is the first to descend, a rifle slung over his shoulder. The second, much to my surprise, is Joseph Williamson. He turns and looks at me. And he nods, as if he has just been proved more right than even he expected.

Chapter Twenty-Five

'Good afternoon, John,' he says. 'The Captain informed us most emphatically that we should not find you here, but it would seem that he has made an honest mistake. I shall explain to him that you are now safe, and invite him to think again to see if he now remembers the manner of your arrival.'

The soldier is already cutting through my ropes with a knife and I am able to move my hands to the front of my body for the first time since yesterday evening.

'How did you know I was here?' I ask.

'You may thank your clerk, who is even now descending the ladder.'

'I don't quite understand . . .'

'You told me to go to Lord Ashley if you didn't return, sir,' says Will, turning to face me. 'But I wasn't sure how much I trusted him. So first I went to see if I could find Mr Sparrow. He was putting together his remaining goods before leaving London. He confirmed my worst fears, sir – that it was Lord Ashley who employed the man who tried to kill you before. So, I went to see the one person that I do trust – Mr Williamson here. We agreed that I should watch Lord Ashley and see where he went. I waited outside the Palace until he came out. I followed him to the river and he took a boat downstream, so I followed in a second boat. I was worried when I saw him heading for the bridge, but it was slack water and he passed under easily enough, so I gave my boatman instructions to do the same. We stayed a bit behind him until he reached this miserable-looking ship and boarded it. That was enough for me. We headed back and just made it under the bridge again before the tide turned properly. Then we rowed back to Westminster and I reported to Mr Williamson, who had already told Lord Arlington of our problem. My Lord had obtained a detachment of guards for us. The tide was running fast by now but, not knowing how things were with you, we shot the bridge again – an exciting experience, sir – and so reached the ship again well before Lord Ashley. There was some dispute as to whether you were on board, so we fired a shot across their bows, as it were, and they saw sense. We're within range of the guns at the Tower, so they weren't going to be allowed just to sail away, whatever they did to us. The crew are all under arrest, though it will take a couple of trips ashore to get them into the Tower where they belong.'

'I am not sure how to thank either of you,' I say.

'How you reward your clerk is your affair,' says Williamson. 'I've no doubt that Lord Arlington would find a way of billing you for the rescue if he could. But I think you should regard it as payment for your work in Devon. You owe his Lordship nothing. Indeed, I rather think he is still in your debt.'

'I hoped you'd say that,' I say. 'Because I may need to ask a further favour of him.'

*

Lord Arlington is very pleased with himself. He has a somewhat contrite lawyer in front of him and the prospect of
bringing down a rival. He takes a pinch of snuff and inhales it
with great satisfaction.

'I hope, Mr Grey, that in future you will learn to trust my
judgement. I told you to stay out of this, but you persisted and
almost got yourself killed. It was fortunate that your clerk and
Mr Williamson had the good sense to come and consult me
and that I was able to obtain half a dozen men from the King.'

'I apologise unreservedly,' I say.

Arlington smiles benignly. 'The outcome is, however, satisfactory, I think, for all concerned. I am not displeased with
you.'

'Good,' I say, 'because I have a favour to ask.'

'I shall grant it if I can, Mr Grey.' Arlington's pleasure at my
having to grovel is such that I almost wish Ashley had been
successful in dumping me in the Thames loaded with chains.
It would be preferable in one or two ways.

'Sir Felix Clifford anticipated your orders to release him
from the Tower,' I say. 'I ask that he should be pardoned for
leaving his cell without seeking permission first.'

Arlington nods. 'I always said he was there only for his
own protection. Ashley was keen to get his hands on him.
He thought that, with a little pressure, Sir Felix would give
evidence against a friend of mine.'

'Then there is no need to report it to the King?'

'I have already reported it. His Majesty was inclined to
make Sir Felix a viscount or at least baron for his audacity. I
had to inform him that that would be excessive. Most of us
have had to earn our peerages through years of devoted loyalty
to His Majesty, not because of a single piece of play-acting.'

'I'm sure Sir Felix will be quite content to remain a mere baronet,' I say.

'Will he?' says Arlington. 'Very well. What are your own plans now?'

'I had intended to ride back to Essex,' I say. 'There is a matter of some importance that I needed to attend to, but having had my arms tied behind my back for many hours, I am not sure that I have the strength in them even to hold the reins. I must wait a day or so. There is time.'

'Good,' says Arlington, without enquiring time for what. 'I shall need to talk to you again – particularly about what to do with Mr Hubert – but it is not urgent. Go to Essex and inform me once you are back in London.'

'I shall wait upon you on my return,' I say.

I bow to him. He does not protest that this is excessive homage. Under the circumstances it may not be.

Will serves me tea.

'There's no need to reward me, sir,' he says. 'None at all. You pay me well enough anyway. Lawyers' clerks don't often get to shoot London Bridge in a wherry, then board a ship with half a dozen soldiers at their command. Anyway, the news that you are going to ask Lady Pole to marry you is reward enough. I congratulate you, sir.'

'Not yet,' I say. 'I'm sure it must be bad luck to congratulate somebody before the deed is done.'

'You were always meant for each other, sir. In that sense the deed was done long ago.'

'Still, if you don't mind, I'll leave accepting those good wishes until I can do so on behalf of both of us.'

'Of course, sir. You'll need an early start tomorrow if you are to reach Clavershall West before nightfall. And I would advise returning here as soon as you can afterwards.'

'Arlington wishes to discuss Hubert with me, but that will wait. Fortunately I can now testify to his innocence of both fire-raising and murder. Arlington will continue to hold him in prison until he is cleared by a trial or released without charges. There is no urgency there.'

'You are right that Lord Arlington was never anxious to take action – one way or the other. He prefers the easy path, whatever that is. I am sure Mr Hubert is safe for a while, but if you wish him to take action against Lord Ashley, it would be as well that you were there to remind him what he needs to do.'

This sounds like further good advice from Will, but he has overlooked one thing.

'Joseph Williamson will do that in my absence, Will. He at least is trustworthy. I shall return engaged to Lady Pole to find Ashley in gaol and Hubert free.'

Will nods. 'I hope so, sir,' he says.

Chapter Twenty-Six

'I trust you enjoyed your visit to London,' my mother says, 'and that your Mr Sparrow proved to be in considerable danger.'

'Sadly he was in no danger at all,' I say. 'In the end, I spent a lot of my time on a boat on the Thames and I talked to two of the King's ministers.'

'You seem to think of nothing but your own pleasure. You are fortunate that I was here to speak to Aminta on her return from Royston.'

'She's back already? What did you say to her?'

'Oh, there's no need to look so horrified. I didn't propose on your behalf. I merely reminded her that you were, in some ways, an excellent choice as a husband – not quite as malleable as one might like, but at least in possession of the good looks of my side of the family and with the prospects of inheriting the manor in due course. As a playwright, she's unlikely to get a better offer. Men don't like wives cleverer than they are – they are always at such a disadvantage in domestic matters that too clever a wife is not to be recommended. But if she gave up the theatre, then you and she might get along well enough.'

'You said all that?'

'Of course not. As a woman she would be aware of these things. It is only to you and Sir Felix that I need to spell them out.'

'Thank you,' I say. 'And what did she reply?'

'She looked very thoughtful indeed. I think that you only need remind her of what I said and then ask her formally. If you discuss dates, then a wedding in the spring would be very nice.'

I find Aminta in the garden of the New House. It has become a little overgrown since my mother moved to the manor. The walk of pleached limes, once broad enough for two to stroll side by side, has become a tunnel of tangled branches that must be negotiated with great care. The topiary birds have grown plump and amorphous.

She too enquires about London. She seems grateful for my intervention on her father's behalf. Like Will, she fears Arlington will stray from the straight and narrow path in my absence. We start a second tour of the leaf-covered lawn, arm in arm. But I am putting off what I came to say. I take a very deep breath.

'Aminta,' I say. 'You will be aware that I have always held you in the greatest honour and respect and have been ex-tremely fond of you since we first played in this garden as children . . .'

She gently disentangles herself from my arm and holds up her hand. 'Is that the beginning of a proposal of marriage, by any chance?'

'If you let me continue for a little longer, you would find out,' I say.

'And if I said that you would have to seek the permission of my father?'

'I am pleased to say that I have discussed it with him. He raises no objections.'

'Does he not? How thoughtful. And you have talked to your mother? She gives you a very good reference, by the way. If she were selling me a puppy, she could not have spoken more highly in its favour.'

'I'm sorry – I told my mother not to say anything to you.'

'But she was clearly aware of your intentions?'

'Yes,' I say.

'And Will, your clerk? What does *he* think about it?'

I pause. I am aware that it will not do to say either that Will wholeheartedly endorses my plans or that he opposes them.

'There is no need to answer that,' says Aminta. 'It is clear that he also knows far more about your marriage plans than I do. What about Arlington? Would he find it helpful if you were married? What about Mr Sparrow? What about that waterman who tried to drown you? Did he think it was a good idea? I can't believe you didn't mention it to him.'

'Don't be ridiculous,' I say.

'So, if not the waterman, who did recommend your current course of action? You have shown little inclination to propose until now.'

'I'm sorry, Aminta. There were difficulties of which I would rather not speak.'

'Really?'

This is getting me nowhere. I take a very deep breath again. 'I was afraid . . . I was afraid you might be my half-sister.'

'Because you thought Sir Felix might be your father?'

'Yes.'

'But you have now been reassured?'

'Yes.'

'That Matthew Grey is my father and Sir Felix yours?'

'You knew?'

'It didn't take any great intelligence to work it out.'

'Didn't it?'

She looks at me pityingly. 'You had only to ask me. I always thought that you looked like Marius.'

'I see.'

'So, now we've cleared that up, would you like to tell me why should I wish to marry you? Your mother assures me that you can be trained and taught to roll over at my command rather than Arlington's. She points out that you will inherit the manor when your stepfather dies, thus returning me to the house I was born in. She stressed that dull men can actually make very good and loving husbands. She sees us growing old together here in Essex, you managing the estate, me supplying her with grandchildren.'

'As I said, I told my mother . . .'

'You should not blame her. I really think she made the best case possible – certainly much better than your own statement that you honoured and respected me and that nobody you'd spoken to recently thought it was a bad idea.'

'Fine,' I say. 'My mother has described the goods correctly. Do I have a sale or not?'

For the first time Aminta smiles. 'I like you, John. I like you a lot. It's just that . . . do you really think that marriage is all I want? Do you think that my dearest wish is to spend the rest of my days here in Essex, running a house – a very nice house, I grant you – and looking after your children? The London theatres will soon be reopening. A little fire won't stop us. I have a new play almost finished. There are actually people out there looking forward to seeing it, *simply because it will have my name on it*. I think I can be the best playwright of our age – or the best writer of comedies, at least. And if I can't be either of those things, I can still try to be the best writer I can be. But I need to be in London. I need to be at rehearsals. I need my actors and actresses around me. I need to talk to other playwrights. I can't do all that in a nice house in Essex, chastising the maids and wiping up sick.'

'I see,' I say.

'Please don't look like that. One day I may want a puppy not unlike you ... Just give me a little more time to think about it. A few days. Maybe a few weeks. A month or two at the most. I'll stay and finish writing the new play here. Then I'll come back. But you need to go to London now, because in the end Arlington can't be trusted to do the right thing and you can be. Go tomorrow if you can. Then be patient. I'll write to you there.'

'I'm sorry I spoke to my mother first ...'

'If it helps, I have to admit that I consulted my father on what I should do if you did propose.'

'And what did he say?'

'He said it was up to me, but that you couldn't be worse than Roger Pole.'

Chapter Twenty-Seven

'I knew that I should have done it myself.'

'On the contrary, Mother, I made a perfectly good case. Aminta wishes to pursue her craft – or at least, she needs longer to think about whether now is a good time to get married.'

'There is no bad time to get married. Just bad choices of husbands, as many women know to their cost. But get the choice right and all times are good.'

'I am to return to London and await Aminta's decision.'

'I think that very imprudent of both of you. The thing stands on a knife-edge. It would be better you were here when she makes up her mind. The problem is, you see, that you are not very memorable. And your good features are not easy to fix upon. She needs frequent reminders.'

'I have to go. A man's life may depend on it.'

'Well, you might stay until tomorrow at least. Your stepfather still imagines he is dying. I have informed him he is mistaken, but it would oblige him and me if you would remain long enough to see which of us is right.'

*

The following morning my mother is reluctantly forced to admit that she is wrong. Even the doctor cannot disprove my stepfather's conviction that he has hours to live. By midday the matter is resolved beyond any further objections that my mother can raise. Before there can be any wedding, there will have to be a funeral.

'The will is quite clear,' says my mother, tapping the sheet of paper in front of her. 'The house and estate are held in trust for me until my death, when you inherit. I think it would, on reflection, have been wise of me to take a countersigned copy of the will with me when I went to see Aminta. It's much better to have things in writing. I have known mothers lie quite brazenly about such matters, and girls are right to be cautious of husbands who come without a proper warranty. But it might have been difficult to explain to your stepfather why I needed to borrow the will.'

'Aminta is not in any way influenced by money,' I say. 'She will marry, if she marries at all, for love.'

'Then she would be wise to fall in love with somebody who has money. Your father – I mean Matthew Grey in this instance – had very little money. I had hoped that he would make some as a surgeon but he was, in that respect as in so many others, a great disappointment to me. I don't know why he had to sneak away with that Clifford woman in the way he did. Neither Sir Felix nor I would have raised any objections had they done it perfectly openly. I suppose he felt that it was the right way to do it. It would sometimes have been interesting to know what was going on inside his little head.'

*

'So does that make you lord of the manor, Master John?' Ben Bowman asks, pushing an overflowing tankard across the bar.

'I don't think so,' I say. 'I'm just a trustee for my mother.'

'That's a pity, because I wasn't going to charge you for that if you were lord of the manor.'

'I'll inherit it all eventually,' I say. 'But it's my mother who is lady of the manor.'

'That's nice for you both then. And I'm sure your mother will enjoy the free ale whenever she stops by,' he says. 'But in the meantime that'll be a halfpenny, cash only – I'd like to give you credit, but only the lord of the manor gets that. You can't be too careful with common folk, can you?'

'As you know, I've been the Colonel's steward since he moved here, sir. The Colonel was a good man, sir, but the estate could have been managed better. He never wanted to drain that big lower field. But we'd be able to grow a lot more corn if we did. It would be worth an extra fifty pounds a year to you. Maybe you might consider . . .'

'Just do it,' I say.

'Thank you, sir. I shall. And I'd fell some of the timber in your wood over yonder, if I were you. That's good English oak, that is. It would more than pay the cost of drainage.'

'Do that too then,' I say.

'Thank you, sir. I think we'll have the estate profitable again by the time you inherit it.'

Well, at least I do have options other than drafting wills and sneaking down dark alleyways for Arlington.

'That won't be for a long time,' I say. 'My mother's family has been waiting almost eighty years to get the manor back. She won't be letting go of it before she has to.'

'I'm pleased to hear it. My great-grandfather worked for hers. Are you going back to London soon, Mr Grey?'

'Yes, the estate seems to be in good hands with you here. I have comforted my mother, to the extent that it was required, for some weeks. I really must go back.'

'Lady Pole used to live here, I think, sir?'

'Yes, before the Colonel bought it from her father . . . from Sir Felix.'

'I saw her walking in the grounds the other day. You've no objection, I assume?'

'Of course not. Oh, and I think you can stop locking the gate to the Park. It shouldn't inconvenience us much if the villagers want to take a short cut.'

'I'll do that, sir. Said she was writing a play, Lady Pole did. Have you ever heard of that before, sir? A lady writing a play?'

'She writes them very well. She's quite famous for it in London.'

He shakes his head. It confirms his worst suspicions about the capital.

'She had no message for me, I suppose?'

'No, Mr Grey. She did not. She stopped and exchanged a few words, but she had no messages. So will I see you here tomorrow, sir?'

'No. I think I'll hire one of Ben's horses and get an early start in the morning. It's a long way from here to London.'

'You are a good agent, Grey,' says Lord Arlington, 'but I do understand the ways of the court better than you. I've had time to think about things since I last saw you. Ashley is a difficult man, it is true, but he is not an enemy. The Earl of

Clarendon conversely *is* an enemy, and one against whom one cannot have too many allies. I can't afford to drive Ashley into Clarendon's camp. Not if we are to bring Clarendon down and free the King from his influence.'

'But if Ashley were in the Tower or in exile it would not matter whose camp he was in,' I say.

'The King is reluctant to have him arrested for encouraging a Catholic plot. It might suggest that the fire was not an accident as the King has claimed.'

'I can see the difficulty. But Ashley did plot with Peidloe and the other conspirators to burn London down.'

'The fire started in Farynor's bakery. Everyone knows that. Mr Graunt's actions in cutting off the water supply may have made life more difficult for the firemen, but Farynor and our Lord Mayor between them could probably have managed to destroy London very well without his assistance. It would not be convenient to take action against Lord Ashley at the present time.'

'So, you place expediency above justice?'

'I'm glad we understand each other so well.'

'Then I see no point in continuing this conversation,' I say.

'Excellent. We can let the matter rest,' says Arlington. 'That is certainly the King's wish.'

'And Mr Graunt . . . ?'

'. . . was quietly released last week.'

'Will it not seem odd,' I say, 'that no action has been taken when people learn that the water supply from the New River Head was cut off on the night of the fire?'

'There is a rumour that it was, but no proof.'

'But we know it was.'

'You won't find it in writing anywhere.'

'Surely the minutes of the New River Company meetings will show it?'

'Why would they wish to do that?'

Arlington, as so often, has a point there.

'And Hubert?' I ask. 'Will he also be quietly released?'

'That would be difficult, since he was hanged yesterday.'

'Hanged?'

'That is what happens if you are found guilty of a serious crime such as setting fire to a city.'

'But we've just agreed – it was an accident. Surely the judge could see that Hubert was mad?'

'Of course he could. So did Lord Chancellor Clarendon – even that fool didn't believe a word Hubert said. Everyone who met Hubert knows he was innocent. But he pleaded guilty. There is no mechanism for the court to dispute that. And Lowman's evidence was damning. Of course, it was mainly about how clever Lowman had been to trick Hubert into showing him how he set fire to the bakery. And how clever Lowman had been in disproving Hubert's ludicrous story about the Swedish ship. But all that combined with the confession – Hubert could only be convicted and hang. It's unfortunate, but there it is.'

'Lord Ashley had told him that as long as he insisted on his guilt, no harm would come to him.'

'Ah, that would explain it then,' says Arlington. 'I'm informed that, at the very last, Hubert seemed to change his mind, just as the rope was placed round his neck. Perhaps he'd finally worked out that Ashley was not going to help him. But it was, of course, much too late then.'

'The King could still have pardoned him,' I say.

'The hanging took place very shortly after the trial. The

following day, in fact. Parliament was due to meet and discuss the causes of the fire, and having Hubert condemned but not yet executed might have been a . . . distraction, shall we say? It was felt that it was better things were tidied up.'

'Hubert was thus unable to give evidence to Parliament? Evidence in which he might have mentioned Lord Ashley?'

'I thought I'd made that clear: he was dead. He couldn't give evidence at all.'

'That was Ashley's price for his support against Lord Clarendon?'

'Rarely has a thing been done so economically.'

'And that's all Ashley wanted?'

'No. He'd also like a plaque put up.' Arlington consults a paper on his desk. '"Here by the permission of heaven, hell broke loose upon this Protestant City from the malicious hearts of barbarous Papists by the hand of their agent Hubert . . ." and so on and so on. It's brief enough. It won't be too expensive to have cut. And it stops short of claiming that there was a plot as such. The King is content with the compromise.'

'Hubert was a Huguenot, not a Catholic,' I say.

'Yes, of course. But it only says he was their agent – not that he was Catholic himself.'

'And you really have no compassion for the poor man?' I say.

Arlington, who has started to read a document on his desk, looks up. 'Sorry – who are you talking about?' he asks.

'Nobody important,' I say.

When I arrive back at Lincoln's Inn, Will thrusts a letter into my hands. 'Arrived an hour ago, sir. From Essex.'

I look at the writing. It is Aminta's.

'Won't you open it, sir?'

I think of Abigail Farley, not wanting the answers to her questions about her husband.

'As long as it's still sealed, she hasn't yet turned me down,' I say.

'I know Lady Pole,' says Will. 'If it was "no", she'd tell you to your face. She wouldn't entrust it to a letter.'

'You never know what you'll do until the moment comes,' I say.

'Well, I'd open it now,' says Will. 'You'll have to do it sooner or later.'

I look at the paper and at Aminta's writing, and at the bright red blob of wax, applied in far-away Essex. Then, very carefully, I break the seal . . .

Notes and Acknowledgements

As ever, this book is a mixture of real events, guesswork and pure invention. The broad account of the burning of London, and of the chaos and confusion of the early stages of the fire, is as true as I can make it. It is also true that the Clerkenwell fire engine was taken down into the City, only to fall into the river, though the surrounding detail falls into the invention category. Likewise, the turning off of the water supply at New River Head on the first night of the fire was described in Bishop Burnet's *History of My Own Time.* John Graunt, the Director whom Burnet accused of cutting off the supply, is perhaps better known as a pioneer of the science of demography. He died in 1674 'lamented by all good men that had the happinesse to knowe him.' If he was responsible, as Burnet claimed, then it should be noted that Graunt also lost his own house in the fire. He was never formally charged and biographies of him refer to his purported role only in passing, if at all. The New River Company records make no reference to any interruption of supply on the night in question. But corporate cover-ups are not unknown.

Londoners did, as I describe, spend more time blaming and attacking the French (or anyone who looked a bit French) than fighting the conflagration. Some foreign residents, such as the King's French firework maker, barely escaped with their lives. When troops were sent in to help fight the fire, they spent a great deal of their time rescuing foreigners from the mob. London had a surprising number of French residents at the time, bearing in mind that we were (as Arlington points out in the book) nominally at war with France in 1666. Robert Hubert's confession was a godsend to those who wanted to blame the French or the Catholics or both. It is difficult to decide whether, in reality, he had anything to do with starting the fire or not. He confessed to it, but changed his story more than once. The chronology that he set out – his trip to Sweden in particular – made (and makes) little sense. But he did succeed, when taken on a walk round the City by Lowman, in identifying the bakery as the scene of his crime – or that's what Lowman later told the court. Almost nobody believed Hubert, but nobody could persuade him to withdraw his confession. That, and Lowman's evidence, pretty much did for him. He was convicted and then hanged with great haste – 'The Commons resolving to examine Hubert ... next day he was hanged before the House sate, and so he could tell no further tales.' Nobody now really doubts that it was Thomas Farynor's carelessness that started the blaze. So it is worth noting that the jury that convicted Hubert included three members of Farynor's family. It is also related that, after Hubert's death, a Swedish sea captain appeared and claimed that Hubert was still on board his ship when the fire broke out, which also may or may not have been true. At all events, it was much too late to make any difference to anything.

My only real invention (and it is admittedly quite a large one in terms of the plot) is the murder of Peidloe. Stephen Peidloe was a shadowy figure at best, though one witness at Hubert's trial claimed to know him and said he was 'a very debauched person and apt to any wicked designs'. Nobody else, apart from Hubert, seems to have ever heard of him. Hubert was adamant that Peidloe had recruited him to set fire to London. In spite of this, the authorities apparently made little effort to find Peidloe. He simply vanishes from records, to the extent that he features in them at all.

The description of London after the fire is based on contemporary accounts, such as that of Samuel Pepys, and illustrations made just after the fire showing the extent of the damage. Most of the City within the old walls was destroyed and the population decamped, as I have said, to the fields around London, before being absorbed, quite quickly, into the suburbs and surrounding countryside. Contemporary accounts describe a strange resignation to their plight. The resettlement of the burnt area seems to have begun almost at once, but it would be twenty years or more until the rebuilding was complete. Citizens, including Pepys, crossed the ruins with great caution.

Other events are based more loosely on fact. Sir Felix's improbable escape from the Tower is modelled (as some will have spotted) on that of the Fifth Earl of Nithsdale, whose wife masterminded the scheme. John Grey's escape through the cesspit was inspired by a problem that Pepys had with his neighbour's privy, built too close to his own cellar.

Anthony Ashley Cooper, Lord Ashley (later Earl of Shaftesbury), was, with Lord Arlington, one of the two As in the celebrated CABAL government of Charles II (the remaining letters denoted Sir Thomas Clifford, the Duke of Buckingham and the Duke of Lauderdale). In a court that leaned towards Catholicism, Ashley represented the Protestant cause. Though vehemently anti-Catholic in public, in private he seems a far more reasonable man. One of the better-known anecdotes about him is his remark that 'all wise men are of the same religion'. When asked by a lady what religion that was, he replied: 'Madam, wise men never tell.' But at the same time he was a professional rabble-rouser, with a large power base amongst the citizens of London. He was later involved in the infamous Popish Plot, where he 'drove on Oates's original revelations, interrogated informants, schooled witnesses, manipulated the fears of doomed men in the cells of Newgate and ferreted out further plots within plots'. Charles II, a good judge of character, described him as the 'Plott Hunter'. His downfall came with his involvement in the Rye House Plot in 1682, when he encouraged the Duke of Monmouth to stake his claim to the throne and threatened to seize London himself with an army of 'brisk Protestant boys'. He badly overplayed his hand and died in exile. I have no evidence that he did any of the things I claim he did in 1666, but he was quite capable of most of them. His contemporaries did not like him much. When he had to have an operation to insert a permanent drain for a liver cyst, his rivals cruelly nicknamed him 'Tapski'. John Caryll wrote of him:

> The silver pipe is no sufficient drain
> For the corruption of this little man
> Who though he ulcers has in ev'ry part
> Is nowhere so corrupt as in his heart

But I have a sneaking regard for him, for all that. He was a man of principle, at least by the fairly low standard of the times.

Arlington, as noted above, was a real minister of Charles II, as was Sir Thomas (later Lord) Clifford. Joseph Williamson became in due course a senior statesman in his own right, was knighted, and later founded a mathematical school in Rochester that still bears his name.

The other characters in the book are my own invention and I am wholly to blame for any imperfections they possess and their success or failure in marrying each other.

I consulted a number of sources when researching this book, the most useful of which are as follows. *Pepys's Diaries*, as already noted, are invaluable, and the best contemporary description of the fire. It is interesting to compare this with the account of William Taswell, who was then a fourteen-year-old schoolboy at Westminster School and was involved in fighting the blaze. Other contemporary sources included John Evelyn's diaries, Bishop Burnet's *History of My Own Time* and Cobbett's *State Trials* (volume 6, 1661–78), which contains much of the verbatim evidence presented at Hubert's trial and at the Parliamentary enquiry. Of the books relating to the fire itself, Walter George Bell's *The Great Fire of London in 1666* is one of the earliest. I also consulted Stephen Porter's *The Great Fire of London*, James Leasor's *The Plague and the Fire* and Adrian Tinniswood's *By Permission of Heaven*. I am grateful to Adrian Tinniswood for his prompt and helpful answers to my questions about The Precious Man. John Spurr's *Anthony Ashley Cooper* is a comprehensive account of the life and times of the slippery Lord Ashley. On espionage during the period, an important source (as with earlier books) was Alan Marshall's *Intelligence and Espionage in the Reign of Charles II*. On conditions more generally, Lisa Picard's *Restoration London* and Alexander Larman's *Restoration: 1666: A Year in Britain* are recommended reading. The Museum of London's exhibition on the Great Fire coincided with the early stages of writing this book and allowed me to see many actual artefacts from the fire.

I must also thank David Headley and everyone at DHH for their continuing support and encouragement, Krystyna Green, Amanda Keats, Ellie Russell and everyone at Constable for continuing to publish me, Penny Isaac for making copy-editing so efficient and painless, Jan McCann for her careful proof-reading, and fellow writer of Restoration fiction, Deborah Swift, for her insightful comments on a late draft of the manuscript. And of course my family, without whose love, patience and forbearance none of these books would get written at all.

Finally, and coincidentally, I completed this book just as another London fire – that at Grenfell Tower – was making headlines. Not for the first time, the present seemed tragically to be imitating the very same past that I was writing about. By the time you read this, you will know much more than I do now about the causes of the more recent fire. Already, however, there are echoes of the accusations of incompetence on the part of the civic authorities in 1666, shock that it could happen at all and a desire to find somebody to blame. Sadly, the loss of life in 2017 was much greater than in the earlier fire that destroyed almost all of the City of London. But it would have been greater still had it not been for the bravery and skill of the London firefighters. *Fire* is therefore dedicated to them.

London, July 2017